GIRLS 'N THE HOOD

"You're back in time, too?" Kat squeals so loudly I think my eardrums will burst. "Oh my god! How crazy is that? Now you believe me, right? The gypsy sent me back in time to the days of King Arthur. I met this totally hot knight, Lancelot, who's now my boyfriend. Him and Queen Guenevere are here in the future with me now."

"Uh, right. Yeah. Cool. But remember the no-babbling rule? I don't have a lot of time. I have to go catch up with the men."

"Sorry. Go on."

"So I'm back in twelfth-century England, but the problem is, there is no Grail. King Richard hasn't come back from the crusades yet, and no one knows when he's expected back. For all I know, I could have to wait around for years."

"Ooh, that sucks," Kat says. "I had to hang at Camelot for like nine months, so I totally know what you're going through. What are you doing while you're waiting? Have you learned to ride a horse yet?"

I pause. "You won't believe it, but I'm actually hanging out with Robin Hood."

A Hoboken
Hipster in
Sherwood
Forest

Marianne Mancusi

LOVE SPELL NEW YORK CITY

LOVE SPELL®

February 2007

Published by

Dorchester Publishing Co., Inc.
200 Madison Avenue
New York, NY 10016

ISBN 0-505-52674-3

Printed in the United States of America.

Visit us on the web at www.dorchesterpub.com.

A Hoboken
Hipster in
Sherwood
Forest

Chapter One

King Arthur's Faire—Upstate New York
Present day

Kat Jones is so dead!

Seriously, when I find that Park Avenue princess I'm going to wring her Burberry-clad neck. The girl has been nothing but a pain in the ass since we arrived at King Arthur's Renaissance Faire a few hours ago. Nonstop whining and complaining—worse than Scarlett O'Hara and Heather Locklear's character on Melrose Place put together. I mean, she even bitched out a poor old gypsy who was just trying to eke out a living by reading palms. And now I turn my back for one second and she's disappeared.

I'm Chrissie Hayward, by the way, a simple fashion magazine photographer not normally given to violent tendencies. In fact, I've even been called a hippie by some. But hey, just because I prefer tofu to tuna and

1

peaceful politics to unjust occupation of third-world countries that pose absolutely no threat to the United States, that doesn't mean I'm some unwashed, patchouli-drenched flower child, does it?

But enough about me. Right now I need to find my slacker coworker. Last I saw her, she was watching the jousting match. I offered to get her some water since she said she had a headache. Now I realize that was most likely her ruse to get rid of me so she could take off early.

I push past the throngs of people, many dressed in authentic-looking medieval garb. I myself am wearing a capped-sleeved, royal blue velvet gown I made from a pattern I got off eBay. I know it's a little silly, but when in Rome, right? I certainly fit in here a lot better than Kat does, what with her couture clothing and stiletto heels. Who the hell wears stilettos to traipse through upstate New York mud?

When my *La Style* magazine editor boss first e-mailed me today's assignment, I was over the moon. After all, how many times does one have the opportunity to get paid to hang out at a medieval faire all day, taking photos? Then I read the P.S.—I'd be working with *her*: *La Style*'s resident fashionista and all-around shallow bitch. Sure enough, the second we got here, Kat started complaining. You'd have thought our editor asked her to go to the front lines of Fallujah the way she's been moaning and groaning. I've tried to make the best of it, to ignore her and enjoy the faire, but let me tell you, that girl could put a damper on Pollyanna's day.

"Excuse me," I say, tapping a random knight in shining armor on the shoulder. He turns around and gives me a dazzling smile. Delicious. "I'm looking for a girl. Blonde. About this tall." I hold up a hand to illustrate approximate Kat hight. "Dressed in Armani—"

"Me too." He grins. "All my life, in fact. Be sure to introduce us when you find her."

I roll my eyes. "I'm serious."

He laughs, then shakes his head, black curls tossing from side to side. "Sorry. Haven't seen her." I try to ignore his thick Brooklyn accent, which seriously detracts from the medieval authenticity level of his costume, and concentrate on his tempting backside as he turns to walk away. Not that I should be looking at a knight in shining armor's backside; I am still technically married, though those 'til-death-do-us-part vows don't really mean anything to me anymore. After all, they certainly meant diddlysquat to Danny when he was off screwing that coffee house waitress after the poetry slam in the West Village last month.

I'll never forget the moment I caught the bastard, naked and writhing and spouting bad verse in the women's bathroom stall. It was like a cheesy Lifetime movie, except for the fact that in made-for-TV land, the husband's usually a successful businessman in corporate America. Someone with assets the jilted wife can acquire to get her revenge. Danny's assets consist of a beat-up Harley from the '60s and a signed, first-edition copy of his hero Jack Kerouac's *On the Road*. You don't end up a rich divorcée on the Riviera from that.

Shaking unpleasant thoughts from my head, I squint and scan the crowd some more. Where could

Kat be? Maybe she went back to the car. I make my way to the front gates of the faire and into the parking lot, finding my old-school yellow Volkswagen Bug still parked where I left her.

"Have you seen the bitch, Flower?" I ask the car, patting her hood. Unfortunately, for all her cuteness, Flower is more the strong silent type, and if she's seen Kat she's not telling.

Suddenly, as if on cue, my camera bag bursts into song. After listening to a few polyphonic bars of the Jefferson Airplane ringtone, I reach in and pull out my phone.

"Hello?" I say, putting the receiver to my ear.

There's static on the other end of the line. Typical upstate New York reception. At least the residents' babies won't die of cancer from living in close proximity to countless cell phone towers like the rest of us probably will. I'm totally anti-cell phone and wouldn't even own one if work didn't require it.

"Hello?" I repeat, walking a few steps away from the car, seeking a better signal. "Can you hear me now?" I ask, unintentionally mimicking the Verizon commercial.

"Chrissie?" A tinny voice registers from deep within the static.

"Kat?" I pull the phone away from my ear to glance at the screen. Full bars. That's weird. Must be on her end. I raise the antenna on the phone, just in case. "Is that you, Kat? Where are you?"

"I need your help." The crackling grows louder. Her voice sounds like it's a million miles away, even though I know she's probably somewhere within a block radius. The faire's just not that big.

"Um, okay," I say, though I'm more than a bit wary of what she's going to ask me to do. Knowing her, she's probably having a broken heel crisis and wants me to swing by the nearest Neiman Marcus to grab her a replacement Manolo. "I can barely hear you."

"I know. Sorry. Evidently they're still working out the kinks in this time-cell continuum thing. Actually, it's pretty amazing they can do it at all. I mean, think of the practical applications! You could call your dead grandmother, for example. Though, of course, that might freak her out a little. I guess it'd only work if you had a dead grandmother that didn't have a weak heart—"

I pull the phone away from my ear again, staring at it in confusion. Is the static distorting her words so much that I'm mishearing them?

"—but I suppose you could always call your dead grandmother and not tell her it's you, or pretend that it's the you that existed when she was still alive— What?" I hear muffled voices on the other end. "Oh, okay. Sorry. Chrissie, I've got to go in a sec. Sorry. Evidently these time-cell calls cost like a million dollars a minute. Literally. Stupid twenty-second century inflation. And there's no nights and weekends plan, either."

"Kat, what the hell are you talking about?" I ask, trying to gain some semblance of control over the conversation. "And where are you? I've been looking everywhere."

"Well, that's sort of why I'm calling. You're never going to believe this, but I'm in the future. Like, a thousand years in the future."

I let out a frustrated breath. "Kat, stop screwing around. We need to get going soon if we're going to beat traffic back into the city."

"I'm not joking, Chris. Believe me, I wish I were. I'm really stuck in the future. Well, first I went to the past. To the days of King Arthur if you can believe that. The land of knights, damsels and no flush toilets. That was a little rough, let me tell you. Then Lancelot and Guenevere and I went through this time portal at Stonehenge to get back to the twenty-first century, but Mordred and his army showed up and Guenevere must have messed up the spell in her rush to cast it. 'Cause now we're stuck in the twenty-second century. And I need your help."

I can't believe I'm actually listening to this BS. "Kat, I'm hanging up the phone now. I'm tired and ready to go home. Go prank call someone else."

"No, wait! You have to believe me."

I pause, the desperation in her voice making me reconsider hitting the End button.

"What, Kat?" I ask, tight-lipped.

"Please, Chrissie, I need your help! I know it sounds bizarre. I didn't believe it myself at first. But I'm desperate! I have to get word to Nimue and you're the only one I know in close proximity to her. I can't call the medieval Nimue 'cause they didn't have cell phones then and the time-cell continuum thing only works through cell phones."

"Nimue? As in, the Lady of the Lake from the King

Arthur legend?" I shake my head in disbelief. Kat has lost it. Seriously and utterly lost it.

"Yeah, her. She's disguised as that gypsy we went to visit. The one who cast the spell on me to send me back in time to begin with. Just go and tell her that Lancelot, Guenevere and I are stuck in the twenty-second century and we need to know how to get back. She'll know what to do."

I roll my eyes. "Let me get this straight. You want me to go ask the Renn Faire gypsy how you can travel back in time?"

"Yes."

"No."

"No?"

"No way. Kat, just stop screwing around and meet me at the car."

"I can't, Chris!" Even through the static I can hear my coworker's anguish. "You have no idea how much I wish I could." However deranged she sounds, I can tell she seriously believes everything she's saying. Which means she's not joking. She's simply snapped.

"Maybe you've had too much sun," I suggest in my gentlest voice. The one I used as a child to talk my mom down from her bad acid trips. "Tell me where you are and I'll send the medic. I'm sure there's a first-aid tent somewhere around here."

"I don't need first aid. I need Nimue. Find her, Chris. Please. I'll do anything. I'll . . . I'll give you all the shoes in my closet!" Even through the static I can hear her hard swallow on the other end of the line. "Even the limited-edition gold Louboutins I got at that sample sale last year."

I raise an eyebrow. Even an insane Kat Jones wouldn't give away those shoes.

"Fine," I mutter. "But you owe me. Big-time. And when the gypsy laughs me out of her tent, you'd better give up this act and meet me at the car." I pause then add, "And I'm holding you to that shoe promise." Not that I'd ever wear such uncomfortable shoes, but surely there's a market on eBay for them.

"She won't laugh. Seriously. Just tell her."

"Okay, okay. Call me back in ten." I click the End button on the phone and trudge back to the faire. I reveal my wristband to the ticket taker, halfway hoping she'll tell me there's no readmission. But she simply waves me through. I push past the turnstile and take a left toward the gypsy tent.

Insane. Kat is truly insane. Either that or she's playing some kind of mean trick on me. I should report her to our boss when we get back. In fact, I'm going to demand that I never have to work with her again. I'll even volunteer to work with Talking Tabitha, the gossip editor. No one wants to work with Talking Tabitha. But I'll do it. As long as I never have to cross paths with Kat again, it'll be worth the risk of permanent Tabitha-induced hearing loss.

I duck into the gypsy's tent, blinking a few times as my eyes grow accustomed to the darkness.

"May I read thy palm, milady?"

The gypsy is sitting at her little crystal ball table, right where we left her. A tiny gnarled woman dressed in gaudy mauve robes and dripping with heavy gold jewelry, she's hunched over, perhaps suffering from some serious rheumatoid arthritis. Poor soul. Hopefully she doesn't have a heart condition or anything, because what I'm going to say next could send an elephant into cardiac arrest.

"Um, hi." I plop down on the stool across from her, trying to act casual. "I'm Chrissie. Remember me from before? I was with that other girl. The blonde, annoying one?"

The gypsy nods slowly. "Aye. Katherine Jones."

"Uh, yeah. Right. Her." Wait a sec. How does she know Kat's name? I don't remember Kat introducing herself when we were here before; she was too busy insulting the woman. Curiouser and curiouser. "Well, this is going to sound really crazy, but . . . um, she called me and wanted me to give you a message . . . and . . . um . . ." I glance around the tent, sure I'll locate hidden cameras. I'm being Punk'd, I know it. There's no other explanation. At least this means I might get to meet Ashton Kutcher. . . .

I glance up at the gypsy, searching for the hint of a smile playing at the corners of her mouth. The smile that would give away the game. But I see no hidden amusement on her face. Instead, she's peering back at me with great concern.

"What is the message?" she asks.

"She says . . ." Ah, what the hell. The sooner I get it out, the sooner I can meet Ashton. "She says that she and Lancelot and Guenevere are stuck in the future and they need your help to get back." I can feel my face flush with embarrassment as I await her response. That's one thing I hate about being a pale-faced, freckled redhead: major blush-age at the drop of a hat. Well, that and all those Little Orphan Annie jokes I endured as a kid.

So I blush and I wait, expecting anything—laughter, disbelief, anger for wasting her time even. Maybe all of the above. What I don't expect is the sheer horror that washes over her wrinkled face.

"Thou art serious?" she demands, her voice losing its serene tone. "But that cannot be!" She stares at me, her eyes wide with apparent fright.

Feeling a little uncomfortable under that intense gaze, I shrug. "Look, don't kill the messenger. I have no idea. Kat just told me to tell you. That's all I know."

The gypsy seems to regain control, rising from her seat and making her way over to a small bookcase at the far end of the tent. For someone so hobbled and old, I'm surprised at how fast she moves. From my seated position at the table I can just make out her mutterings.

"I know I gave Queen Guenevere the correct spell. I am sure of it," she's saying to herself.

I glance around the tent, looking for those candid cameras again. I feel like I'm on a lost episode of *The Twilight Zone*. Or *X-Files* maybe. But unfortunately without sexy Agent Mulder.

The gypsy returns to the table with a dusty tome that looks a thousand years older than the Bible. Kind of reminds me of that *Book of Shadows* they have on *Charmed*. I watch, unsure what I'm supposed to do, as she flips through the book pages at a desperate pace. I contemplate leaving the tent, but it seems rude to simply walk, especially since I'm the one who's apparently caused her this upset. Though, technically it's Kat's fault.

After a moment of page-flipping, she looks up from the book. "I fear something has gone dreadfully wrong for thy friend and her companions," she informs me in a strained voice.

"Technically, she's my coworker, not my friend," I say, not quite sure why I feel the urge to remind her of this.

"I can get them back," the gypsy continues, ignoring my correction, "but I will need thy help."

Why does everyone suddenly seem to need my help? I mean, when did I draw the short straw in the Helper Girl lottery?

"Sorry," I say, feeling kind of guilty for turning her down when she looks so upset. But really, I did my good deed for the day; I delivered Kat's stupid message. And now, since it doesn't appear Ashton's going to be popping out with a camera anytime soon, I'm done with all the weirdness. "I can't help. I need to get home. There's a new *Twenty-four* on tonight." I rise from the table, preparing to leave. "So, if you see Kat, tell her I'll catch her at work on Monday morning, okay?"

I don't know why, but something makes me pause, almost like I'm expecting the gypsy to object. To force me to stay. Instead, her face softens.

"Thou art in pain," she says simply.

"What?"

She reaches out and takes my hand in her gnarled one, tracing the lines of my palm with a bony finger. For some reason, I find I can't pull away.

"Yes. I see. The man thou thought a lamb has been

revealed to be a wolf," she murmurs almost under her breath as she studies my palm.

I stare at her in disbelief. Is she talking about Danny? How the hell does she know about Danny? I haven't told anyone about the waitress incident. I've been too embarrassed. I mean, getting cheated on by the only man you've ever slept with? Your childhood sweetheart who you were supposed to live happily ever after with? Let me tell you, it doesn't get more humiliating than that. My mother doesn't even know.

The gypsy looks up, meeting my eyes with a piercing gaze so intense it's as if she's seeing into my soul. *She knows,* I realize with an odd certainty. *I have no idea how, but she knows.*

"I haven't told anyone," I whisper, feeling tears prick the corners of my eyes. I brush them away with my free hand. The last thing I need is to start crying in front of a stranger. Especially since I'm still not quite convinced this isn't some bizarre reality TV show. I can just imagine my misery being broadcast to twenty million people. Danny and his waitress slut, on the couch, having a good laugh over my torment before jumping each other's bones again. No thanks.

"Thou shouldst not fret, little one," the gypsy says in a soothing voice. She squeezes my hand. "Like thy companion, perhaps thy destiny too lies elsewhere." She opens my hand again and peers at it with rheumy eyes. "Yes. I see it. A lover true awaits thy gentle soul across the sea of time." She looks up at me. "Thou alone can tame his unquenchable thirst for vengeance, I am sure of it."

"Well, okay then. That's good to know," I reply, not sure what else to say. This has got to be, without a doubt, the weirdest conversation I've ever had in my whole life. Even weirder than the time I happened across my mother's stash of acid, tried a tab and chatted with God for about six hours. Well, okay, maybe not quite *that* weird; but still.

I remember how freaked out Kat was when the gypsy read her palm. At the time I'd thought she was overreacting. Now I'm not so sure.

"The stars sometimes align themselves in mysterious ways," the gypsy continues, motioning for me to sit. I lower myself onto the stool, lightheaded, almost as if I've fallen into some kind of semiconscious trance. "I think we can—how do you say it in your world? Kill two birds with a single stone?"

"Huh?"

"Listen carefully and I will explain," the old woman says, her eyes shining with a new enthusiasm. "Time is a slippery slope. A wheel, ever turning. To bring Kat and her companions back from the future requires a complicated spell to bend the wheel. The spell requires many a rare ingredient, including the rarest of all—a drop of pure blood from the cup of the Christ."

I raise an eyebrow. "The cup of Christ? You mean, like, the Holy Grail?"

"Aye," the gypsy agrees. "A vessel long lost to this world. The last time it was seen was when Richard the Lionhearted, King of England, secretly brought it back from the Holy Land when he returned from the Crusades."

I frown. What, does she think I was born yesterday? I mean, someone ignorant like Kat might buy such a fantastical tale, but not me.

"No offense, but I must have missed that day in history class. Sure, I know the English knights went to the Holy Land to seek the Grail and all, but as far as I've read no one ever found it. In fact, I'm pretty sure its whole existence is a myth created by the Catholic Church."

"History is but an abridged record of truth," the gypsy responds patiently, "and only reveals what its writers have knowledge of. I tell thee true. King Richard *did* bring back the Grail. But, deciding he cared not to donate it to the Church, he hoarded it secretly in his castle and spoke not of it until his dying day."

"Okay, fine. I suppose that's possible," I grudgingly agree. "But what does this have to do with me?"

"I need thee to traverse time to the day Richard comes back from his crusade. Thou must convince him to give thee a single drop of blood from the Grail. Put it in this." From her robe, she pulls out a glass vial hanging from a golden chain, and she hands it to me.

"Even if I believed you, which I'm not saying I do," I say, still completely skeptical, "why me? Why not just go yourself?"

"Travel through time can be harsh on one's physical body. I have already traveled far to be here today, and I must travel back to mine own time before I am missed. Another voyage would likely be the end of me."

"Okay, fine," I say. I sympathized. I was tired from my trip from the city, and if she believed she'd traveled through time she'd be exhausted. Besides, I was quite ready to throw question number two at her. "So then, how come if you're so good at sending people through time, you can't just get Kat back on your own? I don't remember you using some random Grail blood to cast your spell the first time around."

Ah-ha! Answer that! I think, before coming to the realization that I'm actually sitting in a gypsy tent arguing the technicalities of time travel. And here I was thinking *Kat* had lost it.

"When the physical body traverses a spoke in the wheel of time, a locator spell is needed before they can be pulled back to the hub."

In plain English, I believe this means time travel doesn't work via remote control. Jeez Louise. This woman's got an answer for everything!

"Well, then how come you can't just—"

"My time grows short, little one," the gypsy interrupts, sounding decidedly less sympathetic than she had been a few minutes before. "I must return to Avalon. Wilt thou question me to death, or accept thy destiny and retrieve the Grail?"

"Well, since you're giving me the choice, I think I'll go with door number one," I say. " 'Cause you haven't exactly convinced me of the whole destiny thing. Or the time-travel thing, if it comes to that."

The gypsy shakes her head. "In my day, women were much less difficult than you twenty-first century girls. We never spoke back, always married the lords our fathers chose and wouldn't ever even *consider* burning our undergarments in protest."

"Hello? You're talking about sending me back in time on some ridiculous quest to save a person I don't even like! That's a little different than lighting my bra on fire, don't you think?"

"I grow tired of thy resistance," the gypsy snaps. "'Tis for the best, my child. You will see." And she suddenly waves her hands in the air. I leap back, but there's no avoiding her spell. "Abu Solstice Nottingham!" she cries in a loud, overly dramatic voice.

Thunder cracks in the sky, shaking the very ground. The already dim tent lanterns fade into gray shadows, and I blink my eyes in an attempt to keep conscious. *What has she done to me? Am I going back in time?*

"Wait!" I cry, fading fast. I suddenly realize I've forgotten the most important question of all. "If I do get the Grail, how do I get back?"

I black out before she can answer.

Chapter Two

When I open my eyes, I realize I'm lying flat on my back in the middle of a dense forest. For a moment I don't move, staring up at the tall oak trees, whose leafy green branches provide a tattered canopy from the bright sunshine. Could make a pretty photo.

Then I remember what happened, and sit up with a start. The King Arthur's Faire. The gypsy. The command to go back in time to find the Grail. The quest to rescue Kat Jones, who for some inexplicable reason is supposedly stuck a thousand years in the future.

At this moment, major freak-outage takes hold and my heart starts pounding way too fast against my ribcage. I take a deep breath and concentrate on the breathing exercises I learned in yoga to steady my pulse. Panic-induced heart attacks, however justified, are not going to help me at this juncture.

I scramble to my feet and take stock of my surroundings. Where am I? Have I really been sent back in time? Or did I only pass out and get dumped in an area that's supposed to represent Sherwood Forest in my reality TV nightmare? Either scenario seems far-fetched, but they're all my frazzled brain can come up with on short notice. Of course, since there's nothing but trees as far as my eyes can see, I don't have much to go on. My only options appear to be two footpaths headed in opposite directions.

If I'd known this morning I'd have to go back in time to save a girl I don't even like, I'd definitely have worn better shoes. These satin slippers may scream medieval maiden, but they aren't exactly forest friendly. Neither is this stupid medieval dress, for that matter. I unlace the corset and let it fall to the ground. It's way too hard to breathe with that thing crushing my ribs. Then I pull the gown over my head to reveal my much more practical yoga Capri pants and long thermal undershirt. Thank God I decided to wear real clothes under my costume.

I roll up the gown and corset and set them behind a tree—too bulky to walk around in, I'll have to come back for them later. I scan the area. Now that I'm properly outfitted for traveling, which way should I go? I scratch my head. I guess since I'm supposed to be looking for King Richard, I should try to find a castle. That, at least, seems obvious. But where the heck do I even begin?

Man, Danny's portable GPS system sure would come in handy right about now. So would Danny himself, for that matter. He's so good with all these nature things—and at taking control when life goes all crazy.

Oh, why did I have go start thinking about Danny?

As always happens when my thoughts wander into the "closed for construction" part of my brain, tears start to threaten. No matter how much I try not to care, I always end up a total basket case when I think about my soon-to-be-ex husband. I always start missing the bastard with a vengeance.

I swallow hard and tell myself to stop being such a dumbass. After all, he betrayed me. The only man I ever loved. My high school sweetheart. The one I gave up my virginity to in the back of his mother's station wagon. The one who ditched me like a bad habit after seven years of marriage for a slut with big boobs. I hate him. And I have to keep hating him if I want to respect myself in the morning.

Forcing thoughts of Danny from my mind, I try to replace the void by drawing on lessons I learned at Camp Fireside back in elementary school days. Which side of the tree did they say moss grew on again?

Then I realize sadly that it doesn't matter. Knowing which way is north doesn't make a bit of difference when you have no idea if your objective is north, south, east or west from your current position.

The whole scenario strikes me as rather unorganized. I mean, if I were going to send a girl back in time, I'd definitely have done a better job prepping her beforehand. "Go find the Holy Grail" isn't exactly a step-by-step procedural, now is it? Not to mention I have no idea how I'm going to get back if/when I find the thing. That in itself is more than a bit frightening.

Of course, this is all if indeed I really *am* back in

time to begin with. It's much more likely that this whole scenario is part of some freakish reality show. One of the more out-there ones, to be sure. It's probably airing on Fox.

"Long live Hillary Clinton!" I cry, hoping to flush one of the Fox News producers out of hiding.

Nothing. Complete silence. Maybe it's airing on Bravo.

I look up and down the path. Should I go left or right? I kind of feel like Jennifer Connelly's character in that movie *Labyrinth*, when she's trying to get to the Goblin King's castle, except in my adventure there's no cockney-accented Muppet worm to ask for directions.

Okay, Chrissie, enough with the pop culture references. Decision time. Pick a path.

Hmm. Well, I know Robert Frost would prefer the one less traveled, but most likely he had on better shoes. I have no interest in twisting my ankle on an uprooted tree stump, so I make the executive decision to go the wide grassy path instead. Besides, with great respect to Mr. Frost, in my opinion it's much more likely that wide grassy paths lead to castles, even if they don't make all the difference.

I saunter down the path, constantly on the lookout for TV cameras. If this is a reality show, the producers really need to up the drama factor. I mean, walking down a path—how boring can you get? And since it appears I'm the only castaway in shouting distance, how does one get voted off the island?

The further down the trail I go, the more worried I

become. Reality shows don't usually hide the cameras, do they? In fact, I bet that could lead to some kind of lawsuit.

"I don't consent to be videotaped!" I cry. "So you're wasting your time filming me."

No answer. Only the whistling wind through the oak trees, creeping me out. I swallow hard and force myself to keep moving. At this point, that's all I can do.

The trees thin and I come to a rushing river. While it's not that wide, it appears pretty deep and the current seems strong. From the looks of it, there used to be a crude wooden bridge, but it's been destroyed. Wonderful. Luck is *so* not being a lady to me tonight. The wide, grassy path continues on the other side, mocking me from a distance.

Against my better judgment, I decide to leave the path and head upriver, searching for another way across. The underbrush thickens and bramble bushes scrape at my skin as I weed-whack through. *Oh, my kingdom for some bug spray.* I'm getting eaten alive by midges. I'm going to look like Colleen on *Survivor* by the end of this ordeal.

Several yards away, I come to an enormously wide log lying lengthways across the river. Saved! But before I can rejoice in my fortune and make the journey to the other side, a male voice stops me dead in my tracks.

"Who dares cross my bridge?" it calls out in a strong English accent.

For some reason all I can think of is that story about the Billy Goats Gruff trying to cross the bridge

owned by the evil troll. Problem is, I can't remember
how the whole thing played out, so I have no way to
apply fairy-tale wisdom to my current situation.
Which, now that I think about it, is probably not a
bad thing.

Before I can answer, a man leaps from the bushes
on the other side of the river and nimbly hops onto
the log bridge. My eyes widen as I stare in disbelief.
The man is dressed almost entirely in green. Green
tunic, belted and hanging to mid thigh. Tight leather
leggings. A green cap with a green feather. He's carrying a long wooden pole in his hands and has another
strapped to his back.

Let me tell you, he's certainly no troll. With thick
chestnut-colored hair pulled back in a ponytail and a
strong, chiseled jaw, he's quite possibly the most stunning man I've ever laid eyes on. And as a fashion photographer, I've checked out more than my share of
male models. The man is ripped under his costume,
and I can clearly see his impressive thigh muscles under his tights.

Could it be . . . ? No, that's crazy. There's no way
this man could be who I'm thinking he is. Could
there? Of course, if I'm here to hang with King
Richard, then I am in the right time period, but
still . . . what are the chances I've stumbled upon the
legendary Robin Hood in the flesh? Maybe Kat's wild
talk of hanging around with Lancelot and Guenevere
wasn't so crazy after all. . . .

"Um," I say, not knowing how to begin. "I think I'm
lost. Is there a castle around here by any chance?"

The man nods. "Castle? Aye, of course. 'Tis not a

quarter day's walk down yonder path, on the far side of this river."

"Oh. Okay." I pause, assuming he'll step out of the way and let me across. But he simply stands there, studying me with cool eyes. "Um, do you mind if I cross over this log then?" I add at last, realizing he's not going to move.

"I'm afraid 'tis impossible," the man says, a solemn look on his face. "Unless you are willing to pay the tax."

I raise an eyebrow. "You've imposed a tax on a log? Jeez. Where are we, Sherwood Forest, Massachusetts?"

He frowns. "My good sir, if you refuse to pay, then I am afraid I must challenge you to a match of skill."

A match of . . . ? Hold on a sec. Sir? Did he just call me *sir*? He thinks I'm a guy? Man! I mean, I know I'm flat-chested and built like a boy and all, but give me a freaking break! Does he not notice my ponytail of red curly hair? Then again, he has long hair too, so I guess that doesn't mean much. Sigh. And I do have on pants. If he's really from the twelfth century, or pretending to be, he may think girls all dress in satin gowns and stuff.

I consider using defensive tactic number one—my feminine charm—to win an instant victory . . . then quickly reconsider. Let's say for a moment that I'm really (gulp!) back in time. Who knows what this man could do to me if he finds out I'm a girl? After everything that's already happened today, I'm so not interested in getting ravaged to top it off. Even if the potential ravager is sexy as hell.

"What kind of a match of skill?" I ask, giving in to my curiosity.

He waves the staff he's carrying. " 'Tis simple," he says. "If you are able to knock me off the log with this staff, I will reward you with the right of passage, along with my utmost respect. If you cannot, I dare say, my fine sir, you are likely to get rather wet."

He wants to have a staff duel? He's got to be kidding!

"Come on, man," I plead. "Can't you just let me cross?"

He shakes his head and I notice a smile playing at the corner of his mouth. He's toying with me. He thinks he'll easily knock me off the log. I can feel my hackles rise to the challenge. What he doesn't know is that I used to be a champion gymnast in high school. And I'm pretty nimble on narrow surfaces like that log. Maybe I have a chance to take him. And I *do* need to cross the river. . . .

"All right, I accept your challenge," I say. "Give me your staff."

Heh heh, the Beavis and Butthead voices in my head chuckle. *She wants his staff.*

The man tosses the long piece of wood at me, and I almost fall backwards under its weight. It's a little heavier than I'd thought. And with this guy outweighing me by about seventy pounds he definitely has the advantage. But I'm determined not to let him get the best of me. After all, this could very likely be the first challenge in the reality show. And if I *am* stuck on a reality show, I'm so not going to suffer the embarrassment of being kicked off on the first day.

I nimbly hop onto the log, all my gymnastic training coming back to me. Mr. I-Challenge-You looks surprised as I twirl my staff and move toward him as best I can. Then he smiles wickedly, as if looking forward to the fight, and pulls out the second staff that was strapped to his back. He swings it back and forth with ease, looking pretty darn comfortable navigating the log's width himself. Suddenly I feel more than a little nervous. Now that I think about it, I've always been way too brave for my own good.

Oh well, too late now.

The man darts forward and I thrust my staff in front of my face to block his charge. Then I swing at him and he deftly parries.

Hey, I'm pretty good at this!

He swings again, and I imagine he's Darth Vader and I, the brave Luke Skywalker, must resist turning to the Dark Side. I block him, then dance forward two steps and swing again. He deflects my pole and follows up with a swing so hard I nearly lose my balance. Summoning all my gymnastics training, I take a few steps back to center myself.

I realize if I'm going to beat this guy, I'll need to use some unconventional methodology. He's way too good with his staff, and too strong. I'll have to use my brains to combat his brawn. As he waits, urging me on with a smirk, I formulate a plan and take action.

I toss my stick to the side and leap into a cartwheel, just like I used to do on the balance beam during gymnastics meets. The moment my feet touch the log, I swing them backward, launching into a backhandspring. I haven't done this move for a few years and my muscles strain in protest.

But it's worth it. My feet smack into flesh as I make contact and I hear him cry out as he loses his balance. Next thing I feel is a splash as he falls into the water, followed by piercing pain as my feet miss the log and I slam chest first into the wood. The wind knocked out of me, I grip the log with all my might to keep from falling off.

Woohoo! I won!

Once I've regained my balance and breath, I look around, watching and waiting for the reality TV EMTs to pop out of the bushes and rescue my vanquished foe. I wonder what luxury item I'll get for this challenge. Bug spray or a pillow would be nice.

Um, why isn't anyone coming to rescue him?

I watch, growing concerned as the man thrashes around in the raging river, helplessly dragged down by the current. My heart leaps into my throat. I didn't want the poor guy dead! What if he can't swim? What if he hit his head and is unconscious?

What if I really am back in time and I just murdered Robin Hood?

Without giving common sense the time of day, I dive off the log and into the river, paddling as fast as I can with the weight of my clothes dragging me down, trying to catch up with him. In the distance, I can see his head bobbing up and then disappearing into the foamy waters.

As I finally reach him I grab him from behind, my arm wrapping around his solid chest as I've seen them do on *Baywatch*. I start the struggle to pull him to shore, which isn't an easy task by any means. My slippered feet find it nearly impossible to get a grip on the slick river rocks, so I kick them off and attempt to gain purchase barefoot.

Midway there, Robin, or whoever he is, regains his senses, turns around and grabs me. I scream, struggling to get away. Is he trying to drown me? Then I realize he's laughing.

"By God, you fight like a tiger, boy," he says, as he plants his feet on the river floor. I realize then that he's tall enough to effortlessly walk to shore. And here I thought I was saving his life. D'oh.

"I kicked your ass, didn't I?" I say grouchily as he proceeds to dump me unceremoniously on the riverbank. At least I'm on the other side. Soaking wet and in major pain, but on the other side.

He grins and looks down at his privates, which I can't help but notice stand out rather prominently beneath his soaking wet tunic and leggings. Has he stuffed a sock in there or what? "I wish you had. 'Twould have hurt a lot less."

My face heats as I realize exactly where my backhandspring kick made contact. But still, he asked for it. Trying to tax a log? Puh-leeze.

"What is your name, boy?" he asks, wringing out his tunic.

Hmm. He still thinks I'm male. Okay. Distressing, yes. But probably a good thing. Especially since I'm getting the sneaking suspicion that, like it or not, realistic or not, insanely crazy or not, I've somehow been sent back in time.

I'm going to kill Kat if I ever see her again.

I realize the man's waiting for an answer. "Uh, Chriss . . . tian," I tell him, making it up on the fly.

27

Christian is a close enough boyish equivalent to Chrissie, so I'm sure I'll have no trouble answering to it. "Christian Hayward. What's yours?"

"Why do you want to know?"

I frown. What's with the secrecy here? "Er, I don't know. You asked me mine. Just trying to keep up ye olde conversation."

The man pauses for a moment, then says, "You may call me Robin." He pauses and, as if measuring my reaction, adds: "Of Locksley."

My eyes widen. Robin of Locksley? Could it really be? Could the man I just bested in this fight actually be the legendary Robin Hood, for real? I mean, we're in the right time period. He's dressed all in green. And heck, how many guys besides Batman's friend go by the name Robin?

Should I ask him if he's who I think he is? Or will that totally freak him out? After all, he is an outlaw. Probably has to keep his true identity on the down-low. I'd want to as well if I were a regular on the medieval version of *America's Most Wanted*. Yes, best not to push him.

I take a moment to study him closer. He's certainly as handsome as I imagined Robin Hood to be. Much better-looking than Kevin Costner, though that's not saying much. And what do you know, he actually speaks with a British accent (unlike Mr. Costner).

"Look, Robin of *Locksley*," I continue, emphasizing the Locksley part. "I need to find King Richard. You got any idea where he is?"

Robin's eyes darken and the laughter fades from

his face, replaced by a scowl. "Do you mock me, lad?" he asks.

Huh? "Uh, no," I say carefully. I certainly hadn't been expecting *that* reaction. "I really need to talk to the guy. Can you direct me to his castle?"

"To his castle, aye," Robin says with a sigh. "I could direct ye. 'Tis not far off, in fact. But you will scarce have luck in finding His Majesty, the King of England, behind its walls."

"What, is he on vacation or something?" That'd totally be my luck.

"Nay. He is lost. Gone a year too long from the crusades in the east. He left to fight in the Holy War, taking with him England's finest men, and has ne'er been heard from again."

Oh, that's just freaking great. Nimue sent me back in time to the wrong year? I mean, we all know that King Richard shows up eventually. Comes back and boots the sniveling—and thumb-sucking in the Disney version—Prince John from his throne. But how close am I now to that time? Does this mean I'm stuck here until the King shows up? That completely blows. I mean, I can't be hanging out in the Middle Ages for the next year. I have things to do. Anorexic models to photograph. A cheating husband to divorce. An apartment to get evicted from.

Okay, maybe it wouldn't be *so* terrible to spend a few months away from my present-day hell. I hope Kat's cool with being stuck in the future a bit longer. . . .

In any case, what am I supposed to do now? Go to

the castle and hang out there, wait for the King to come home? That seems potentially on the dull side. I mean, if I've really traveled back in time, I should go exploring, have adventures, right? Maybe take some photos. I wonder how much photos of the real-life Robin Hood would fetch on eBay? Oh shoot, I left my camera on the other side of the river. Have to remember to go get that.

I turn my attention back to Robin. "If you seek an audience with Prince John," he is saying, "I will gladly direct you to the castle. But I cannot offer you escort to its gates. You see, I am an outlawed man and less than welcomed." He laughs, a bit bitterly. "Well, my head would be welcome, forsooth, but I cannot guarantee 'twould stay attached to my body come sunup."

"I guess there's no reason to go to the castle if the King isn't there," I tell him, making up my mind. "How about I come hang with you in Sherwood Forest instead? Meet your merry men and all that jazz." After all, how many chances does one get to chill with a living legend? Like I said, if I'm stuck back in time, I'm going to take full advantage. I could even write a Robin Hood biography when I got back to the 21st century. Get a book deal. Retire.

Robin's face darkens. "How do you know about my men?"

Oh, good one Chrissie. He hasn't mentioned his men yet. "Uh, well, I just assumed, I guess. Though, I suppose we all know what assuming does. Makes an ass out of you and—"

"Who are you?" the outlaw demands, rising to his feet. "Did the Sheriff send you to spy on us?"

"What? No!" I cry, completely taken aback. "Of course not! I'm one of the good guys. And totally for the good old 'rob from the rich, give to the poor' concept. After all, I'm a Democrat."

"Rob from the rich?" Robin repeats, looking completely confused.

"Yeah, you know," I say, scrambling to my feet. "The whole Robin Hood legend thing."

"Lad, I tell you true, I know not of what you speak. Nor am I familiar with the name Robin Hood."

I raise an eyebrow. "You mean to tell me you don't steal from rich people and give the money to the poor?" Did I get it wrong? Is he not the infamous outlaw after all?

No, he has to be. He's Robin of Locksley. He's wearing green, he lives in Sherwood Forest, he has merry men. I've got to be right. Maybe he just doesn't want to admit it in front of me. He does suspect I work for the Sheriff, after all.

"We are not thieves, no matter what the Sheriff might brand us. We forage from the land and keep to ourselves in the forest," Robin insists.

"Okay. My bad. Never mind then."

He fixes me with a stare. "But you have not answered my question. Who are you and from whence do you hail? You dress strangely and speak with the oddest tongue."

Hm. How am I supposed to answer this one? And should I tell him I'm actually a girl? I mean, it would be easier to come clean about my rightful sex. Then again, I know nothing about this guy except that I think he might be Robin Hood. What if I'm wrong and he's really Robin the Rapist or something? That would be bad, to say the least. Better to hide the truth a bit longer, I think.

"I come from a kingdom far, far away," I say at last. "The kingdom of . . . Hoboken. English is not my first language, which is why I speak it so badly." There, that ought to explain the American accent and improper Ye Olde English terms and phrases. I just have to hope he doesn't ask me to speak my native tongue or it'll be a lot of *Leasepay ontday askay emay nymoray estionsquay.*

"And how did you find yourself in the forest Sherwood?" he asks. *Phew.*

"I um, ran away. From . . . the church." The church was pretty powerful back then, right? They'd be someone you ran from. I still run from the ones in the airport. "They wanted to make me an altar boy. Er, I mean, a choir boy. They—"

"Made you a eunuch?" Robin gasps.

Ewww. Isn't that a guy who got his you-know-whats cut off? What makes him think I'm one of those? As I remain silent, Robin adds thoughtfully, "A choir boy. I thought perhaps you were actually a woman. You stand tall as a man, yet have no hint of a beard. Your voice is fair sweet . . ."

I decide to run with his suggestion. "Ha, ha, ha!" I slap my knee in hysterics over his ridiculous statement. "Me? A woman? That's a good one. How could anyone think I'm a woman? Ha, ha, ha!" I hawk a loogie into the river and let out a loud belch. "Nope,

I'm about as manly as they come. Well, as manly as anyone who got his balls cut off by the church." I fake a dispirited look.

Robin pats me on the back. "Indeed you are, lad, I meant no insult."

Suddenly a scream cuts through the forest. Robin's body tenses and he motions silently toward the bushes. We dive in and take shelter underneath the thick overgrowth. I can hear my heart pounding as fast and heavy as the horses' galloping hooves. What now?

Suddenly a young boy dashes past us, stopping at the riverbank. He can't be more than ten years old, barefoot and dressed in gray rags, with a shock of blond hair atop his head. He looks a little like Macaulay Culkin from the *Home Alone* era. Strapped to his back is a crude bow and arrow. His eyes are wide and frightened as he realizes he's trapped.

The horses show up next. Coal-black steeds, three in all, that remind me of Black Beauty. Atop the horses are soldiers, each dressed in chain mail with a scary-looking sword strapped to his waist.

One of the soldiers, the biggest and ugliest—think Tom Arnold on steroids—urges his horse forward. He draws his sword and points it at the boy's throat. "It seems the hounds have snared this hart," he says with an evil-sounding chuckle. The other two men laugh appreciatively at what I guess they consider a joke. I glance at Robin. He puts a finger to his lips, warning me to be silent.

"Now answer me, boy," the soldier continues. "Did ye or did ye not kill the king's deer?"

"I was starving, sire," the boy protests in an adorable little English accent. Like the kid in Oliver Twist. Or Tiny Tim without the crutches. "We all are. I dunna mind going without, but me sister is sick. She needs food and we 'aven't any."

Well, I'll be darned. I totally remember this scene from the Robin Hood stories. They try to cut off the kid's hand and then Robin comes dashing in to save him. I glance over at the outlaw, grinning in anticipation. Adventure number one, coming right up. I can't wait to see this.

"Do ye know the price of your trespass?" one of the other guards asks. His mouth twists in a sinister smile. "By order of the Sheriff of Nottingham, thieves like you are to have their hands severed from their arms. 'Twill prove rather difficult to shoot a deer with one hand, will it not?"

Yup. Just as I remembered it. How very cool to be living a legend. I can't wait to see Robin swoop in to save the kid's day. This back-in-time stuff is almost better than Must See TV.

Go for it! I mouth.

"Please. I beg you!" the boy sobs. He falls to his knees, hands clasped together, pleading for mercy.

The soldier with the sword looks impatient. "Hold out your hand, boy, or I will run you through."

"Aye. Be quick about it. We've wasted enough time already."

Seeming to gain some resolve, the little boy bravely rises to his feet, sticking out his hand, palm up, with unmasked defiance on his face. The soldier chuckles and turns to his friends.

Um, okay, Robin. Any time now would be good.

"Who would like the honor?" the man asks.

I look back at Robin, who for some reason doesn't seem to be rearing into action. "Aren't you going to do something?" I hiss.

Robin gives me another stare of disbelief. "Risk my life to save the hand of a peasant boy?"

I stare at him for a moment, not sure I heard right. Could Robin Hood actually be refusing to help the helpless? In order to save his own neck?

"So, let me get this straight," I whisper back. "You not only don't do the whole 'rob from the rich, give to the poor' thing, but you're refusing to help this helpless kid?"

He shrugs. "He will surely live with one hand. If they catch me, 'twould be my head they sever from my body."

"Oh, you're pathetic!" I can't believe how lame the real Robin Hood has turned out to be. "Well, screw you. If you won't do something, I will."

I search the ground and find a good-sized stone. I wrap my hands around it and, just as the soldier starts his blade's descent, I huck the stone as hard as I can. It slams into the man's horse's flank, and the beast bucks in surprise and pain, dismounting his rider.

The other two guards stare in the direction of my throw.

Damn. I don't think I quite thought this through.

"Nice," Robin says, with more than a hint of sarcasm. He grabs my hand, drags me to a standing position, and motions for me to start running. "Congratulations. Now you're an outlaw like the rest of us."

Chapter Three

Way to go, Chrissie. Real smooth.

We race through the forest, dodging trees and diving into bushes. Brambles scrape my face, my arms, and rocks stab into my bare feet, but I can barely feel them, I'm so scared. It's like I'm living *The Blair Witch Project* or something. I can hear the soldiers' cries as they attempt to follow. Luckily the underbrush is so thick in this part of the forest, where Robin leads, the horses seem to be having a hard time navigating through it. Otherwise we'd be so dead right now.

"This way," Robin says, grabbing my arm. Maybe it's due to my frazzled emotions or the lack of breath in my lungs, but his fingertips burn my skin and the whole thing suddenly seems oddly romantic. Not that he intends the gesture that way, I suppose, seeing as he thinks I'm a guy. I mean, I can accept the fact that the legendary outlaw hasn't lived up to all my expectations so far, but I'm still pretty positive he's hetero.

We take a sharp left and then Robin stops short. He glances from side to side, searching for something, then his eyes light up and he pulls back some hanging vines. Behind them lies a dark, tiny cave cut into the hillside, not even big enough to stand up in.

"Get in," he instructs.

I stare at him, wide-eyed. "I can't go in there. I'm claustrophobic."

"They will kill you if you do not." He shrugs, as if my state of existence doesn't mean jack to him. Which it probably doesn't, now that I think about it. In all honesty, I've ruined the guy's peaceful morning and forced him to run for his life. Yeah, he's psyched to have me around, I'm sure.

"Fine." I stomp into the cave, realizing I'm acting as spoiled as a five-year-old who's been denied Wedding Dress Barbie. The only reason we're here is because of my foolish heroics. And, like the method or not, Robin *is* trying to save my life.

He ducks in behind me and pulls the vines down over the entrance. We're now stuck in a damp darkness that clings to my bones and twists my stomach into knots. I try to steady my breath with those yoga breathing exercises again as the blackness seems to close in.

I can feel Robin squashed beside me, breathing hard, and for some reason this makes me feel a little better. He shuffles to crouch in a more comfortable position and his leg brushes against mine. Again, his touch sends electric sparks up into me and I suppress a shiver. Just great. The first guy I'm attracted to after my cheating husband is a legendary outlaw from the

12th century who thinks I'm a guy. I sure know how to pick them.

"Which way did they go?" The soldiers' cries get louder as they grow nearer. My heart pounds triple-time as I realize they're now right outside the clearing. I can see their horses' hooves stamping from behind the vines. I swallow hard, fear of caves replaced by a much more rational fear of evil medieval men-at-arms with big scary swords.

"This way, I think," says one of the soldiers, who sounds a bit further off than the others. "I see some trampled branches."

"Excellent." The first soldier urges his horse on and gallops away, leaving Robin and me to squat in silent relief.

"We stay here a bit longer," he whispers. "To be sure they do not come back around."

For a brief moment, I feel exhilarated by our daring escape and don't even mind staying crouched in cramped darkness with a sexy outlaw for a few more minutes. Then I have to pee. The situation seems a lot less comfy-cozy.

I suppress my bladder's urges as long as possible before speaking. "Um, Rob? You think the coast is clear? 'Cause I got to pee like a racehorse."

He laughs softly. "You speak with the strangest tongue, lad." He pats my knee. "I will check. Stay here." He crawls out of the cave, giving me a good view of his muscular backside. I know I shouldn't be staring, but trust me, if you saw a butt like this guy's you'd stare too.

"Are we good?" I ask, crossing my fingers for an affirmative answer. There's no way I'll be able to hold out much longer.

"Aye," he says.

Grateful, I pop out of the cave and dive into the bushes to pee. I wonder if eunuchs usually pee standing up or sitting down. I would assume still standing up, right?

I glance back at Robin. He's got his back respectably turned, so I decide to squat. I grab random leaves to wipe, praying that none of them are medieval species of poison ivy. I'm deathly allergic to the stuff and there's no cortisone here to bring down the swelling.

When finished, I approach Robin.

"So you think we're safe?" I ask.

He shrugs. "For now." He paces a few steps, then turns to look at me. "You have put yourself in danger, boy. If either of those guards remembers your face, they will put a price on your head and declare you an outlaw."

Oh, great. First day in medieval times and I've managed to get myself on a Most Wanted poster. Nice one, Chris.

"But I couldn't just sit there and let them cut off his hand!" I say.

Robin's face softens. "Aye. Forsooth, 'twas a selfless deed." He places a hand on my shoulder. "You are a brave lad."

"Thanks," I say, feeling my face heat at his compliment. Or maybe at his touch—it's hard to tell at this point. I wonder if now's a good time to reveal my inner female.

"Well, fellow outlaw, will you join us for supper?" Robin asks. "I could introduce you to my men."

Ooh. An invite to hang with the Merry Men. Now we're talking.

"Sure," I say. "I'd be up for that."

I decide to skip telling him I'm a chick. At least for now. He might get all protective and want to drop me off at a village where I'll be safe. After all, in these days, women were seen as fragile, delicate flowers not suited for cavorting with outlaws. If I have to be stuck in the 12th century until King Richard returns from his crusades, I at least want to live more of the legend before I'm relegated to some medieval kitchen.

Argh. My feet kill. I would give absolutely anything right now, even my rent-stabilized apartment, for a pair of Nikes. You won't ever know the pain of walking barefoot through a dense English forest for miles on end, but to give you an idea, it's worse than walking the length of Manhattan in two-sizes-too-small stilettos. Really. I've done both now, so I know.

"Who goes there?"

I jump back with a start as a man leaps from the bushes, bow and arrow drawn. Robin only laughs.

"A bit jumpy are you, Much?" he asks.

The man lowers his bow and flashes a toothy grin. He's tall and scrawny, with wild blond hair that sticks up in tufts. He wears a gray hooded cloak over a battered leather tunic and trousers.

"Well, Robin, you canna be too careful," Much

40

says. "The sheriff's men have been in the forest all day—searching for some poor bastard who avoided his taxes, I wager."

Robin gives me a pointed look. "Much, I'd like you to meet Christian," he says, motioning to me. "Our guest for supper. We shall be roasting one of His Majesty's deer in his honor. If you care to join us, you would be most welcome at our table."

Much's eyes light up as my heart sinks. Is this a good time to tell them I'm vegetarian? Or that I watched Bambi fifty-four times as a kid and have no desire to leave some poor fawn to face the winter without his mother?

"Well met, Christian," Much says to me, bobbing up and down in a sort of half bow, half curtsey.

"Well met," I repeat, deciding to keep quiet about the impending Bambi massacre. My situation is precarious here, and I don't want to appear ungrateful. I won't go as far as actually eating the deer, though; I don't want my PETA membership revoked.

"We must be off," Robin says. "If we are to reach the lair by nightfall."

"Hold on a second. Aren't we almost there?" I ask, peering up at the sun, which is still quite high in the sky.

Robin shakes his head. "Nay, we have some distance still."

Oh, man. More walking. I don't know if my feet can handle it. I lift my right leg and peer at the sole of my foot. It's black and bleeding. Lovely.

Robin catches my examination and to my surprise pulls off his own leather boots. "Might be a bit large for you," he says, handing them to me. "But they are all I have with me. When we arrive at camp, I will find you some proper footwear."

"But what are you going to wear?" I ask, trying to be fair even though I desperately want those shoes.

He shrugs. "My feet are tough and used to walking." He holds out the shoes and I take them with immense relief.

"Thank you so much." I crouch down to put them on my aching feet. They're almost four sizes too big and have no Dr. Scholl's shock-absorbing gel inserts, but they're a great improvement over my barefoot status. I can't believe the guy's literally given me the shoes off his feet. Danny would never even give me half the blankets in bed on a cold winter's night.

Much waves good-bye as Robin and I continue our journey. "I will send an arrow to announce yer arrival to the men," he says in an eager-to-please-the-boss voice. Then he tilts his bow skyward and affixes an arrow with some sort of circular barrel attached to its tip. I stop to watch, intrigued. He sends the arrow skyward and it makes a whistling noise that echoes through the forest. So that's what people did before Nextels. Far less annoying, for sure. *Can you hear my arrow now?*

Robin nods to Much, then pulls a long white rag from his sack and turns to me. "I am afraid I must blindfold you for the remainder of the journey," he says apologetically. "We cannot have strangers knowing the way to our hideout."

"You think you're going to put *that* over my eyes?" I say, staring at the nasty, stained piece of cloth. Ewh.

I take back all my "isn't he nice to give me shoes" thoughts.

Robin laughs. " 'Twill not kill you."

Maybe not, but I can only imagine the potential zit factor. I mean, who wore this before me? So help me if I get a sty. But I sigh and give in. After all, I don't have a lot of alternatives at this point.

Robin moves behind me and places the rag around my head, tying it in the back. I can feel his breath on the back of my neck as he concentrates on the knot. Instant goose bumps.

Why the heck am I so damned attracted to this guy? Is it simply the bad-boy factor? He's an infamous outlaw, after all. Or maybe it's my practically single status. I can't exactly remember the last time Danny and I made love. He'd come home saying he was too tired and I, the good wife, had bought it and gone without. I hadn't realized the fatigue came from banging Wanda Waitress, or I'd have gone out and gotten tired myself.

With my vision now completely obscured by the nasty and probably unsanitary rag, Robin takes hold of my elbow and leads me down the path. It reminds me of those old team-building games they used to make you play at work. Where you had to trust the other person. Being blindly led by a practical stranger who every once in a while whispers for me to step up, step down, veer left or right. It feels rather intimate, actually.

After about a half hour it's no longer intimate or sexy or fun. In fact, it sucks. His camp or lair or whatever he calls it is evidently in the East Bumfuck zone of Sherwood Forest. Either that or he's taking me the long way round to make sure I really have no clue where the place is.

"Are we there yet?" I ask.

"Almost."

I'm relieved at that until I realize, five minutes later, we're still walking. What's his definition of almost, anyhow? Almost, a few more paces? Or almost, just a mile or two more down the path?

"Are we there yet?" I can't help but ask again. I know, I know. I sound like Donkey in *Shrek 2* when they're traveling to the kingdom of Far, Far Away.

I can hear his exasperated sigh. "Almost."

But still we walk. And walk. And walk. You know, when I said I wanted to swing by and check out his camp, I had no idea it'd be located in another time zone.

"Are we there ye—?"

He huffs, stops walking, and whips off my blindfold. I blink a few times as my eyes adjust to my surroundings. "Are we here?" I ask, looking around. If we are, it's not much of a camp. In fact, it doesn't look like any camp at all. Just a bunch of trees.

"I . . ." Robin turns around, shielding his eyes as he looks to his left and then right. "I think I might have taken a wrong turn somewhere."

"What?" I cry. "You mean we're lost?"

"Nay!" he retorts. "We are not lost."

Oh, no. Of course we're not lost. No man on the planet, medieval or modern, would ever admit he doesn't have the slightest clue where we were.

"Look, there's a hut over there." I point to a building in the distance. "Why don't we ask them where we are?"

"Nay, I will not."

I don't know why I even bothered suggesting it. Of course he's going to refuse to ask for directions.

"Oh, quit being such a baby," I chide, making strides to the small dwelling. "We'll just ask them approximately where we are. Get your bearings. Then you can play woodsman again."

He doesn't answer, but falls into step behind me. I guess that's something. Men are so damn stubborn sometimes. Okay, most of the time.

We reach the cottage and I lift a hand to knock on the door. Calling it a cottage is being kind, by the way. It's made of rotted logs and features big gaping slats caked with crumbling mud and a thatched roof which seems a total fire hazard. Does someone really live here?

"Go away!" cries a raspy female voice from inside. "I already paid me tithe."

I glance over at Robin, who shrugs back.

"Ma'am, we aren't tax collectors," I say. "We're travelers and we're lost. We were hoping you could help us figure out where we are."

The door opens a crack and I can see an eyeball. A woman glances outside. "Yer not with the sheriff?" the voice asks, still suspicious.

"Hell no!" I say. "His men tried to kill me earlier today. I can't stand the guy."

The door swings open, revealing an extremely pregnant woman dressed in gray rags. Two little barefoot rugrats cling to her legs.

"I beg yer pardon," she says, and she motions us inside. "But as ye know, these are desperate times."

"Aye," says Robin. "They are indeed."

Easy for him to say, I think, as we walk into the hut. He's going to be chowing down on roast deer tonight. Selfish jerk.

The hut's interior is depressing, to say the least. It's tiny, for one thing. Way too tiny for a woman and two kids. The floor's made of dirt and there's a straw pallet in one corner with a few ratty blankets on top. Is that where they sleep? A large earthen pot sits atop a smoky, smoldering fire. Church mice would feel well-off if they saw this woman.

I feel so bad for her. Talk about extreme poverty! I mean, I thought *I* had it hard when they shut off our cable after Danny was laid off and we couldn't pay the bill. I can't imagine living in this squalor. And worse, having *children* live in this squalor.

As Robin asks the peasant woman for details on where we are in the forest, I feel a tugging on my leg. I crouch down to eye level of the dirty but sweet-faced little girl in front of me.

"D'you have any food?" she says, sticking a grimy index finger in her mouth. I wish I had found time to retrieve my camera bag from the other side of the river before running for our lives. I know I had some sanitary wipes in there. That and granola bars. "I'm hungry."

Poor kid. My heart aches for her. If the others in Nottingham are half as bad off as this family . . . How could the Prince allow this to happen? How can he sit in his castle, enjoying his jewels and servants and fine dinners while these children die of starvation?

I can see why Robin Hood felt it so important to re-distribute the wealth in this godforsaken place. Well, the Robin Hood of legends, anyhow. The real life Robin seems much more interested in getting back to his camp so he can fry up a nice fat deer and pig out. I decide that if we're anywhere near his camp now, I'll sneak out and determine a way to return to this hut with my portion of meat.

"Hang in there, sweetie," I say, kissing the little girl on her forehead. "I'll try to bring you some food."

That's it!

Inspiration strikes as I rise from my stooped position. That's how I'll spend my time in Sherwood Forest while I'm waiting for the King to return. If Robin's not up to the task, fine. I can organize a little robbing from the rich and giving to the poor myself. Maybe I can even recruit some of the less selfish merry men to help me.

I can see it now: Chrissie Hayward, Princess of Thieves.

I kind of like the sound of that.

Chapter Four

The blindfold goes back on as soon as we leave the vicinity of the hut. I try to protest, saying if *he* doesn't even know where we are, how the heck does he expect me to? But I might as well be trying to talk to a Patriots fan on Superbowl Sunday while Brady has the ball for all the attention I get.

"If I were to lead you to my lair without a cloth 'round your eyes, my men will think I've gone soft," Robin explains, sounding almost apologetic. "And power is such a tricky lass—to be kept under a tight lead. Should I show weakness, some other man, perhaps, would rise in challenge. And we do not want that, now do we young Christian?"

Okay, fine. I guess he's got a point there. So I let him lead me, praying we won't get lost again and that the camp isn't too far from here. I've only got so many miles left in these shoes. And when I say "so many," I mean less than one. If that.

But luck thankfully has gone from über bitch to a lady once more. Not ten minutes later, Robin lifts the cloth from my eyes.

"Behold," he says, with a gallant sweep of his arm. "My forest home."

I blink my eyes a few times, getting used to the light filtering through the birch trees, then scan the area. It's a small camp. Below me lie dozens of weather-beaten grey tents and dilapidated wooden huts with thatched roofs. Ladders built into the trees lead to crudely built lookout posts above. In the center, a huge stone fire pit boasts a blaze that's currently giving off way more smoke than fire. It's not half as impressive as the Robin Hood secret hideouts I've seen in movies, but hey, the apartment in *Friends* doesn't look much like my East Village place, either. Real life can be depressing like that.

Dozens of men mill about the camp. A few tend the fire, others chop wood at the outskirts. A stablehand feeds oats to a few chestnut-brown mares who stand tied to a tree munching contentedly. At one end of the camp someone's set up some targets and several men are honing their bow and arrow skills. Others are being less productive, sitting around with what appears to be a beer keg, mugs of frothy brew in their hands. That'd be Danny if anyone ever sent him back in time. He'd figure out a way to spend the entire trip drunk as a skunk.

Not that I'm thinking about Danny. After all, I'm back in time a thousand years with a legendary outlaw who thinks I'm a choirboy. Not to mention my mission to find the Holy Grail. That's gonna take a bit of focus, most likely, seeing as it's only the most insurmountable quest in the history of the world. Therefore, all thoughts of ex-husbands, positive or negative, need to, like Elvis, leave the building pronto.

Robin grabs the curved horn that dangles from his leather belt and blows into it. At the deep, almost mournful sound, the men drop what they're doing and direct their attention to the hill where we're standing. Power may be a "tricky lass," but as Mick Jagger says, Robin's currently got them under his thumb.

"We have a visitor," Robin announces to the group—in case, I guess, they assumed the strange person standing next to him was a dear friend they'd forgotten they had. "Young Christian has succeeded in angering the good Sheriff of Nottingham this fine day, and has thus been invited to dinner."

His words spark cheers from the gang. Cheers for me! How cool is that? I pissed off the sheriff and now I'm instantly the It girl (er, boy) with the outlaw contingent.

"Does this mean we eat venison tonight?" calls out one man from the back.

Hm. Then again, maybe they don't give a damn about me and my adventures and are just hungry. Oh well.

Robin chuckles, his green eyes flashing with amusement. He really does have great eyes. Not that I'm staring at them or anything.

"But of course, my good sir," he says. "We'd be ill hosts indeed to have an enemy of the Sheriff of Nottingham dining on berries we foraged from the forest."

Even though in this case she'd *prefer* berries foraged from the forest. Or, I think wistfully, some Franken Berry cereal to munch on. . . .

The camp erupts in excited murmurs—probably arguing who gets the leg meat and who's dining on the vital organs. Robin narrows his eyes, seemingly displeased by the ruckus.

"Did your mothers raise you as Saxons?" he demands, which I'm assuming he means as an insult. The camp falls silent again, the men properly rebuked. "Or would you care to introduce yourselves to our guest?"

I hear a few muttered apologies amidst a few more muttered protests over the Saxon barb. Finally, one man steps forward. And when I say man, I mean a jolly green giant. If he had been born in the 21st century he'd be a linebacker for the Miami Dolphins. He's got to be at least seven feet tall with the broadest shoulders I've ever encountered. He has bushy black hair that's probably never seen a comb, chubby cheeks, and a beard so thick a bird could build a nest in it. He's wearing a belted leather tunic that must have taken the skins of a half dozen deer to fit all the way around his massive circumference.

I smile to myself. That's got to be—

"I am John Little," he says, patting himself on his burly chest with large hands. "Though thanks to Robin here, most now call me Little John."

Aha! I was right. Little John. Robin's right-hand

man. His lieutenant. A big and burly oaf, good-hearted if none too bright. Played by a bear in the Disney cartoon.

"And I am Allan a Dale," says the next man. He's tall and thin, with an almost effeminate face and beaklike nose. He wears a feathered cap and carries some kind of harplike instrument in his delicate hands. He strums a chord before speaking again, the notes decidedly out of tune, though I'm no Jimi Hendrix myself, so I shouldn't judge. "The minstrel who entertains this ragged band of thieves."

And then, out of the blue, he breaks into song:

"Good Christian has come to our lair,
He has not been eaten by a bear.
He angered the good Sheriff of Nottingham
A man that likely has no mum."

Huh. Well, not exactly something Simon Cowell would thumbs-up—actually, I think even sweet Paula Abdul would have a problem with this English Idol wannabe—but I guess I should cut him some slack, seeing as he made it up on the fly.

I clap my hands, all good vibes, and he bows low. "Thank you, sir," he says, and I can see he's blushing a bit. Makes me glad I didn't go with my initial reaction of hands over my ears to stop the pain. But hey, I've sat through worse on open mic night down at EarthMatters.

I wonder if he ever sings songs about what a coward Robin is, like his *Monty Python and the Holy*

Grail counterpart. I could totally give him the 'defeated on the log by a simple gymnastics trick' anecdote if he needs new material.

"I'm—*hiccup*—Friar Tuck," bellows another man, not moving from his spot by the keg. He's short and bald and extremely fat, wearing a long brown robe with a loose tie around his waist. He lifts his mug in way of greeting. "If it's praying ye need, I be yer man."

"If it's beer ye need, more like," Little John quips. The camp breaks out in laughter. At first Friar Tuck looks offended, but then he just laughs and raises his glass to the group and downs a mammoth gulp of ale.

"The Good Lord asks that we enjoy all the fine gifts he has given us," he says after swallowing, "and I always like to do what the Good Lord asks." He sets down the mug on a nearby tree stump and belches loudly.

"If you are quite finished, my dear drunken friar, may I go next?" A richly dressed boy of about eighteen steps into the open. While the others are clothed in mainly gray rags and rugged leather, he wears a scarlet tunic of fine silk. Not so suitable for hiding out in the woods, mind you, it's very expensive-looking.

"Will Scarlet I am," he says gallantly, sweeping off his feathered hat and bowing low. "And 'tis a great honor to make thy acquaintance."

Hm. While I'd never want to make judgments of sexual preference based on someone's dandyish dress—he could very well be a medieval metrosexual, after all—the sly once-over he gives me as he rises

53

from his bow does make me a little curious as to what team the boy's batting for.

Others step forward then, introducing themselves one by one. There are probably fifty merry men all together, though I'm not quite sure "merry" is the appropriate term. Overall, they seem kind of a beaten-down lot. I guess being outlawed and forced to live in the middle of nowhere in 12th-century England will do that to a person. And, thanks to Robin "Slacker" Hood here, they don't have any robbing the rich/feeding the poor distraction to while away the hours.

"Enough loafing around for you all," Robin says, clapping his hands after introductions. "Let us prepare for the feast."

They all spring into action, and soon the camp is crawling with very productive men. It's like a mini factory. Everyone seems to have a job to do. Makes me feel a bit slackerish, myself, and I realize I should pitch in. After all, I'm not some princess who needs to be waited on hand and foot. Not like Kat probably demands, wherever in time she is. I, Chrissie Hayward, can pull my own weight.

"Anything I can do to help?" I ask Robin, wondering what kind of task I'd be good at. Anything, I suppose, except preparing tonight's dinner. Skinning the deer.

"You could skin the deer," Robin replies automatically.

Of course.

My stomach roils at the thought. They really expect me to jump in and start disemboweling without a care in the world? I'm supposed to actually scoop out the bloody innards of an innocent forest creature that was forced to sacrifice his life in celebration of my untimely arrival to 12th-century Britain? Lovely.

"Um, anything else available? I make a mean salad, you know." Actually, my specialty is this amazing vegan Jell-O mold, but I highly doubt that's on the menu tonight.

Robin chuckles. "Too fancy to get your hands dirty, eh lad? Perhaps you'd like to entertain the men with a church hymn instead? Sad truth be told, I think they enjoy bawdier tunes—music I'm sure 'twould offend your delicate ears."

I narrow my eyes. Hmph. I see how it is. He thinks I'm some total wimp. Some church boy who won't be able to survive an outlaw's life. Well, I'll show him.

"I'm not too fancy for anything," I growl. "Pass me the knife and bring on Bambi." Robin shoots me a confused look. "Uh, the deer," I clarify. "The one for dinner. I nicknamed him Bambi. Seems like a deer-ish name, don't you think? I mean, much better than, say, Fred." Man, I've got to stay in character here. Not be so stupid. The last thing I need is for it to be found out that I'm not only a chick, but a chick from the future. I'm sure that would go over *real* well.

Robin snorts. "Very well then," he says, his eyes sparkling. He knows he's trapped me in a dare and is way too amused by it for my liking. "Go see Little John then. He will offer you the proper tools you need."

I head down the little hill and into the bowels of the camp. Ew. My nose wrinkles in protest as I near the fire. They are so not using Glade Plug-ins or washing with Irish Spring here in Sherwood. The place reeks of sweat, rot, and some other unidentified substances that I would prefer stay that way. And I haven't even gotten to the deer carcass yet. Great.

I shake my head to clear my 21st-century thoughts. So Febreeze has yet to be invented. Big effing deal. You probably don't smell of roses either, toots, I remind myself.

When in Rome, smell like the Romans do, I guess. Or the medieval Britons, in this case.

"Excuse me?" I say as I approach the giant called Little. He's bending over to tend to the fire, and his butt looks bigger than a cow's, his tunic straining at the seams. The guy is not only tall, he's in dire need of Jenny Craig. I guess whatever the starvation state of the rest of the kingdom, Robin keeps his men well fed.

Little John turns, a wide grin on his face. His hair sticks out in the weirdest places and he's missing several teeth. But his smile is friendly. Infectious, even, and I grin back at him. Definitely a gentle giant, though I still would not like to get on his bad side.

"I'm here to help you clean the deer," I announce, uneasily shifting from foot to foot. I really can't believe what I've gotten myself into this time.

Neither can John, evidently. He raises a skeptical eyebrow and gives me a once-over from head to toe. "Are ye sure ye want to be dirtying your hands, boy?" he asks, though much more genuinely in tone than dear Robin did. "I dunna mean to insult you, but it's a bloody job, it is. Not one meant for a squeamish stomach."

"Sure I'm sure," I say, mustering up a bit of false

bravado after a quick glance up the hill to where Robin is still standing. He's watching me closely, a smirk on his otherwise handsome face.

Little John shrugs and nods toward the woods. "The men have just returned." He hands me a knife caked with blood and gristle or something. I feel my stomach gurgle just at the sight. I can only imagine how it's going to react to slicing flesh. My kingdom for an Amy's California Veggie Burger.

But it's too late to turn back now. I sit down on a rock and watch as two men carry a large brown deer over to us. It's upside down, its legs tied to a long wooden pole, and its head flops to one side, its glassy eyes staring at me accusingly. As if I were to blame for its early demise. Which I am, in a way. Bleh.

The men stick one end of the pole into the dirt and the deer is now hanging vertically. Little John motions for me to make the first cut.

"Just slice down its stomach," he says, tracing a pudgy finger down the deer's furry belly.

I take a deep breath and squeeze my eyes shut, then open them again. *I can do this. I can do this. I can do this.* I lift the blade, realizing my right hand is trembling like crazy.

Come on, Chrissie, this is your big test. You've got to prove you're one of the men.

"Sure you don't want to go wash pans down by the lake instead?" a voice behind me jeers. I whirl around. Robin's come down the hill and is watching me, arms folded across his chest. "Or gather berries in the woods?"

What a jerk. He knows this is totally uncomfortable for me and yet he still feels he has the right to tease. I guess after I bested him in a fight, saved the little boy's hand, and witnessed him getting lost in his own forest, he's probably dying for me to fail at something.

I grit my teeth. Failure is not an option. I *will* skin this deer, and I will skin it without running screaming into the woods.

"Do you mind? We're trying to prepare dinner here," I say.

Robin holds up his hands in front of him, his eyes glittering with even more amusement than before. "By all means, young Chris, please continue."

Angry now, I jab the blade into the deer. Blood pools instantly around the dagger, gushing out in spurts. It's redder than I imagined it would be, coating the fur in crimson. Coating my hand with some horrible steaming goo.

It's red. It's hot. It's disgusting. I've never been good with blood. Not since the time my friend and I hosted a Friday the 13th marathon party when we were eight. Now I'm stuck playing a real-life Jason to this poor sweet deer who did nothing wrong.

My head starts to swim. I can feel myself swaying and I struggle to keep consciousness while holding on to the blade with both hands, dragging it down the deer's stomach. It sounds like ripping fabric and little wet drops spatter my face. I swallow back the vomit that threatens to spew from me like Linda Blair in *The Exorcist*.

"Are you all right?" I can hear Robin's voice from a distance. He doesn't sound amused anymore, at least.

But still, I'm going to see this thing through. Is the cut long enough? What next?

The deer's entrails suddenly flop out of its body in a tangle of what looks like sauce-covered spaghetti.

Eff this. I'm so fainting.

Chapter Five

I wake up under a large pile of soft fur. I open one eye, then the other. Where am I? It looks like I'm in a tent. How did I get in a tent? Was there camping at King Arthur's Faire? Where's Kat? What time is it?

Then it all comes rushing back to me. The phone call from Kat. My mission impossible—to retrieve the Holy Grail and thus help my coworker get back from the future. Meeting Robin Hood and his not-so-merry men. My volunteering to help clean out a deer carcass just to prove I'm a man. My fainting at the sight of the deer carcass, proving perhaps that I am not.

My stomach heaves as my mind replays the vision of the disemboweled creature and dangling entrails. What had I been thinking? Did I really need to prove my point that badly?

"Ah, awake, are you?"

I look over to the tent entrance. Robin pulls back

the flap to step inside. The tent's tall enough that he only has to crouch down a little.

"How do you fare?" he asks. "Do you think you would be able to hold down a bit of stew?"

My stomach growls and I realize I'm starving. At the same time, I'm pretty sure the main entrée on the menu is slaughterhouse deer, not tofu. Can we say, *No thank you?*

"I'm okay," I lie, sitting up. "Don't really have my appetite back yet."

Robin nods—without condemnation, thank goodness. "Aye," he agrees. "You did well, though," he says, squatting down to my level. "When my father first showed me how to skin a deer I ran screaming at the first cut."

"Really?" I ask, surprised by his admission. Here I was ready for him to make fun of me some more. Tear me down so he could build himself up. Like Danny used to.

He laughs. "I know 'tis hard to picture, but I was not always the strong, strapping man you see before you," he says, patting his chest with a silly grin.

"I see." I say, smiling back despite myself. "So what's your story, anyway? How did you turn into this big bad outlaw guy?"

The smile fades from his face. "Eh, 'tis a long sad tale," he says with a shrug. "Surely you'd rather go out to the fire and hear Alan a Dale spin a song of adventure."

"Maybe in a bit," I say, not willing to drop it. I want to hear his story and no song or dance is going to

tempt me away. Especially not by that William Hung
wannabe. So many things about the Robin Hood legend have turned out different than what you read in
the storybooks or see in the movies. I'm all about
gathering the real truth while I'm here. After all, if I'm
stuck back in time waiting for King Richard's return,
I might as well learn something. Unlike Kat, who I'm
sure whittled away her hours drunk and dancing at
the local pubs. Probably charming the knights with a
rousing adaptation of the Pussycat Dolls' "Don't You
Wish Your 'Damsel' was Hot like Me?"

Bleh.

"I'm kind of cozy here, to tell you the truth." I stretch
out my arms and run my hands down the soft furs to
prove my point. That is, until I realize what I'm doing.
Ew. I pull my hands away. Essentially, I'm lying in a pile
of dead animals. Cozy would not be the right word.

"Well, don't be getting used to it," Robin says. " 'Tis
my bed you lie in. And I plan to take it back when I'm
ready to lay my own head down."

"Sure. It's all good," I say as casually as possible,
feeling my eyes burn a bit as I realize I've taken over
his bed. I don't know why; I mean, it's just a pile of
skins on the floor. But still . . . Kind of intimate, I
guess. Thinking about him curling up underneath the
furs. Relaxing his muscles as sleep overtakes his body.
I wonder if he sleeps naked. Not that I care. Really.

"Uh, how about you tell me your story?" I say, suddenly desperate to change the subject. At the very
least I want to stop the blush that I can feel heating
my pale face. It's dark, but not that dark.

He stares at the far side of the tent for a moment,

his eyes glazed and his expression contemplative. I study him in the semi-darkness. He really is a good-looking guy, and his close proximity is doing funny rolly things to my insides. Half of me (the brave, lusty Paris Hilton-esque half) wants to grab him and drag him down into the bed and have my way with him. After all, thanks to Danny's infidelity, it's been awhile. But the other half (the pathetic, cowardly, not-like-any-movie-star-I-can-think-of half) manages to restrain my inner Paris. After all, I don't know this guy or anything about him, save the legends—which, so far, have proven sadly inaccurate. Not to mention he thinks I'm a eunuch, which would, I'd imagine, make him a bit squeamish if not running-screaming-from-the-tent-all-together-ish were I to suddenly attempt to molest him.

Still, he does smell good. Musky. Smoky. Of the earth, yet with a hint of sky. *Eau du Outlaw*. Not something they'd stock at Neiman's, but it's certainly turning me on. He stretches his arms above his head and his tunic tightens across his chest. I steeple my fingers to restrain myself from reaching out and touching someone. Him. I imagine tearing off his tunic, tracing his six-pack abs with eager fingers. Pushing him down onto the furs. Feeling him. Tasting him. Having him. His body growing hard as his desire for me builds. Pressing against that hardness, rejoicing in the effect I'm having on him. Until he can take no more. Until he pushes me roughly onto my back and tears off my clothes just enough so he can push himself inside of me. So he can take me as I've never been taken before.

Robin clears his throat, breaking through the thick walls of my ridiculous fantasy. I shake my head in disgust. What am I doing, going on about this guy? Sexually frustrated much, Chris? After all, I'm not even technically divorced yet. Not that Danny waited for such technicalities. Heck, he didn't even wait for the honeymoon credit card bills to be paid off. (Yes, we were married seven years, but paying the minimum each month doesn't exactly bring down your balance.) Still, I'm certainly not ready for a new relationship. I should be healing. Learning to live on my own, not going and jumping the first sexy legendary outlaw that crosses my path. Even were this guy Brad Pitt himself, I'd do best to stay clear. (Actually, even more so with Brad, given his track record. . . .)

Then again, there is that whole theory of rebound relationships. Maybe a romp in the forest with someone who lived and died eight hundred years before me could be just what the doctor ordered. After all, it's not like he could go all *Fatal Attraction* on me once I went back to the 21st century.

But it seems it's not meant to be. At least not tonight. Because, before I can say anything or do anything that I'd probably end up regretting, catcalls from the merry men suddenly erupt outside. Cheering, jeering, an all-around ruckus really. Loud as Red Sox fans after a game, and I half expect a "Yankees Suck!" chant to fly through the night. Robin's face lights up and he grabs me by the hand, pulling me to my feet.

"Something's afoot," he says gleefully, his somber

spell broken. He's funny that way—his moods change from one to the other with hardly any warning. "Shall we see what it could be?"

I crawl out from under the blankets and scramble to my feet, following him through the tent curtains (no, I do not steal another glance at his butt, really!) into the outside air. It's gotten quite cold now that the sun has gone down, and I wrap my arms around my body in a feeble attempt to garner some warmth. It had been summer back in New York; it's cold enough to be late autumn here. And there's no central heating in Sherwood Forest. Just like when my mother "forgot" to pay the gas bill for six months straight and they turned off our heat. I remember the ice crystals forming on the inside of the windows of our tiny Hoboken apartment, my little brother and I crawling under piles of ratty blankets, desperate to get warm. It wasn't long after that the DSS showed up. But once I got to my warm foster home, I realized I hadn't minded the cold that much.

The cooking fire's been built up to blazing proportions, reminding me of Woodstock 1999, where festival-goers gleefully burned down the Rome, New York, concert grounds during the Red Hot Chili Peppers set. However, this fire, while just as raging, thankfully seems under control. A good thing, too, since we can't exactly call 911 were it to suddenly start burning down the camp. Sure, I could then rightfully teach Alan a Dale the "Roof is on Fire" song, but I'm thinking the "burn motherfucker burn" lyrics might just blow my cover as a choirboy.

The men stand around the fire, but the flames are sure not what's got their attention. Every last pair of eyes is focused on whatever's behind the crackling blaze. I follow Robin around the pit for a better glimpse of what all the men have found so enthralling. My eyes widen when I realize what it is. Or rather who it is.

A woman.

I'd peg her as thirty, though the wrinkles around her watery blue eyes make her seem much older. She's blonde, on the heavy side and certainly blessed in the chest department. Sort of a medieval Anna Nicole Smith, pre-Trim Spa. She's wearing a thin, low-cut peasant's dress, her stringy hair pulled back into a bun. Not exactly your stereotypical Penthouse Pet, but the men seem pretty excited all the same. Guess they don't get women much in Sherwood Forest.

Next to her is a small boy. I recognize him immediately as the one I saved earlier from the Sheriff's men. Small world.

"What is the meaning of this?" Robin demands. I glance over at him. His mischievous expression is gone, replaced by a distinctly annoyed scowl. Whoever this woman is, she's clearly not welcome here. A spurned lover, perhaps? Nah, Robin wouldn't date anyone so skanky. Would he?

The woman looks nervous as she bows low to Robin. "I beg yer pardon, good sir," she says in a quavering voice. "But I be the wife of Much the Miller, one of yer men." She points over to the far corner of the camp where the lookout guy I met earlier is trying to blend into the shadows. I guess his wife's visit was an unexpected surprise for him as well.

"That may be so, but what brings you to my lair?" Robin asks, folding his arms across his chest. "You should know strangers are not welcome here. It troubles me greatly that you knew the way to the secret lair to begin with." He shoots an accusatory glance in Much's direction. The miller jumps behind a tree. He is *so* busted.

"But good sir, I came to thank ye. For savin' the life of me son when the sheriff's men went after him this day. He came home tellin' tales of ye riskin' yer life by attacking one of the sheriff's men's horses, allowin' him his escape."

Robin narrows his eyes, glancing back at me this time. I know what he's thinking: no good deed goes unpunished. But still. I shrug. I mean, what's the big deal? I think it's sweet that the boy's mom came all this way to thank him. Even though technically I should be getting the credit here. Good old heroic Robin was more than ready to let little Much Jr. go through life as Captain Hook to save his own neck. But does he give props to me? Uh, no. Typical man.

" 'Twas nothing," the outlaw says with a shrug. Yeah, nothing for him, exactly, considering he did nothing. "All in a day's work. Now was that all ye came for? And will ye be leaving soon?"

"Aw, come on, Robin, let them stay for a drink," cajoles Friar Tuck. "We should toast her son's health, we should. Or yours, for being such a brave man and risking yer life to save a lad."

"Aye, Robin, let them stay for a bit of stew." This

from Little John. Always thinking about his stomach, this guy. "We have enough left over to feed the entire kingdom and I'm fair sure they must be starving from their long journey."

"A grand idea. And I'll compose a song of your brave rescue," Allan a Dale declares, grabbing his instrument from a nearby rock and strumming an impromptu tune.

"Much the Miller's son attacked a deer,
I think he shot it in the rear.
So the sheriff wanted to cut off his arm
He'd then be useless on the farm—"

"Quiet!" Robin says, looking seriously annoyed at this point. Jeez Louise! What crawled up his ass and died? "We have rules here, and rules for a reason. They shall not be broken nor excepted to. We all signed the sacred code when we first banded together, did we not?"

"But Robin, it's just—"

"No women!" he declares, his eyes flashing. "The Good Lord says they tempted Adam with the apple and surely, if given the option, they will tempt you all as well. They will make you weak and will divide your loyalty. Not to mention, they never come as one. If I let her stay, tomorrow I am sure the place will be crawling with your wives and girl children. *No.* You have said your piece, milady. Now please, go back to your village and leave us be."

Wow. This is an interesting morsel. I stare at Robin.

He really has a thing against chicks, huh? Thank goodness he doesn't know what I really am or I'd so be tossed out into the wild. And then where would I be? No safe place to go. With all the poverty here I doubt anyone else would agree to take me in and feed me. And it's not like I have a good skill-set to fall back on to get any sort of job. Magazine photographer isn't exactly a lucrative 12th-century career.

Nope. If I don't keep up this eunuch charade, I'm toast.

Much the Miller steps out feebly from the shadows. "Come along, my dears," he mumbles, trying to take his wife by the arm. "I will lead ye home."

But the woman stands fast and the boy stubbornly clings to her skirts. "Nonsense, my dear husband," she says, crossing her meaty arms on her chest. The move succeeds in accentuating her cleavage— something not lost on a single merry man in camp, I'd wager, judging by the wide eyes around me. " 'Tis late and the roads are dark and dangerous—crawling with thieves and wild beasts," she says, evidently the only one willing to stand up to Robin. I guess it makes sense. She has the least to lose. Though Much is looking like he'd be perfectly happy to crawl under a rock and die at this point. "Would you save the child one moment, only to kill his family the next? Would that please you? To have my son grow up without a mother?"

Woot! I smile to myself, admiring the woman's courage. Score one for Mrs. Much.

"If you truly cared for your safety, you should not

have come in the first place," Robin counters stubbornly.

Grr. He's clearly not going to give in without more persuasion. And while it's not exactly my strong point, I suddenly feel compelled to come to the aid of my fellow sister soul.

"Duh. She came to *thank* you," I find myself interjecting. Not that I have much hope it'll work. I mean, if he won't even listen to his own men, how can I really expect Rob to listen to me, a virtual stranger? "She appreciates what you did to save her son's life. And do you say, 'You're welcome'?" I ask. "Do you say, 'Stay and have a drink with the men'? No, you ungrateful bastard. You think it's totally fine to just send her away, even though you know for a fact she could end up being eaten by a lion, a tiger or bear—"

Oh my! I stop talking and hold my breath, realizing I just came off way too strong for my own good. I mean, what if Robin decides to throw me out of the camp with her? Then where will I be? Probably dead. I wonder what happens if I die back in the 12th century. Will I zip back to the 21st? Or is it game over? And if I die, what will happen to Kat? Will Nimue send someone else to get the Grail? Or is the fashionista SOL?

This time-travel stuff is way confusing.

I gather my courage and steal a glance at Robin. I offer him a sheepish smile, praying it will work.

"Sorry. Got carried away," I say with a small shrug. "All that church learning, I guess. Do unto others, turn the other cheek, all that jazz."

Robin continues to glower at me for a moment, then his expression lightens and he starts to laugh.

"You are brave and outspoken, young Christian," he says, shaking his head. "I would surely kill you—if you did not remind me so much of myself."

He slaps me on the back, almost knocking me over. Then he turns back to Much and his wife. "Very well then," he says. "You may stay. But I want you gone at first light, woman. The moment the sun peeks through the trees and you deem it is safe to travel. And do *not* return," he adds. "Next time I shall not be so generous."

The camp erupts in cheers. Several of the men pat me on the back as we make our way again to the firepit. Allan a Dale picks up his harp and strums a few chords, and soon the camp is alive with the sounds of music, bawdy singing, and laughter.

And I'm clearly the hero of Sherwood Forest.

After a time, the music dwindles and the fire smolders in its ashes. The mead has made us dull and lazy, and talk replaces song. I lay my head down on a patch of grassy leaves, wishing I'd brought my comfy camping chair with me or my memory foam pillow. Not to mention some kind of portable shower device with good steamy hot water pressure. And deodorant sure wouldn't go amiss. One day in medieval England and I'm filthy, sweaty, and reek of smoke. Good thing they think I'm one of the guys, 'cause I certainly don't feel very girly.

"How goes it in the villages these days?" Little John asks the Miller's wife.

"Bad and getting worse, I'd say," she answers glumly. "I'd give me right arm for King Richard to return, I would. My left too, if he could knock that bastard Prince John and the Sheriff of Nottingham from power."

"That bad, eh?" I ask.

"We are starving, lad, while Prince John sits on a throne and stuffs himself with roast quail, fruits and cheeses. He grows fat while our children die of starvation all around him. And does he care? No, he does not."

"Me wife says the same," pipes up another man. "The taxmen raid the villages daily, taking bread from the mouths of babes."

" 'Tis a damn shame, to be sure."

"If only King Richard were to return."

"Aye! Now there's a thought—King Richard back on the throne. We would all be free men. Pardoned for the crimes we did not commit."

"Outlaws no longer. We would be back with our families."

"We would regain our lands. Plow our own fields."

"I remember moaning about plowing a field. What I would not give to have the chance to moan about it again."

The bitching goes on and on 'til I can't stand it any more. These guys are as useless as my Democratic neighbors who moaned about Bush but voted for Nader. What happened to the brave outlaws of the storybooks, the ones who risked their lives to better those of their countrymen? The Robin Hood I knew didn't hide away like a coward in the forest, drinking mead, chowing on roast deer and complaining about the government. He helped people. He stood up to The Man. Did the storybooks get it wrong? Or am I now in some kind of parallel back-in-time universe where Robin Hood was simply Prince of Pansies?

I think back to the little girl in the hut earlier today. Her grubby hands, her gaunt, half-starved face. Parallel universe or not, I can't just sit around and let that happen. Besides, I've got time to kill while I wait for King Richard to show up with the Grail. Might as well make myself useful. Change history for the better and all that.

"Why don't you stop complaining about the situation and do something about it?" I demand, making my decision. I just hope it doesn't get me kicked out of the camp. I'm likely on thin ice as it is, after defending Mrs. Much.

"But what can we do?" asks Little John, with a shrug of his linebacker shoulders. "We are outlaws. We cannot live in the villages. Therefore we cannot take jobs to earn bread for our families."

"Besides, even if we did manage to find work, all the wages we earned would be taxed until there's nothing left."

"Bah, forget work," I say, scrambling to my feet. "I've got a better plan."

I'm getting a bunch of skeptical looks, and half of me wants to just sit down and shut up, but I swallow hard and continue.

"Together, you've got a small army here," I say, gesturing to the group. "And I bet you know Sherwood Forest a lot better than any of the sheriff's men."

"Aye," agree a couple of the men.

"And I'm sure you're *much* cleverer than all of those bozos put together." I add. It's funny how easy it is to rouse men to action by playing on their egos.

"Aye!" I get a few cheers and chuckles this time.

"And who's better with a bow than our dear old Robin here?" I say, looking down on the outlaw, praying that at least the legends didn't get that part wrong.

"He's the best in the land!" calls out Allan a Dale, strumming his harp. "I always sing about it.

There once was a man named Robin,
Whose skill with a bow made grown men go
*   sobbin'.*
He'd hit a bullseye from a mile away
And then go find a woman to—"

"Anyway . . ." I interrupt, glancing at the wide-eyed Much Jr. "A bit TMI, but I get the point. Robin's an ace with a bow. You guys rock in the forest. So there you go. Use your resources. When the kings' men raid the villages, taking your families' money, steal the money back!"

"*Aye!*" The men cheer, raising their cups of mead, their eyes shining in the firelight. I smile. Cool! They're totally on board. Little old Chrissie's somehow succeeded in stirring these legendary men into action. I'm so good! Maybe when I go back to the 21st century I could become a motivational speaker or something. Eat your heart out, Tony Robbins.

"If we steal the money, how, pray tell, are we any

different than the sheriff himself?" Robin asks point-edly, after the initial cheers subside. He's apparently the only skeptical one left in the bunch. Figures. But luckily I've got an answer.

"Because you give it back!" I say triumphantly. "All the money you steal from the rich, you shower on the poor. You'll be heroes. Legendary. They'll sing songs about your good deeds for centuries to come. The renowned Robin Hood and his merry men."

More cheers and catcalls, drowning out Robin's next round of protest. He looks seriously annoyed.

"Hey, Friar! We'd be even merrier if you would not be so stingy with the mead," notes Much the Miller, staring into his empty cup.

The man of God pauses mid-slurp, then raises his own mug into the air. "The Good Lord giveth and the Good Lord taketh away!" he cries. "So we'd be doing the Good Lord's work." He belches loudly and laughs and passes his cup to the man on his right, then proceeds to fill another, passing it along.

"Here's to Christian!" says Will Scarlet, raising his own mug. "And his plan to defeat the evil Sheriff of Nottingham!"

"To Christian!" the men chorus, raising their cups and downing their brew.

"This inspires me to song," Allan a Dale threatens.

"Good Christian came to Sherwood land,
His ideas 'twere sharp, though he 'twas not
*   quite man.*
He suggested we go and rob from the rich.
If only I didn't have that pesky groin—"

"Stop. Stop all this nonsense at once!" Robin cries, suddenly scrambling to his feet, anger flashing in his eyes. "This talk is madness." He paces toward the waning fire and back again, then turns to face his men. "When I found you lot, you were a sorry sight to be had. Starving, outlawed, nothing to call your own. I brought you here to this haven and we made a life for ourselves. We may not be rich, we may still be outlaws, but we have fresh meat every night and no longer fear for our lives at every turn." He places his hands on his hips and scans the crowd. "Do you really wish to abandon everything we've worked for just because a stranger suggests it? It sounds a grand plan, to be sure, but is any one of you willing to die like that? To risk all we've gained?"

"*You* may be safe and sound here, Robin," I say, furious that he's undermining me again. Selfish bastard. "But what about these men's wives? Their children? Heck, what about their father's brother's nephew's cousin's former roommates?" (Yes, I've seen *Spaceballs* three too many times.) "They're starving. Dying. And we have a means to stop that. How can you just sit back and not do anything?"

Robin shakes his head. "The church has sheltered you from reality, young Christian. You do not know what the Sheriff is capable of. He will hang every man here, and their limp bodies and broken necks will not slacken his appetite for the morning meal."

"But—"

"I will hear no more of this," Robin says. "You have disrespected me once, pleading for the woman. And you nearly made me lose my own neck by defending the Miller's son earlier this day. You are lucky I do not throw you out of the forest or deliver you to the Sheriff of Nottingham myself. So be still and enjoy this night of sanctuary I offer you, or fend for yourself out in the wilds. I do not care which."

And with that, he storms off into the night. I stare after him, extremely pissed. How dare he? No one talks to me like that. What a jerk!

"Do not mind him, lad," Little John says, interrupting my internal rant. "He will come back."

"What's his problem?" I growl.

"He is angry because he knows you speak true," Little John says with a shrug. "But he is afraid."

Afraid? The big bad outlaw is afraid? I'm in the freaking 12th century here and I'm not scared. Well, maybe a little, but still. "He doesn't seem afraid. He just seems like a stubborn old goat to me," I complain, hoping they won't take offense to me bashing their head guy, even though he obviously deserves it.

Luckily the men just laugh. "Aye," Friar Tuck says, raising his glass. "He can be at that!"

"A right bastard at times," agrees Allan a Dale. "I've penned many a song about it."

I shake my head. "So why do you guys follow him? I mean, he is your leader, right?"

The laughter dies away and Little John turns to me with a serious expression on his burly face. "Because, young Christian, beneath that prickly shell lies a truly great man. A man who saved us all."

"We were nothing before Robin came along," Will Scarlet continues. "Penniless outlaws who'd all but lost the will to live. We roamed the countryside, starving and alone, unable to show our faces in the villages for more than a day or two, lest the sheriff get wind of our location. But Robin saw the good in us."

"He pulled us from the taverns where we drowned our sorrows in watery brews and bade us follow him," chimes in Friar Tuck. "He offered us a sanctuary here in this forest—a simple hideaway where we can live freely and without fear of being caught. Here we can await the true king's return, and there is always enough to eat and, of course, to drink." He holds up his mug with a smirk. "In Sherwood Forest we work together and never want for any creature comfort."

"So you see, Christian, Robin may seem as unbending as a mighty oak, but his heart is true," Little John concludes. "He cares more for us then he does his own life. And he will gladly die to protect what he has built here."

Wow. And here I just thought he was a pig-headed jerk. Serves me right for jumping to conclusions. "I'm going to go talk to him," I say.

"Perhaps 'tis better to wait," Little John suggests gently. "He is a good man and will see that you are right once he thinks upon it a bit."

"Meh, I've never been one to let the sun go down on an argument," I say. "I'll be right back."

I head away from the fire, its warmth fading with its glow. It takes a moment for my eyes to adjust to the darkness. When they do, I see that there is a small pond not far from the camp. I walk toward it, pulling branches away and letting them snap back behind me. I hope there are no ticks in Sherwood Forest. Or that lyme disease has yet to be invented.

I find Robin seated on a rock by the shoreline. The

full moon illuminates half of his face. He's throwing pebbles into the water, watching them skip before sinking into the depths of the pond.

I walk over and sit down on an adjacent rock. It's not the most comfortable seat in the universe, but better than the damp ground, I guess. Seriously, my kingdom for a La-Z Boy recliner.

"I'm sorry," I say in my sweetest voice—the non-threatening one I used to reserve for calming my third foster father down when he was in one of his drunken rages. "I was out of line. I'm a guest here and I over-stepped my bounds."

"Aye," Robin says, kicking at the muddy ground with his leather-clad toe. "But you said only what needed to be said. And bravely too, I might add. With little thought to your own situation. I admire your courage."

"Huh?" I was not expecting this. Was he actually apologizing?

He sighs before speaking. "Do not think for one moment I am unaware of the poverty and injustice that surrounds this forest, lad. I am not blind. 'Twere it in my power to make a difference—to do something good—I'd be the first to attempt it."

"Then why not? Why not give my idea a try?"

"It sounds simple, but there is risk," he says. "I have seen what Prince John is capable of, and 'tis not pretty. I want to protect my men, and I do not like the idea of putting them in danger."

"They're grown men, Robin. Surely they should de-cide for themselves."

Robin stares up at the moon, as if lost in thought.

"I fought overseas during the Third Crusade," he says at last, turning back to look at me, though his green eyes still seem distant, "with many a valiant English knight and our brave King Richard. We fought hard and long, and were in sight of the Holy City of Jerusalem. We thought God had given us victory."

"But . . . not so much, I take it?"

"The climate is unmercifully harsh. And water, scarce. We ran out of food and had no way to replenish our stores. We weakened day by day, until one morning our band was attacked and those not killed were captured. I spent three months in a Muslim prison. Tortured. Barely fed. I thought I would die there."

"But you didn't."

"Nay, I managed to escape and make my way back to England. When I got here, I realized I should have allowed them to kill me back in the East."

"What do you mean?"

"I introduced myself to you as Robin of Locksley, and so I am—by birth, lord of that land. But when I arrived back from the Crusades, weary and ready to return to the comfort of my castle and people, I realized I had neither left to me.

"My father was killed, hung as a traitor in his own castle courtyard. A loyal subject to King Richard to his dying breath, he was too outspoken for his own good. Prince John felt threatened by my father's loyalty, his unwavering support for our brave true king and his rash words against the injustices of the current rule. So the prince had him executed." Robin squeezes his hands into fists, a scowl washing over his otherwise handsome face. "The bastard prince then seized our lands, ruling that a traitor's kingdom should be handed over to the throne."

"That's terrible," I cry. No wonder the guy's so bitter.

"Yes. When I returned and found my lands taken and my father murdered, I flew into a rage. I was blind with fury—my only thoughts were those of revenge. I gathered up a small army of men who had returned from the crusades with me. Many of them had also lost their lands and were as bloodthirsty as I. We planned an attack on a small castle south of here, where it was rumored Prince John had taken up residence after growing bored of the court at Nottingham. Our spies said he had only a handful of guards watching him, and we thought 'twould be an easy victory."

"But again not so much, right?"

Robin's face darkens as he relives what must have been a nightmare for him. "Nay. We were betrayed. Two nights before we planned to attack, I allowed the men to go home to their villages—to lie with their wives and play with their children. I thought 'twould do them good, give them a reason to fight. But 'twas just the opposite. Robert of Appleby, one of my best men and a good friend throughout the crusades, met up with his mistress, and after she plied him with ale he confessed to our plan—aiming to impress her, he said. And impress her he did. Enough to send her straight to the sheriff. When we arrived at the castle two mornings later, they were waiting to ambush us."

"Wow." That sucks. No wonder Robin's so pissed off at females.

"For lust of a woman, dozens of fine Englishmen were lost that day," Robin continues bitterly. " 'Twas a massacre, and I barely escaped with my life. Most of the others were killed."

"And that's when you became an outlaw."

"Aye. For weeks I wandered, half dead in my sorrow. I drank too much and barely ate. But then I began to meet men—lost men, like me, outlawed for remaining loyal to King Richard. Unable to go home to their families, or to work to earn their bread. It dawned on me that while alone we were all weak and powerless, together we might create some sort of life. So I gathered them to me and we set up this small village deep in Sherwood Forest. No one knows that we are here, and thus we can live safely, gathering from the land what we need to survive."

"You do have a sweet setup, I must say."

"So you see, Christian, while I think your ideas are noble and brave and good, I worry that by becoming champions of the poor, we will lose the little peace we have created for ourselves. And with no hope of victory."

"I understand," I say. "But I'm not talking an all-out war on Nottingham this time. Just a few small robberies here and there. I mean, sure, you and your men are all hooked up here in the forest. But what about the others? Your men's families? The little girl we saw earlier in that cottage? The little boy who almost had his hand cut off? It's in your power to ease their suffering. Do you want to just sit around in the woods, chowing on deer and letting them suffer?"

He stares out into the water for another moment, grabbing another rock in his fist and flipping it into the pond. It skims the surface a moment before sinking.

"Mayhap you are right," he says at last. "Those who lived in Locksley, peasants who were always loyal and true, now die of starvation and disease. And I sit, a coward in the forest allowing it to happen." He hangs his head. "My father would be ashamed."

"So let's do something about it," I urge. "Let's give the sheriff a run for his money. I'll help. It'll be fun, in a way. Outwitting the bad guys and making them look like fools. Showing up in the villages armed with bread and meat. Showering the children with silver."

Robin smiles a little. "You are right. I can no longer sit by selfishly and watch my people suffer. I am not that man." He turns to look at me, and if I didn't know better, I'd say his eyes look a bit moist. "Thank you, young Christian," he says. "You come to my camp a stranger, but teach me more truth in one night than I have been willing to hear in a year."

I'm glad it's dark, 'cause I know I'm blushing. And the worst part is, he's looking at me all goofy and grateful. Like, if I were a girl, I bet this is the point where he'd kiss me. But he can't. He thinks I'm a boy. And while some legends have been proven wrong, I'm still guessing Robin probably digs chicks.

He shakes his head and the intimate moment breaks. He scrambles to his feet.

"We had better get some sleep," he says, back to his old cocky self, "if in the morn we are going to outwit the sheriff and Prince John."

I grin. "Sounds like a plan."

Chapter Six

Whoooooosh!

The arrow whistling through the trees announces the arrival of the carriage. We'd been tipped off of their schedule by some friends of Will Scarlet's, and now we're all in place. Ready to rob. I, myself, am lodged quite uncomfortably in a nearby tree, small sword in hand. I've been practicing alongside the men for the last three days, but I don't think this blade will be a deadly weapon in my hands anytime soon. Ah well. We're not out to kill anyway. Just to scare. And rob.

This had better work. Especially since I'm the one who came up with the plan. Robin's men now think I'm some sort of tactical genius. Of course I can't take complete credit—especially since technically I ripped the entire thing off from a rescue scene in *Tristan and Isolde*, this medieval movie I watched last month. But hey, I'd bet my Birkenstocks that no one in the approaching coach Netflixed the film, so to them it'll be a complete surprise.

Then again, Hollywood could have gotten it completely wrong and we'll be screwed. Guess we'll have to wait and see.

"Wait for it," a hidden Robin hisses to the men across the dirt road. For as much as he didn't want to do this in the first place, all morning he's been like a kid in a candy store. I think deep down thievery agrees with him.

I'm not so sure about myself, however. To tell the truth, I'm just not adjusting to medieval life in Sherwood Forest as easily as I thought I would. Not that I'm some girlie girl—I'm not afraid to get my hands dirty or anything. But still! There are no beds here. No toothbrushes. And very few vegetarian entrees beyond wheat bread. I'm sore from sleeping on the ground and my stomach keeps growling its displeasure at the food I send its way. Let's just say I have a medieval version of Montezuma's Revenge and there are no bathrooms to hide and be sick in.

It's kind of disappointing, actually. I figured I'd be the perfect girl to go back in time. I'm not like Kat—all princess-and-the-pea–like I don't mind living at one with nature. Not that there was a lot of nature in my hometown of Hoboken, but still. Danny and I went to the Catskills a ton of times and I never had a problem sleeping in a cabin.

But this is much harder than I figured. I'm tired, dirty, depressed and even bored. I feel like I'm attending some horrid summer camp and there's no way to call Mom and beg her to come pick me up. Not that my mom would have ever interrupted one of her drug-induced trances to hop in her Volkswagen bus and retrieve me.

I mean, what am I doing here? Three days and I'm no closer to accomplishing my mission. How long before King Richard returns? What if it's not for a year or something? Am I really going to have to hang out in Sherwood Forest for a year? And what if Robin's right and the sheriff catches us all? Will they hang me? And if they do, will I pop back into the 21st century? Or does death here mean death back home as well? Ugh.

While I'm at it, has time passed in the present? Am I missing work without calling in sick? What if they fire me? Photog jobs are so hard to come by—that's why I'm working at that silly fashion magazine and not, say, *National Geographic*, to begin with. Same with Kat. Monday morning neither one of us will show up to work. Will people think something horrible happened to both of us? Will they call out the National Guard? Will we be featured on milk cartons? Or do you have to be gone at least a year to get on those?

Will *La Style* do a full-page spread on Kat's and my mysterious disappearances—a tribute to their two employees gone missing on the job? Oh, wait, probably the beautiful, stylish Kat will make the front cover. I'll be reduced to a brief mention in the article. So help me, if they call me her sidekick—

"They're here!"

The dusty cloud and thunderous sound of hooves against dirt brings me back to reality. (Though whoever thought I'd call 12th-century England my reality?) No time to mourn my past life now; I got these men into this situation and now I've got to get them out alive. Alive and with gold, hopefully.

"Now!" Robin cries.

The archers in the surrounding trees loose their arrows, which fly past the front of the carriage; causing the horses to come to a screeching halt, rearing up on their hind legs, frothing at the mouth. The two mounted guards riding alongside draw their swords and scan the woods, while the plump, bearded driver wrestles for control of his team.

"What was that?" he cries.

Time for phase two. Will Scarlet urges his white mare out of the woods and into the road. He flashes the guards a big smile and a wave of his red-plumed hat, then turns and gallops off as fast as his horse can carry him.

Sure enough, the guards give pursuit, just as I'd hoped, leaving the carriage completely defenseless. The rest of us jump out of the trees and into the road, surrounding the conveyance, knives out and bows drawn.

"Please, please! I have children at home!" the driver cries, his face pale and his eyes wide with fright. I feel a bit sorry for him—he's just a working stiff, after all. But hey, this is why you don't work for the bad guys.

"Be silent but not afraid. Our aim is not to hurt

you," Robin says, walking around the carriage with a bit of a swagger. "Just to relieve you of all your worldly possessions."

An older fellow with a well-trimmed white beard and a fine red silk tunic pops his head out of the carriage window. "What is the meaning of this?" he demands angrily.

"Consider it a toll," Robin says sweetly. "You have heard of tolls, have you not? Well, to cross through Sherwood Forest, you must now pay one."

"And what is this toll? And by whose order?"

"The toll is every piece of silver you have on you. Jewelry will do as well." Robin grins, grabbing the man's arm through the window and sliding a gaudy jeweled ring off his fat finger. "And who am I?" He lets out a confident laugh and flashes an arrogant grin. "Why, I am Robin Hood, Prince of Sherwood Forest, of course!"

Ooh. I shiver a bit, and not from the cold, either. He sounds so grand when he says that, it gives me goose bumps. Now *this* is the stuff of legends. And I made it happen! Not to mention I convinced him to start calling himself by the infamous "Hood" name. How cool is that?

The rich guy doesn't need too much more persuasion. He gladly hands over the goods. Well, *gladly* might be overstating a bit—he does grumble a bit about thieves and forests and the Sheriff of Nottingham's bloody incompetence as he produces a gold chain, a few more rings, and a large silk bag stuffed full of silver pennies. But all in all he's a pretty good sport about the whole thing. Guess when you're surrounded by men with bows you don't have much choice.

A few minutes later, Will Scarlet trots back into view, a big smirk on his clean-shaven face. He led the guards into a clearing, he says, where some of the merry men were waiting in grass-covered pits, just as I'd told them to. As the guards approached, the men leapt from their hiding spots, bows drawn.

"Your guards are tied to birch trees not far down the road," Will informs the coach driver, who still looks a bit shaken. "You had best rescue them, for they seem quite displeased by their current situation."

"You are letting us go?" the driver asks, his voice betraying his disbelief. Jeez. Did he think we were going to kill him or something? These are definitely harsh times.

"But of course," Robin says, bowing low. "As I said before, 'tis merely a toll to pass through this fine forest. We ask no more than is due to us."

"Thank you, thank you," the driver says, bowing back.

Robin leans over and whispers something to the man, then surreptitiously slips a couple of silver coins into his palm. The driver starts in with even more blubbering thank-yous, until Robin presses a finger against his lips.

"Go and fetch your guards," he instructs.

The man flicks the reins and the horses take off down the road, the sound of hooves and the cloud of dust fading into the distance.

Robin's men erupt in cheers.

"We did it!" cries Little John, raising his meaty arm in triumph.

"That was perfect!" cries Much the Miller, dancing around the road.

"I must sing a song about it," Allan a Dale declares.

Everyone covers their ears.

"Songs and celebration shall come later, lads. Today our quest is far from complete," Robin interrupts, looking flushed and happy. "Now we must take this treasure and bestow it upon starving villagers." He holds up the sack of coins. "Any suggestions as to who should be the first to benefit from our crimes?"

Several villages are named, but in the end it is decided that it will be a small town just outside Sherwood Forest that will get the goods this time around. Several of the men have families there. Not to mention the village is the opposite direction from the way the carriage is headed. Good plan.

We make our way to the village on foot—there aren't enough horses to go around and everyone wants to see the villagers' faces when they're presented their newfound riches. It's a long walk—like the length of Central Park—and I'm soon wishing I'd been more vocal about which village we picked as the recipient of our generosity. Like, sure they loved their families, but I love my feet.

Just as I'm ready to beg for a few minutes of downtime, we step into a clearing, which strikes me as very familiar. Then it hits me. The river where I bested Robin in the log fight is near here.

Ooh, I can go retrieve my camera bag!

"I, um, have to go to the bathroom—er, relieve my-self," I say, gesturing into the woods.

Robin nods. "Very well, Christian."

"You guys can go off ahead, I'll catch up."

Keeping an eye on which way they head, I run over to the shore, walk nimbly across the log, and locate my bag. Thank goodness no one else came along and stole it. I check its contents. Camera, check. Credit cards, check. Vial to fill up with blood from the Holy Grail, check. I stuff the camera bag down the tunic shirt they gave me to wear and hope they don't notice the bulge. The last thing I need is to be forced to ex-plain the inner workings of a Nikon digital camera to a bunch of medieval Britons. I do, however, want to try to secretly take some pictures in case I ever get out of here.

Beep! Beep!

Yikes! My chest starts beeping the second I start back over the log. I run back the other direction, reaching down my shirt, into my bag and pull out my cell phone.

I have a message?

How did I get a message? There's no way a cell phone would work back in medieval times. No cell towers. And I know I didn't have a message before I left; I checked, looking to see if Kat had called me. Not to mention, the phone's been sitting in the woods for three days. Surely that's drained the battery.

I'm about to check voice mail, but before I can, my phone erupts into song and I almost drop it. I hope the merry men took my advice and kept moving, 'cause the Jefferson Airplane tune is going to be a tad hard to explain.

I stare at the phone as it chirps away. How the hell is it ringing? Impossible, yet . . .

"Hello?" I ask, clicking the Send button and putting the receiver to my ear. After all, impossible or not, this could be an important call, right?

"Chrissie? Is that you?" The voice on the other end is static-distorted but most definitely recognizable.

"Kat?" I cry, for once overjoyed to hear my coworker's nasal Brooklyn accent.

"Chrissie, thank god! I've been calling you forever. Where have you been? What did Nimue say? Is she going to get me back from the future?"

"Well, that's kind of a funny—"

" 'Cause we totally need to get back, ASAP. Guenevere's in an awful scandal here and I just think we've worn out our welcome."

"Actually Nimue sent me—"

"Not to mention I've been gone so long. I'm worried about my dog. Gucci's been locked up in the house for almost a year now. What if the SPCA shows up and takes her away? I couldn't bear life without Gucci."

I grip the phone tightly. "Kat," I say, forcing my voice to be calm. "If you will just shut up for one second, I'll tell you everything."

The other end of the phone thankfully goes quiet.

"I did go talk to Nimue. She said she needed a special ingredient to bring you back in time. Blood from the Holy Grail, to be precise."

"The what? Isn't that a Monty Python movie or something? No, wait! Indiana Jones. Now I remember."

I can't believe anyone can be this stupid. "No, dumbass. I mean, yes, those movies featured it, but, well, the Holy Grail was the chalice that Jesus drank from during the Last Supper."

"Oh, wait. This is ringing a bell now. Isn't the chalice really the body of Mary Magdalene after she hooked up with Jesus and was having his kid?"

"Well, sure, if you believe that Da Vinci Code book, but—"

"Yeah, that's the one. But I thought it was a movie . . ."

"Kat!"

"Sorry. Go on."

"Anyway, supposedly the Holy Grail was brought back after the Crusades by King Richard—"

"King Richard hooked up with Mary Magdalene, too? What a slut! And wouldn't she have been pretty old by then?"

"It's a *cup,* Kat," I say through gritted teeth. "Dan Brown was wrong."

"Who's Dan Brown? I thought that was a Tom Hanks movie."

"Oh my god, Kat. If you don't be quiet I'll leave you there in the future forever."

"Uh, please don't do that. I mean, sure there are some cool things about the future. They have these coffeemakers that instantly make you the perfect cappuccino. No waiting in line at Starbucks anymore. But the fashions—ugh! Can you believe pointy-toed shoes are out of style? And they love high-waisted pants? Isn't that so sad?"

"I'm hanging up now."

"Wait! Please don't. I'm sorry. I don't mean to babble. It's just so nice to talk to someone from my century."

She has a point. As annoying and vapid as she is, like it or not, we're in this together.

"Fine. But please listen to me. In order to get back from the future, Nimue needs the Holy Grail. So she sent me back in time to recover it."

"You're back in time, too?" Kat squeals so loudly I think my eardrums will burst. "Oh my god! How crazy is that? Now you believe me, right? She sent *me* back in time to the days of King Arthur. I met this totally hot knight, Lancelot, who's now my boyfriend. Him and Queen Guenevere are here in the future with me now."

"Uh, right. Yeah. Cool. But remember the no-babbling rule? I don't have a lot of time. I have to go catch up with the men."

"Sorry. Go on."

"So I'm back in 12th-century England, but the problem is, there is no Grail. King Richard hasn't come back from the Crusades yet, and no one knows when he's expected back. For all I know, I could have to wait around for years."

"Ooh, that sucks," Kat says. "I had to hang at Camelot for like nine months, so I totally know what you're going through. What are you doing while you're waiting? Have you learned to ride a horse yet?"

"You won't believe it, but I'm actually hanging out with Robin Hood."

"Robin Hood?" Kat sounds impressed. I guess even she has heard of the legendary outlaw. "Does he look as sexy as Carey Elwes did in that *Men in Tights* movie?"

"He's pretty good-looking, yeah," I say, trying to sound nonchalant, while my face heats in a blush. Thank goodness these aren't videophones.

"Too bad you're married. You could totally hook up with the guy while you were waiting for the Grail. Have some rocking medieval sex action."

"Actually . . ." I pause. Do I really want to tell her I'm not happily married anymore? I haven't even told my own mother yet. Not that she will stay sober long enough to care. "Actually, he thinks I'm a boy." Better to go the less painful follow-up questions route.

"A boy? How can he think you're a boy? I mean, sure you've never been exactly stacked, but still!"

Sigh. "Thanks, Kat," I mutter. "Anyway, he thinks I'm a eunuch. Like a choirboy. Sort of gender neutral, if you know what I mean."

"Ew. And he thinks you're that? How come? Why not tell him the truth?"

"Because he doesn't allow women in his camp. No exceptions. And I have no place else to go while waiting for King Richard. The villagers are all starving and I don't dare go meet up with the evil Prince John at the palace."

"Ah. Good plan then. Though sucky in the sex potential."

"I'm not here to get laid, Kat. I'm here to rescue you, remember?"

"I know. But there's no reason not to have some fun in the process. I had a blast back in Camelot. Even though I did get kidnapped a bunch. That kind of blew. But then Lancey rescued me. My hero. A genuine knight in shining armor—with actual armor! I totally want you to meet him. I hope it all works out. Maybe you and me and Lance and Danny could all go out for drinks one night when we're back. Someplace quiet. Maybe in the West Village? I don't think Lance is ready for Times Square just yet. Though you should see the guy on a computer. He's totally addicted to *World of Warcraft 10*."

She keeps babbling on, but I almost don't mind. It's refreshing to talk to someone who knows who I really am, where I really belong, and what gender I was born into. Even if she is an airhead, she's the only friend I've got in this place. The only one who would believe I'm really here.

"Anyway, Chris, I've got to go. They're going to kill me when they get their phone bill. I'll call you later if I get a chance to see where you stand."

"Okay," I say, actually feeling a little sad to let her go. "I understand."

"Oh, and Chrissie?"

"Yeah?"

"Try to have some fun while you're there. You only go back in time once. I think, anyway. Make the most of it."

"Okay. Thanks, Kat."

"Cool. Adios. I'm ghost." And with that, the line goes dead.

I let out a sigh and stuff the phone back in my bag. Have fun indeed. Easy for her to say. She went back in time and got to hang out in a castle—with knights and ladies and probably court jesters. I, on the other hand, am stuck in the middle of the filthy woods with a group of ragged outlaws and their mopey leader, who has a thing against girls. She got to wear fine medieval dresses and make love to a legendary knight in shining armor. I have to pretend I'm some dude or I'll be kicked out of camp. So sure, Kat, it's easy for you to say "have fun." Reality is much bleaker on this side of the cell phone.

It's not surprising, really. People like Kat always end up going through life with no problems at all. They don't have husbands who cheat on them with coffeehouse waitresses. They flit around from one social event to the next, their biggest worry being whether their shoes will match their camisole tops. They don't worry whether they will be able to make the rent next month on their studio apartment that was always too small for two people, but too expensive for one. They don't bounce checks or have creditors calling them.

Maybe it's better that I'm back in time with the other downtrodden. I'd feel sick living it up in the castle knowing others were starving down in the villages. These are my people. The ones without hope.

I rush down the path to catch up with the men. I come to a small village surrounded by a stone wall, and from the excited cries coming from inside I realize I must have the right place.

I walk down the narrow dirt streets until I come to a small town square. It must be market day; little wooden stands flank the sides of the road with pitiful offerings of moldy bread and cracked eggs. Slabs of meat give off a slightly rotten scent. There are woven baskets and crude knives.

But no one's shopping. The whole crowd of dirty peasants has gathered around Robin and his men.

"Long enough have you been persecuted and taxed to the point of starvation by the evil man who dares rule in his brother's place," Robin is saying. "But keep your faith, good people. Soon our blessed King Richard, rightful lord of England, shall return, cast the usurper from his throne, and restore the riches of our great land to the people who toil on it."

Cheers erupt from the crowd. Not surprisingly, Prince John doesn't seem to have a large fan base.

"But until that day comes, your children must eat. They must grow to be strong men and women who can fight for their country. Therefore, we have brought you some silver to buy seed for your farms, bread and milk for the mouths of your babes." He lifts up the bag of silver and waves it in the air. All the peasants' eyes light up like someone flipped a switch.

"Silver?" one old hunchbacked man breathes.

"For us?" asks a small blond boy in the front, his big blue eyes wide with amazement.

"Where did ye get it?" asks a suspicious middle-aged brunette.

"We took it from a man who had much to spare," Robin says with a grin. "And are giving it to you who have so little. I think 'tis a fair trade, do you not?"

Judging from the general whoops of cheer, I'd say the idea is pretty unanimously accepted. Robin appoints one villager as a treasurer, and gives him the silver to dole out to each peasant.

"Now we must take our leave," he says, removing his hat and bowing with a flourish.

"Stay for dinner!" begs a pretty maiden in the front, batting her eyelashes at our hero. Robin is *so* a rock star here. "I'm told I make a very lovely stew."

"Aye," agrees a man in the back, leaning on a crooked cane. "We want to thank you for all you've done."

Robin shakes his head. " 'Tis not necessary," he says. "We must take our leave. I am afraid soon there may be those who will come looking for us. And I like keeping my head on my neck, thank you very much."

The crowd giggles at this.

"Farewell, brave and noble sirs," says the man who Robin appointed treasurer. "We will not forget this day, nor the men who made it so glorious."

Robin can't help but smile. I can tell—he's digging the hero stuff in spite of himself.

Chapter Seven

That night there's a big celebration at Camp Sherwood. More venison (the king is going to run out of deer the way the outlaws go through it!), more beer and more songs.

I'm very happy that the whole thing worked out, but I can't shake the sadness I felt earlier. I feel so alone here, and the longer I stay the more it weighs on me. Everyone's been nice and accepting and all, but I just don't fit in.

I slip away from the festivities and head down to the pond. I sit on the shore, staring out into the water. Why am I here? Sure, I guess I have a mission: to retrieve the Holy Grail. But then what? How will I get back to the 21st century? And if I do, what then? Go back to my pathetic life? My stupid dead-end, low-paying job? My cheating husband?

And what was it Nimue said about me finding love here? She called me the gentle soul that would tame an outlaw's thirst for revenge or something. Obviously she must be talking about Robin Hood. But do I really want to go there? Reveal my feminine side and start a relationship with a guy who lived and died hundreds of years before I was born? Sure, I could see Robin as a pretty de-lish boyfriend. But the whole scenario seems a bit shortsighted. Like, what—we fall in love, start doing the happily-ever-after thing, then King Richard shows up with the Grail and I get my chance to go back to the 21st century? What then? Will I be forced to choose my love over my life? Give up everything I've worked so hard for in order to be with this other person? Uh, been there. Done that. And I don't much like the T-shirt I got from it.

A noise behind me makes me turn around. Robin appears through the trees, his eyebrows lifting in surprise when he sees me sitting here. I probably should have picked another spot. Or maybe I subconsciously was hoping he'd show up.

He says nothing and simply sits down beside me, close enough to touch were one of us to reach out our hand. The proximity does funny things to my insides. His scent, perhaps. A bit smoky from the fire, and musky. You'd think someone who spent his entire lifetime camping in the woods would smell sweaty and gross. But he doesn't, for some reason. I almost wish he did. Would make it a bit easier.

" 'Tis a good spot for thinking deep thoughts, is it not?" he remarks quietly, staring out into the water.

"Yeah."

We both fall silent. But it's not the uncomfortable silence you get on a first date. In fact, it's nice in a way. Intimate. Danny was always talk, talk, talk. He couldn't stand the quiet parts of life.

"Must be a bit unsettling for you to be here," Robin says after a while.

I turn to look at him, surprised. "What do you mean?" There's no way he could know I'm not from 12th-century England, is there?

"An outlaw's life, mayhap, was not one you thought you'd lead. Your abbey likely had warm beds and hot meals."

Ah, he's talking about my supposed great escape from the church. "You got that right." Funny. He isn't far off the mark, though he's talking about some 12th-century cathedral, not 21st-century Jersey.

"I understand more than perhaps you know. I grew up in a small castle, myself. I had many servants and loyal subjects and never had to lift a finger for anything. I thought 'twould be the only life I ever knew. I would inherit our small fiefdom when my father died and be a fair and kind ruler to my people. Those who worked hard would always have meat on the table under my rule. I would marry Maid Marion, King Richard's niece and my childhood playmate, and produce an heir. All very simple wishes, I thought."

"But things obviously didn't work out that way."

"Nay," he says, kicking at the ground with the toe of his boot. "King Richard launched the third Crusade, asking that all able-bodied men join him on his quest to seek the Holy Grail. My father loved King Richard so. And for him to provide his king with his only son—well, he was only too happy to do it."

"And it all went to pot from there I take it."

"I am loyal to my king," Robin says with a shrug. "And we should not question the decisions he makes. But to abandon his country, to fight in a foreign land for some religious cause and leave his own people unprotected from his evil blood relative—well, that seems an unwise decision to me."

"Yeah, pretty dumb. He should have at least left some sort of force behind. Like the Knights of Homeland Security or something."

"So you see, Christian, this forest existence is not the life I hoped to lead. Or one I could ever be truly content with. I was born to lead knights, not a band of ragamuffins. I was born to sit on a throne, not a stump of wood." He fidgets, trying to get comfortable. "At the same time, in many ways, this forest life agrees with me. It's simple. Honest. And I know, forsooth, my men are true. They would stand with me in the face of death, should I ask it. You do not often win such true friendships in a castle court, where the power-hungry vie for control."

Hm. Sounds a lot like the fashion-mag biz, if you ask me. A bunch of skinny, Gucci-clad prima donnas fighting as if their life depended on getting that cover-story byline. So often I've imagined a simpler life. A less glamorous job in a small town. One where people know their neighbors. Where families help each other out. Where you can make trustworthy friends. Marry trustworthy people.

"What about Maid Marion?" I ask, curious. I've been wondering about her: a major character in the Robin Hood legend, but completely absent from what

I've seen. And after all, if I were to decide to start something with Robin Hood, I've got to size up the competition.

Robin scowls. "She chooses the life of a lady in waiting at Prince John's castle. She has no interest in coming out into the woods and getting her soft white hands dirty."

Ah, I'm starting to see more why the guy's so bitter against women. He lost his titles and riches and his chick went running in the other direction. Stupid gold-digging, uh, wench.

"That's pretty lame," I say. "If you two loved each other . . ."

"I loved her more than anything. Mayhap, I still do. But I cannot say whether she ever loved me or simply what I once had. All I know for certain is that she seems no longer interested in my affections."

"Are you sure? I mean, have you talked to her?" Oh jeez, I am the incurable matchmaker, aren't I? Still, I can't bear to hear the hurt in his voice without at least trying to Dear Abby.

"When I first returned from the Crusades, my only wish was to see her again. But after I became an outlaw, I realized I could not by right walk through the castle gates. So I risked all, sneaked into the city dressed as a beggar and climbed over a back wall into the castle gardens, desperate to find her. And I did find Marion there, but she was in the arms of another." Robin stops for a moment and I can see his hard swallow. "She did not wait for me."

My heart pangs in my chest as I steal a glimpse of

his hurt face. If only he knew how much I understood. That devastating moment when the world as you know it crashes down, when the one you love more than anything betrays you in the worst possible way . . . I will never, ever be able to burn the image of Danny, pants down to his ankles in that bathroom stall, pounding away at that waitress. Him stopping when he heard someone opening the door. The color draining from his scruffy face as he realized it was me.

Time stopped. I don't know if I said anything. If I cried out my horror and surprise. The next thing I remember was running through the coffeehouse, Danny chasing me, still rezipping his trousers. Calling my name. Begging for me to stop. To turn around. To give him a chance to explain.

But how can you explain something like that? Something so obvious? Danny, my first and only love. The one I gave my virginity to. The one who swore on our wedding day that he would be true 'til death. The same man that now saw fit to violate our marriage, our trust, our love, by sticking his cock into another person. Someone who didn't matter. And who knew if that was even the first time he'd done it? Working as a bartender, he'd had plenty of opportunities. Plenty of nights to come home late. Plenty of chances to betray me.

Robin hates women for what Marion did to him. I can see why. I definitely have a thing against certain men.

"Wow. I'm so sorry you had to go through that," I say, realizing I'd been lost in my own angry thoughts and hadn't properly responded. "That really sucks."

"Sucks?"

Oops. Gotta chill with the 21st centuryisms. "That's terrible," I amend. "Very . . . bad."

"Aye."

I look at him thoughtfully. "Would you ever go back to her? If she came out to Sherwood Forest and asked for another chance?" I always wonder this about myself. If Danny begged for forgiveness, would I grant it? Or perhaps more importantly, should I? We vowed through good times and bad. I just never thought the bad would involve a waitress with Pamela Anderson-sized boobs.

Robin shrugs. "To be honest, I do not know. But 'twill never happen, so 'tis useless to talk of it."

Sigh. He's probably right. Why would the gold-digging chick want to live this type of life when she's probably got a sweet setup back at the castle? But that's so sucky. I mean, how could she choose some other random guy over Robin here? Sure, he can be a bit arrogant and pigheaded, but he's really a nice guy. Loyal, brave, confident . . .

Eesh. Now I sound like I'm falling for him. Which I'm totally not. I mean, yes, I'm attracted to him. How could I not be? He's handsome as sin. But that's as far as it goes. I'm not ready for a new relationship yet. Especially not with a 12th-century outlaw who thinks I'm a eunuch. No matter what Nimue predicted, it just ain't happening.

Besides, the history books always have Robin ending up with Maid Marion, right? What would happen if I showed up and inadvertently changed all that? I mean, hey, I've seen *Back to the Future 2* a few times, and changing history is never pretty.

Bottom line? It's totally not worth altering the world as we know it for a quick rebound romance, no matter how hot the guy.

Once again, it seems like my role here is to fix things. Now that I've got Robin stealing from the rich and giving to the poor, it must be time to get his lady friend back. Luckily, I've seen a lot of Dr. Phil.

"Look, Rob. It may feel useless to talk about it, but in a way it could be therapeutic too."

"Thera—?" He cocks his head. Oops, psychobabble terms have probably yet to be invented.

"Um, good for the soul," I amend quickly. "The heart. You know, it's not always healthy to keep your anger wrapped up inside. It'll just eat away at you. Make you bitter and vengeful. Do you really want her having so much power over you?"

"She has no power over me," he retorts—way too strongly.

"Um, yeah, sure." I laugh. "Look. First you need to give yourself permission to feel hurt at her betrayal. Men hardly ever do that, you know. They just push it down deep inside. Pretend it doesn't matter. And then their anger grows to monstrous proportions and they go punch walls. Or start wars. But if they'd just talk about it, get it out . . ."

Ugh. I feel like I'm lecturing myself. I haven't exactly been forthcoming about the whole Danny thing either. In fact, no one knows it even happened. It's just too embarrassing to admit, even to close friends. Not that I have many close friends.

Robin scowls. "I told you everything already."

"Right. Well, how about this? What would you say to Marion if she suddenly showed up to camp?"

He shrugs his shoulders but says nothing. Grr. Men can be such pains in the ass at times.

"You're in a safe place here. You can say anything," I press. "What is said at the lakeshore stays at the lakeshore."

He stares down at his hands, stripping a twig of its bark.

"Come on, man," I say, softening my tone. "I know it's something you've imagined a million times."

He narrows his eyes and presses his lips together firmly before speaking. "I would . . . ," he begins, his voice surprising me with its unsteadiness. "I would . . . ask her why she did it," he says slowly. "Why she did not wait for me."

The pain in his voice makes me ache inside. Poor guy. Poor, poor guy. This Marion chick is a real bitch and a half, isn't she? I know what I'd do if she showed up at camp. I'd smack her upside the head.

"That'd be a good start. What else?"

"I do not know," he says, shrugging his broad shoulders and staring at the ground.

"Yes, you do."

He sighs deeply. "I would . . . I would tell her that I loved her. That I would have done . . . anything." He looks over at me for the first time, his brilliant green eyes clouded. "I would have . . . I would have died for her, Christian."

Tears prick the corners of my eyes as I look back at him. How could Marion do this, blow off a guy who loved her so much? Stupid bitch. She doesn't know how good she had it. A once-in-a-lifetime storybook love. A man willing to lay down his very life for her. And she gave it up for a few pieces of silver.

What I wouldn't give to have someone feel that way about me. But that'll never happen. I'm not the kind of girl who garners that kind of love. Hell, my own mother would have sold me for a nickel bag of pot. Actually I think one time she did. And Danny . . . Oh Danny, why?

"Are you crying?" Robin asks suddenly, cocking his head in confusion. "Did I upset you by my words?"

I swipe at my eyes with my sleeve. "No. Sorry," I say, my face burning with embarrassment. "Your story just . . . affected me. I'm real sensitive. Always crying at movies—er . . . plays." They did have plays in medieval times, right? God, what I wouldn't give for five minutes with Wikipedia to look this stuff up.

Robin reaches over and awkwardly takes my hand in his, giving it a small squeeze. The gesture sends a flood of longing straight to my already aching heart. He's so sweet. So genuine and true. He would have never cheated on Marion with a waitress. Heck, he wouldn't have cheated with the queen of England. He's the type of man who's loyal to a fault. The one who loves with all his soul.

And where does that loyalty leave him? Heartbroken and alone. Just like me.

Love is so overrated.

Robin releases my hand and I look over, catching a small blush on his face. He's probably realizing it might not be too cool to start petting the eunuch. Suddenly the urge to tell him the truth about who I am overwhelms me. What would he do if I told him I was a woman? What would he do if I told him I was from the future? Would he forgive me? Would he fall in love with me? Not that I want that to happen. Well, not really . . .

Get a hold of yourself, Chrissie! This isn't some random encounter with a random guy you met in the woods. You already know how the legend plays out. Who he ends up with. No matter what issues they're having now, Robin marries Maid Marion. End of story. Don't go falling for someone who's destined to hook up with someone else. You'll just be left, once again, heartbroken and alone.

Thankfully Robin changes the subject. "I saw you holding a bow yesterday," he says. "How are you at archery?"

I swallow hard, pushing my emotions back down my throat, just as I instructed him not to do moments earlier. But what choice do I have? If I fall apart here, he'll just freak out and run in the other direction. And where will that leave me? No, it's better to stay in character. A place to sleep and food to eat are more important at the moment than indulging in my mixed-up feelings and sharing them with someone who wouldn't be interested in listening.

I wrinkle my nose and force myself to laugh. "The bow? I'm terrible. I can't seem to get the hang of aiming the damn thing."

"I figured as much," he says, reaching over to ruffle

my hair. His fingers tingle as they lightly scrape against my scalp. "Tomorrow, if you wish, I will aim to teach you the secret."

"Yeah?" I ask, stealing a glance at him. He smiles at me, a gentle sweet smile that breaks my heart. "That would be . . . nice."

God, I'm falling for him. I'm really, truly falling for him. This is very bad. I must stop. I'm going to get hurt. And I can't take any more hurt. Not right now. Not when I've yet to recover from the first round of the stuff.

He nods. "Aye. 'Tis the least I can do. You have brought much joy to my men since your arrival, young Christian. And to . . . me as well."

I have to restrain myself from beaming stupidly at the compliment. Joy. I bring him joy. That's good, right? Chrissie the joy bringer. Making men merry throughout Sherwood Forest.

So why oh why can't I just be content with that?

Chapter Eight

"Stand with your body at a right angle to the target there...."

I shift position a bit, trying to line up with the bull's-eye in front of me. Robin inspects my stance with a critical glare.

"No, no," he says, shaking his head. "Imagine a line connecting from your left shoulder to the target."

"Can't we just get to shooting the arrow?" I ask. Not to be a whiner, but we've been at the positioning thing for the last half hour. I want some target practice, baby!

"Shooting from the right position is half the trick to hitting your mark."

Of course it is. This guy's as bad as Mr. Miyagi in *The Karate Kid*. I'll go ballistic if he starts teaching me the zen of wax on, wax off in a thinly veiled effort to get his horse washed.

"How's this?" I ask, shifting once more.

"Aye, 'tis not bad. Now take the bow." Robin hands me a bow almost the size of my body. "And hold it out with your left hand, like so."

I do as he instructs. I feel pretty cool, holding an actual medieval bow in my hands. I mean, what if I turn out to be a complete natural? I am learning from the best in the land. Maybe I could go do some competitions. Earn a little fame back here in the 12th century.

"Very good. Now 'tis time to nock the arrow," Robin says, pulling one from his quiver.

"Uh, like this?" I ask, knocking once on the wooden shaft. It seems pretty silly to me, but maybe it's some kind of weird tradition around here. Thanking God for arrows, or something. Knocking on wood that they hit their mark?

Robin rolls his eyes. "Not knocking, nocking! Fit the arrow on the string."

Oh. Duh, Chrissie. I take the arrow and slip the string into the groove, holding it in place with my right hand.

"Now hold the bow with your left hand and rest the tip of the arrow on top."

I can do this part. I've seen it in the movies.

"Now, pull the string toward you and when you've lined up your arrow with your target, release."

Yeah, baby. Now we're talking. I start pulling back on the string and . . .

"Uh . . ."

"Pull back on the string, lad," Robin repeats patiently.

"I, um . . ." I can feel sweat beading at my temples. God, this is embarrassing. Come on, Chris! You've never been some girlie-girl, have you?

"Too tough for you, eh?" Robin asks, that patronizing look back on his face. Grr.

"Not. At. All!" I cry, pulling back with all my might. The good news is I manage to pull back the string enough to get some tension on the bow. The bad news is that I completely lose all sense of aim. The arrow goes flying wildly through the air, up into the sky, then downward . . . straight into Little John's big behind, which happens to be sticking out as he tends the fire.

"Ow!" he howls, practically falling head first into the cooking pot. He turns around. "What in God's—?"

Horrified, I drop the bow and rush over. What if it's a bad injury? What if it gets infected and he dies? After all, they don't have penicillin yet. What if I've just inadvertently killed the famous Little John?

"Are you okay?" I ask, trying to get behind him so I can inspect the arrow sticking out of him. "I'm so, so sorry!" He circles around to try to face me. We dance this way for a bit, before he reaches behind him and feels the arrow.

"Ye'd better work on yer aim, boy," he says, shaking his head.

"Are you all right, John?" Robin says, rushing over. His face shows concern, but a closer look reveals a bit of mischief in his sparkling eyes. What do you know, he thinks it's funny! Thank goodness.

"God's teeth! I've got a bloody arrow stuck in my

butt. Aye, I'm just lovely," John growls. "Thanks to your young apprentice here. I'm glad 'tis Will Scarlet who's responsible for training the rest of this sorry lot. For the best shot in the county, you make a lousy teacher." He tries to reach around to grab the arrow from his behind. Unfortunately for him, he's just too round about the middle to reach, and so he ends up circling a few times before stumbling to the ground, luckily not onto the arrow itself.

Oh. My. God. I'm going to die of humiliation.

"I suggest you wander over to Friar Tuck's tent," Robin says, with a face that looks like he's withholding a lot of laughter at his buddy's expense. "He'll yank it out of your backside—and he'll ply you with enough mead afterward to make you forget 'twas ever there."

"Aye, sounds like a plan," Little John agrees, nodding. "At least he didn't puncture the barrel."

"Yea, that'd totally be alcohol abuse!" I say, chuckling. The two men look at me. Sigh. I can't wait to get back to a time where people understand my jokes.

"Now, young Christian," Robin says, "I think it best if we continue our lessons on the morrow. For now, I have something I would like to show you."

"Okay," I say, wondering what on earth it could be. I follow him to the edge of the camp where a chestnut brown mare stands docile, saddled and tied to a tree. Robin slaps her affectionately a few times, then frees her from the tree, sticking his foot in a stirrup and hopping up on her back. Then he reaches down and motions for me to take his hand. I put my hand in his and he scoops me up onto the horse so I'm riding in front of him. He flicks the reins and off we go.

"Where are we headed?" I ask curiously, trying not to notice the way Robin's muscular chest presses against my back. Every movement feels intense. Intimate. And he has no idea.

"I told you about Castle Locksley," he says. "My ancestral home. I thought mayhap you'd care to see it with your own eyes."

Oh cool, a real life castle. And not just any castle, but Robin's. "Nice. I'd love to see where you grew up," I say, smiling. He must really like me if he wants to show me his home, right? "That'd be really great."

"Well, do not expect too much," he adds. "When the sheriff's men invaded it and arrested my father for treason, they looted the treasure and destroyed the rest. Today Locksley Castle is merely a burnt-out husk of the glorious home it once was." His voice is melancholy, and I wish I could turn around and give him a hug. Obviously the place meant a lot to him. By default, it suddenly means a lot to me.

"Well, I still want to see it," I assure him. "Very much."

"Good. Because I'd very much like you to," he says, his voice warming. He flicks the reins and the horse picks up its pace.

"Um, one question though," I add.

"Yes?"

"Aren't there bad guys in it now? I mean, isn't it guarded by anyone?"

"Mayhap a soldier or two is posted there, but there

would be little reason to keep it under heavy guard. The sheriff's men have likely already stolen everything worth stealing, and there are other more strategic castles in the area to occupy."

"Er, right," I say, not sure he's getting my real question. "But two soldiers are not zero soldiers. I mean, how are we going to get past them?"

He laughs. "Ah, wait and see, Christian. I have a plan. Disposing of the guards will be half the fun."

"Fun?" Trips to Walt Disney World are fun. Getting drunk at a baseball game and booing the Yankees is fun. (I know, I know, I'm from Hoboken. But my second foster father was a diehard Yankees fan and so I went for the Red Sox.) Risking our lives by infiltrating a guarded medieval castle? Not so much fun in my book.

Sadly, at this point there's not much I can do about it. I'm on the back of a horse trotting down a narrow forest trail. How do I get myself into this stuff?

I tell myself I shouldn't be scared. After all, I'm with the legendary Robin Hood. Surely no mere mortal man could hurt me with this guy on my team.

Soon we've left Sherwood Forest behind and Robin urges his horse into a gallop across what appears to be a never ending stretch of countryside. The sun shines down upon us, kissing my skin with warmth, and the breeze toys with my hair, coaxing curls to tumble into my face. It's pleasant, actually, galloping through fields of wildflowers and heather, up grassy knolls, past crumbling stone walls. We wave to shepherds sitting idly under trees, watching their sheep munch on sweet-smelling grass; to peasants walking behind ox-driven plows, cultivating their fields, growing food to feed their families and liege lord.

There's a certain sense of peace to the scenery here. A simple life, so to speak, though I can't imagine Paris Hilton and Nicole Richie trying to tackle the day-to-day tasks of medieval serfs during a future season of the show. Still, I wonder what it'd be like to live this way, concerning yourself only with survival and feeding your family. Having no idea how big the world actually is. How confusing it is. How heartbreaking. If you never have hopes and dreams, you'll never be crushed when they fail to come true, right?

Then again, most of these people live a sickly existence full of hard manual labor, lice and disease. Oh, and they die at like forty years old—if they're lucky. So maybe I should stop with the grass is always greener thing and be thankful for the good things that I've got.

We come to the bottom of a hill and Robin slows his horse. "We walk from here," he says, jumping off, then offering me a hand. I hop down from the horse, wriggling the kinks out of my legs. Even that short ride has me a bit creaky; my knees and thighs are screaming for a massage.

"Great," I say, swallowing back my annoyance at the idea of hoofing it again. Seriously, I'm so sick of walking everywhere. My kingdom for my good old Volkswagen Bug, Flower. Though, to stay in glass-half-full mode, I'm sure to get back to the 21st century in record shape, and thighs of steel are never a bad thing. Who knows, maybe I'll be so buff and kick-ass I'll be able to win a marathon or something. Of course I'd never be able to tell the media my winning training strategy. . . .

Robin shields his eyes from the sun and points. "Locksley Castle lies yonder," he says, pointing to the hillside. "Just over that."

"Great. So now what? What's this big plan of yours to defeat the bad guys guarding the place?"

He grins. " 'Tis simple. You will flush them out."

"Uh, what? Me?" Hold on one gosh darned second. "Flush?"

Robin reaches into his saddlebag and pulls out a folded garment. He shakes it loose and I realize it's a dress.

What the . . . ?

"Put this on," he instructs, handing me the outfit. "With your clean face and build, the guards will think you a woman. Go to the front door and knock on it. Beg for food. I'd wager they have not seen a woman so comely and will be more than glad to allow you entrance."

"Yeah, so they can rape and pillage me?" I say. "Thanks, but no thanks." I'm not waltzing up to some enemy castle's front door with nothing more than a medieval gown to protect me, all on the insane hope that the guards inside will find me attractive enough to completely disobey their orders and Open Sesame at my command. But, did Robin call me comely?

"Have no fear. I will follow and lie in wait close behind, bow drawn. Once you lure them outside, I will act."

I narrow my eyes. "Are you sure this will work?"

He laughs. "Not at all. But 'tis half the fun not knowing, is it not?" He slaps me on the shoulder, so hard I almost fall over. Ugh. This guy really needs to get out more, to work on his definition of fun.

"My young Christian," Robin continues, his voice taking on a more serious tone. " 'Twas you who first suggested we rob the rich to feed the poor. Forsooth, I have not returned here since those first days. Mayhap there are a few hidden treasures inside that the sheriff's men have not discovered. Would it not be grand to retrieve them?"

Oh, I see. Use my own words against me, why don't you? How can I refuse now? Very Medieval Psych 101. Eesh. The things I do for the poor people in the land! If only all these charitable works were tax deductible back in the 21st century.

"Okay, then. Let's do it," I agree, against my better judgment. I look at the dress, then at Robin. "Um, do you mind?" I ask. I'm not changing in front of him.

He laughs. "Modest, are ye?" he teases, but thankfully turns around. If only he knew that it wasn't modesty, but my female anatomy that I'm concerned about.

Quickly, before he changes his mind about looking, I slip out of my tunic and throw the gown over my head. The fabric flutters over my skin, draping my body in seductive softness. I run my hands down the front of the garment, rejoicing in the feel of silk against my bare skin. It feels so nice to dress like a girl again. And in such a gown! It's emerald green and empire-waisted, with embroidered cuffs, neck and hemline. I wish I had a full-length mirror so I could experience the full effect. I have the inexplicable urge to twirl around and let the breeze take my skirts. To dance through the field like Julie Andrews and sing about the hills being alive with the sound of music.

But then Robin might get a tad suspicious, I guess. After all, I'm supposed to be a dude. I have to play like this is embarrassing, not glorious.

"Ugh," I say, trying to hide my pleasure at my new apparel. "This thing, uh, smells like perfume or something. Stupid women, always dousing themselves with the stuff."

Robin turns around to inspect me, his green eyes widening as they catch my appearance. His tanned face visibly pales and, to my utter secret delight, his mouth drops open.

"Wow," he murmurs.

I can feel my cheeks heat. "Like it?" I ask, suddenly forgetting I'm supposed to abhor the feminine look. I twirl around to give him the full effect, enjoying his flabbergasted stare. Does he think I'm pretty? Is he attracted to me? Am I turning the legendary Robin Hood on?

He shakes his head, as if trying to break the spell. " 'Tis nothing," he mutters. "Just . . . for a moment there . . ."

"What?" I start, then stop, scolding myself for my vanity. As much as I secretly want him to think I'm hot in the dress, it might prove counterproductive in the long run. I mean, what if he suddenly realizes that I'm really a girl, now that I'm dressed like one? What would he do? Berate me for lying? Kick me out of camp? Then again, maybe he'd be so blown away by my beauty that he wouldn't care that I'd deceived him. He'd simply sweep me into his arms and say—

"I think you need some breasts."

Hmph. Well, there goes that fantasy down the drain.

"Um, breasts?" I ask, raising my eyebrows and trying to ignore the disappointment rolling through my stomach.

"No one's going to believe you're a woman with a chest like that," he says, chuckling. He reaches into the saddlebags again, this time pulling out two apples. Unceremoniously, he grabs the neckline of my dress and plops them inside.

Sigh. I reach up to adjust my newfound cleavage. This is seriously sad. I can't believe I thought for a moment that he was really attracted to me. What had I been thinking?

"Better?" I ask, rolling my eyes.

"Aye." He grins, completely oblivious. "Now you look buxom as Little John's mum."

Oh-kay then. There's an image I didn't care to conjure up.

"Um, great. Super," I mutter. "So, um, you want me to just walk right up to the castle and knock on the front door or something?" Better to concentrate on the mission, I think. Before I strangle him for his stupidity.

"Aye. Tell them you are starving and try to draw them outside. I'll take care of it from there."

I square my shoulders, firming my resolve. "Okay. Let's do this then."

Eager to be away from him and his stupid belief that all women should grow up to look like Little John's mom, evidently the Jenna Jameson of Nottingham, I stalk across the field. I can feel Robin's eyes on my back, following my every move, so I pick up my pace. Flat-chested, indeed! I'm so sick of that. Why are guys so hung up on big boobs, anyway? What good do they really do them?

I walk up a small hill and at the top catch my first glimpse of the castle. It's beautiful. Built entirely of gleaming white stones, it stands tall and majestic on the moor. But as I get closer, I realize that it's in dire need of repair. The stone foundation is crumbling. The banner flags waving from the turrets are tattered. The iron front gate is hanging open, and in the courtyard I discover the dilapidated remnants of a fiefdom torn apart: broken market stands, empty cages, animal bones bleached white from the sun. It's bleak. Depressing. I wonder what Robin will think when he sees the state of his ancestral home. Poor guy.

I reach the massive wooden front door of the keep and knock as instructed. An iron peephole slides open with a loud creak, and a beady eye peers out at me with suspicion.

"Who goes there?"

I bow my head and then look up through my eyelashes, giving my best little-girl-lost look. I'm not as good at it as say, Kat, who has perfected the art of getting whatever she wants in life with a mere batting of her eyelashes, but if Robin's right, this man won't have seen a woman in weeks, so I doubt I have to achieve a Mary Kate and Ashley level of pouting. "Just a poor humble woman," I say, "hoping for a few crumbs of bread from your majesty."

"Beggars are not welcome here," the voice says harshly. "Begone."

"But sir," I say coyly. "I'd be willing to trade a *lot* for just one slice of bread. A lot!"

"A lot? Like what?"

Jeez Louise, this guy is dense. Obviously he's never had the pleasure of a stripper showing up at his front door with a pizza delivery that's, 'Ooh, just too hot.'

I jut out my left hip. "You know, like . . . let's get it on?"

Oh god, I sound like Marvin Gaye. But whatever. I mean, I might as well throw all my cards on the table, right? I need to flush him out—get the door open—and obviously he's not doing so well with the subtle hints.

"I beg your pardon?" he repeats, disbelief in his voice. Not surprising, I suppose. I mean, how many medieval women show up to castles on a daily basis to try to hook up with the guards? I'm guessing about zero.

"Yes. Like, ooh, me so horny," I add, starting to get into the act. "For much . . . rutting." Isn't that what they called it back in medieval times? I mime a few thrusts for good measure, thankful there are no video cameras in medieval times, guaranteeing my actions won't end up on YouTube. "Me love you long time."

I hear a noise behind me and my face heats. No video cameras, but a live audience. Doh. I didn't think Robin would be close enough to hear me. Is he snickering? How embarrassing.

Silence from behind the door. A moment later, it

creaks open. Wow. Robin was right. It's amazing what guys will do for a little nookie.

"Come in, come in," the guard says impatiently. He's a heavyset man with a salt and pepper beard and a bulbous nose. "I'm not supposed to open this door, you know. The sheriff would have my head if he knew."

I step back a few paces instead, trying to lure him out so Robin can do whatever he plans. "I'm shy," I say, swaying side to side. "Maybe you should come and get me."

The guard grins and pulls off his helmet, revealing a shock of unruly black hair and a dire need for modern dentistry. Not exactly knight in shining armor material, this guy. Robin better make good pretty quickly, 'cause I so don't want to follow through with my promise of rutting.

"Ah, my lady. I shall come get you indeed," he says, leering at me. He steps out into the open, meaty arms outstretched, lecherous fingers waggling and ready to probe. In a split second he'll be in grabbing-distance of my breasts. And I so don't want to know how he likes them apples.

Whoosh! I feel the wind change as an arrow flies, seemingly out of nowhere and straight for the charging guard. He realizes this just in time and throws himself to the ground to avoid being pierced. His helmet goes flying, landing at my feet. The arrow harmlessly bounces off the stone wall.

The guard looks up at me, furious to learn this was all a trap. I'm pretty surprised Robin was going to shoot him, too. But I don't think he'll accept my apology.

"Bring it on, bad boy!" I taunt, positioning my hands in front of me. I can *so* take him. After all, the dude's going into this thinking I'm some random medieval maiden, not a 21st-century grad of the Central Park Self Defense Weekend Academy. He's so screwed—and not in the way he was originally hoping.

He lets out a battle cry as he lunges at me. I wait 'til he's close, then calmly knee him in the groin, just like I was taught eight hundred years from now. And just like any 21st-century mugger/serial killer/bad blind date who won't take no for an answer type, the guy buckles over in pain. I grab his dropped helmet and smash it against his skull. It makes a loud thunking sound, kind of like when you crack a coconut, and the guard falls to the ground, losing consciousness. I whack him again, just in case.

I drop the helmet and grab his sword from its sheath and wave it in front of my face. "Woot!" I cry, triumphantly, raising the sword in the air in triumph. "Oh yeah, baby! Who's your daddy?" I look around for Robin.

"My father? Why, the former Lord Locksley, as I told you before. Why do you ask?" Robin says, stepping out from his hiding spot.

I roll my eyes. "Uh, that was sort of a rhetorical question."

Robin shrugs, then takes a look at the incapacitated guard. He grins, throws his arms around me and twirls me in a hug. "Good work, Christian," he praises.

"Thanks!" I cry. I'm enjoying the feel of his body pressed against mine way too much. The sword drops to my feet.

He sets me back on the ground and reaches in to grab the apples out of my bodice. "Most difficult to hug you with these in," he says with a laugh.

Suddenly the whole situation seems so funny and absurd that I start laughing too. He pulls me close to hug me again and this time there's no fruit in our way. I can feel every contour of his body against mine. Every muscle. Shivers trip down my spine. He should not feel so good. He should not feel so—

He releases me from the hug and our eyes meet for a moment. Suddenly the smile fades from his face. His pupils darken and he just stares at me, a shadow crossing his handsome features.

"This may sound absurd, but I must say you look quite lovely in that dress," he murmurs. "It's . . . strange."

Not really, I want to say. Actually it makes perfect sense. *'Cause I'm a girl!* But I chicken out. If I tell him now, he'll totally flip. Why, oh why did I think it was a good idea to lie in the first place? If he knew I was a girl right this moment, I'm pretty sure he'd kiss me. He'd lean down and press those amazing lips against mine . . .

Either that or he'd be really, really pissed that I've been lying to him all this time. Better change the subject.

"Whose dress is it?" I ask, desperate to stop the wildfire heat spontaneously erupting throughout my body. Hugs and compliments are one thing, but I'm pretty sure he'd be freaked out beyond belief if the eunuch suddenly tried to jump his bones.

" 'Tis Marion's," he says with a small shrug. He looks down, kicking the ground with his toe. "One of the few things I still have of hers."

For some reason the spoken reminder of Robin's true love dampens the air and weighs down my former light-headed giddiness. It shouldn't, I know. After all, it's not like Robin and I are some couple. We aren't in a relationship. Heck, he doesn't even know I'm the proper sex.

Still, the hurt in his voice, the pain clouding his emerald eyes, the way his mouth lovingly forms her name sparks a longing ache in my stomach. In my soul. If only someone would love me that strongly. Mourn me when I'm gone. I'm sick of being the one who loves more. The one who stands by her man, only to have him run over her heart with a semi.

Maid Marion is a total stupid idiot. She had someone who loved her. Who wanted to care for her and protect her and marry her and have babies with her. And she threw it all away. Betrayed him, left him, didn't even give an explanation as to why she'd gone.

And what did she gain from trampling this man's tender heart? Money? Power? Prestige?

Puh-leeze.

And now Robin is a broken man. Scared. Angry. Vengeful. Even if he does someday get over Marion, which could take years, it'll be forever before he trusts again. Before he allows someone access to the soft spots. The spots he now knows could get hurt.

A deep part of me, the codependent, needs-a-twelve-step-program part, desperately wants to heal him somehow. I want to wrap my arms around him and somehow absorb the pain. Make him whole again. Make him happy and content. Specifically, happy and content with me.

But I know I can't. He has to heal on his own time schedule. And all I can do is be his friend. Be there for him. And let him feel comfortable talking about another woman, even though each time her name is mentioned it cuts through me like a clichéd knife.

"So, uh, let's check out this castle of yours," I suggest, after swallowing back the lump in my throat.

"What about him?" Robin says, kicking the guard with his toe.

The guard grunts and rolls over. "What? Who?" he asks, shaking his head, trying to regain his senses.

Robin pulls a knife from his belt. "Do not move," he commands.

"Uh, Robin? What are you doing?" I ask, worried. He's not going to try to kill the guy, is he? I mean, it's all fun and games until somebody loses a life.

"This man works for the sheriff, Christian," Robin says, not relinquishing his knife. "Do you know what the sheriff's men did to my fellows? I wish you could have seen the slaughter that day. Blood flowing in rivers down the streets. Brave men left to rot in gutters and be eaten by dogs."

Wow. So much anger and hate. So much thirst for revenge. Suddenly the words that gypsy spoke to me seem to float through my consciousness.

Thou alone can tame his unquenchable thirst for vengeance.

"Yes, I know," I say. "I can't even imagine how it must have felt to be there and see that. To lose your friends and your family. But Robin, killing this guy won't bring them back. It won't make things right. You must get past your anger. Your hate. Otherwise you're as bad as the sheriff himself."

Robin looks torn. "But how can I spare this man's life when his kind took those of my dearest friends?"

"This guy probably wasn't even there. He's just on the sheriff's payroll. Guarding a castle—alone— making a wage to bring home to feed the wife and kids. I'm not saying it's the best occupation he could have chosen, but it doesn't mean he deserves to die for it."

I feel like young John Connor in *Terminator 2,* instructing Arnold not to kill. He may agree, but I'm not sure the reason is really sinking in.

"Christian, your soft heart will be the death of you," Robin says.

"Probably. But this guy isn't really in any shape to do the job, is he? Let's just tie him up or something."

"Please good sir, the lady is right," the guard begs. "I was just doin' what I was told to do here. Following our lord's orders and all."

"I am Robin of Locksley. This is my castle. There is only one person with the right to give orders here."

"Yes, sir. I did not know. Please forgive my ignorance and let me live."

Robin sighs deeply, then motions to a length of

rope tied to a collapsed stanchion lying nearby. I run over and grab it, and together we tie the guard's hands and feet.

"Thank you, good sir," the guard babbles. "You will not regret this day."

"I do already. Thank the boy, for I would not have been so kind should I have come here myself."

"The boy?"

Robin laughs, gesturing to me. "Ah, I forgot you were fooled into thinking him a woman. Perhaps without the apples in his bosom you may better glean the truth."

Argh. If I hear one more boob joke . . .

"Forsooth? She still looks a woman to me. Very beautiful, as well, I might add."

I could kiss that guard. I really could—bad breath, big nose and all. Now I'm doubly glad I saved his life.

Robin shakes his head in disbelief. "In any case, we will let you free when we are done. Shan't be long, I'd expect."

"Thank you, kind lord. I owe you a life someday, and I, Duncan of Carlisle, always repay me debts."

"Then you owe it to young Christian here, not to me," Robin growls. He clearly doesn't like being seen as kind. "For surely I would slash you down without a moment's regret were it not for his merciful heart."

The guard bows his head in my direction. "To Christian, then," he says.

"Um, thanks," I reply, smiling at him. "I appreciate that. Hope your head feels better." Wish I had some aspirin for the guy or something.

I look back at Robin, who's giving me an impatient stare. Once satisfied he has my attention, he turns to the castle gate and makes a sweeping gesture. "I welcome you, young Christian," he says, "to the Castle Locksley."

I step through the open door and into a low-ceilinged, dark stone hallway. Small slits in the walls offer just enough sunlight to see spiders wandering through their dusty webs.

"This way," Robin says, coming up behind me, his hot breath in my ear. He takes me by my shoulders and turns me so I'm headed down a side corridor. It's spooky. Eerily silent. And weirdly intimate, too. I've really got to shake this feeling that we're on a date in Adventureland.

"You, um, don't think there are more guards around, do you?" I ask worriedly. The last thing we need is to be ambushed or something.

"Nay. Prince John is very stingy in all matters," Robin says. "He would not waste paying too many men to guard an outlaw's sacked castle. There is no benefit to it, and 'twould merely serve to drain his purse. Duncan there was likely just a scout."

"Such a shame to let the whole castle just go to pot," I say, stepping into a large open chamber. There's a blackened fire pit in the center of the room, and sunlight streams down from a skylight window. Grandly woven but now moth-eaten floor-to-ceiling tapestries hang from the walls, depicting brave knights on black chargers, flaxen-haired maidens, fire-breathing dragons and snow white unicorns.

"This was our great hall," Robin explains, walking to the far end of the room and stepping up on a dais. "My mother and father's thrones sat here. Prince John must have deemed them valuable when he looted the place. Bastard." He reaches down and picks up an old discarded leather ball. He examines it, a wistful expression on his face, then tosses it up in the air and catches it.

"When I was young, I would play at my parents' feet while my father heard the petitions of the serfs and peasants." He smiles. "He used to kick me with his boot if I got unruly, and I'd run to hide in my mother's skirts."

I smile at his memory, completely able to picture a small boy's innocent play while the politics of the land were argued by chancellors and priests. I can imagine the hall as it must have once been, filled with courtiers and ladies-in-waiting. Court jesters juggling, bards strumming harps. Tables piled high with meats and fruits and cheeses. Knights swigging mead and laughing as the pretty maids batted their eyelashes at them, hoping to gain their favor. A court of the first class—swirling, glittering, noisy, alive.

Now it's just an aching echo of what it once was, painfully quiet, with each word resonating off the vast cobwebbed ceiling, the smell of death and decay replacing that of a fine feast or lady's perfume. The colorful sights are now but a dismal gray.

Robin sinks to the ground, head in his hands. He's reliving it all, overwhelmed by the past and swallowed up by the emptiness of present-day reality. I've got to snap him out of it before he gets lost in his despair.

"Did you have dances here?" I ask.

He looks up, swallowing hard before answering. "Aye," he says, forcing a smile to his lips. "Wonderful banquets with plates overflowing with food and goblets brimming with wine. My mother loved song, and we'd have the most famous minstrels of the land come to our castle to perform. And we'd dance 'til the sun peeked over the hillside."

"Sounds like fun," I say, examining a particularly cool tapestry of a maiden surrounded by unicorns. I think I've seen something similar in the Met gift shop. It's amazing someone could weave this with a loom or whatever it was they used, to reveal such an intricate picture one strand at a time. "I love to dance."

My second foster mother was a ballroom instructor, and she taught me ballet, jazz, tap, the waltz and the tango. You name it, I learned it from Jeanine. And I loved each one. The magic of the dance, the feeling inside when the music takes over your body and soul; living in the moment and not worrying about the past or obsessing about the future. . . .

"Forsooth? I did not know the church would permit you to dance."

My face heats. Damn, I forgot who I'm supposed to be again. I really need to focus. "Oh sure," I say carelessly. "My church was pretty modern. We danced all the time."

He nods. "Of which dances are you most fond?"

Okay, I've really got to stop opening my big mouth. I don't think saying I dug the Macarena (not that I did!) is going to work here, and I certainly don't know the names of any traditional medieval dances.

"Um, I never remember the names," I say with a shrug.

"Then show me. For I feel nostalgic in this ruined hall," Robin says, twirling around as if recalling its former beauty. "I want one more happy moment here."

"Um, okay." Hm, what the hell am I going to show him? The Electric Slide is so not going to work. Nor is the Boot Scoot Boogie.

Then a brainstorm hits me. One day, a few years back, Danny had gone on a "finding himself" weekend trip to the Poconos. (Though thinking back, now I wonder if he managed to "find himself" some female company as well.) Anyway, I was stuck at home bored. I rented *A Knight's Tale* and fell in love with it. So much so, I taught myself the Dance of Gelder that Heath Ledger invents to impress Lady Jocelyn. Silly and pointless, I know, but hey, I was really bored. And now it seems like the perfect option. A true fake medieval dance.

"Okay, then. Here's a traditional dance of my homeland of . . . Hoboken. First you . . . bow," I instruct, demonstrating as I go. "Then you throw your hands to your hips and step several times. Um, then you clap left and bow again."

Robin tries to follow my instructions. It's awkward, but then again it was an awkward made-up dance to begin with.

"Then you hop, hands out, palms up. No, no—like this!" I grab his hands to put them in position.

GET UP TO
4 FREE BOOKS!

You can have the best romance delivered to your door for less than what you'd pay in a bookstore or online. Sign up for one of our book clubs today, and we'll send you **FREE* BOOKS** just for trying it out...**with no obligation to buy, ever!**

HISTORICAL ROMANCE BOOK CLUB

Travel from the Scottish Highlands to the American West, the decadent ballrooms of Regency England to Viking ships. Your shipments will include authors such as CONNIE MASON, CASSIE EDWARDS, LYNSAY SANDS, LEIGH GREENWOOD, and many, many more.

LOVE SPELL BOOK CLUB

Bring a little magic into your life with the romances of Love Spell—fun contemporaries, paranormals, time-travels, futuristics, and more. Your shipments will include authors such as KATIE MACALISTER, SUSAN GRANT, NINA BANGS, SANDRA HILL, and more.

As a book club member you also receive the following special benefits:

- **30% OFF** all orders through our website & telecenter!
  (Plus, you still get 1 book FREE for every 5 books you buy!)
- **Exclusive access to** special discounts!
- **Convenient** home delivery **and 10 days to return any books you don't want to keep.**

There is no minimum number of books to buy, and you may cancel membership at any time. See back to sign up!

*Please include $2.00 for shipping and handling.

YES! ☐

Sign me up for the **Historical Romance Book Club** and send my THREE FREE BOOKS! If I choose to stay in the club, I will pay only $13.50* each month, a savings of $6.47!

YES! ☐

Sign me up for the **Love Spell Book Club** and send my TWO FREE BOOKS! If I choose to stay in the club, I will pay only $8.50* each month, a savings of $5.48!

NAME: _____

ADDRESS: _____

_____

TELEPHONE: _____

E-MAIL: _____

☐ **I WANT TO PAY BY CREDIT CARD.**

☐ VISA   ☐ MasterCard   ☐ DISCOVER

ACCOUNT #: _____

EXPIRATION DATE: _____

SIGNATURE: _____

Send this card along with $2.00 shipping & handling for each club you wish to join, to:

**Romance Book Clubs
1 Mechanic Street
Norwalk, CT 06850-3431**

Or fax (must include credit card information!) to: 610.995.9274. You can also sign up online at www.dorchesterpub.com.

JOIN NOW!

Robin laughs. "This dance is bloody terrible!" he cries.

I shake my head, dropping his hands. "Okay, fine. Give up then," I say in mock disapproval.

"No, no!" he insists. "I will get this! No mere dance can best the great Robin of Locksley."

Bow, step, clap. Bow, step clap. Bow, step—

"Oh, this is silly!" I cry. "Let's just dance freestyle."

"Freestyle?" Robin cocks his head in question.

"Like, make up your own dance. Let the music take you where it will. Well, I guess we don't have any music. Maybe that's our problem." If only I had my iPod with portable speakers. I could pull up David Bowie's "Golden Years" and we'd really be re-living *A Knight's Tale*.

Though, whipping out a device containing twenty gigabytes of modern music might just possibly freak out the 12th-century outlaw a tad, I suppose. Guess I'll have to sing.

" 'Golden Years, wup, wup, wup! Gold-en years!' " I croon, admittedly more than a bit out of tune. I twirl around the makeshift dance floor, grabbing Robin's hand and dragging him with me. " 'Don't let me hear you say . . . life's taking you nowhere. Annngel!' "

"You're mad, Christian! Absolutely stark raving mad!"

"Boo! Don't be a sore sport! Just dance!"

And so he does. Together we whirl around the great hall, Robin's hand in mine, his arm around my waist. It feels so good. So right. I start getting silly (okay, maybe "start" is the wrong word since I've been belting out Bowie for the last couple minutes) and exaggerate the dance steps. I dip myself backward, allowing him to catch me. He fumbles the catch, almost dropping me, and I manage to slam my foot down on his as I step backward to steady myself.

"Oops," I say, consumed by giggles at this point.

"If you step on my feet one more time . . . ," Robin threatens with a laugh.

"You'll what?" I challenge, whirling to face him.

"I shall . . . sentence you to death," he says sternly. "As Lord of Locksley, 'tis perfectly within my rights."

"Death," I say coyly, batting my eyelashes at him. "My good sir, how do you plan to kill me? Poor, innocent, defenseless me."

"Defenseless? Ha! Those feet are a deadly weapon."

I stick out my foot and point my toes, then flex them. "These?" I ask, all innocent. "How could these . . ."—I pretend to slam my foot down on his once more—"hurt you?"

"That's it, now you're dead!" he cries.

Laughing, I turn tail and run across the Great Hall's floor. He pursues me, chasing me down the hall. I come to a set of stairs and scramble up, trying to outrun the footsteps that I hear closing in behind me. At the top, I push open a wooden door and find myself in a tower room. It's empty, save a bale of hay in one corner—probably a makeshift bed for prisoners. Problem is, because of that prisoner thing, there's no escape route.

Robin bursts into the room, his eyes lighting up as he sees I'm trapped. He grabs me by the shoulders and shoves me back into the hay, jumping on top of me and tickling me with relentless fingers.

"Death by tickle!" he cries through his laughter.

"Uncle! Uncle!" I cry, knowing he won't understand my plea. "I surrender! I surrender! No one can withstand tickle torture!"

He stops. His hair has come undone from its ponytail and has fallen into his face as he stares down at me. His laughter fades and his look is dead serious. Dead sexy. I can feel his hot breath on my face, strands of hair tickling my cheeks. Before I can do anything, say anything, he leans down and presses his mouth hard against mine.

Chapter Nine

Oh my god. What is he doing? I mean, it's very apparent what he's doing, crushing me with a kiss, stealing my breath, pinning me to the straw bed. But he thinks I'm a boy. Could he be gay? Is this time-travel trip suddenly turning into an episode of *Brokeback Forest*? God help me if the legendary Robin Hood suddenly wishes he could quit me.

What am I to do? His lips feel amazing. His tongue demands entrance. I can't help it. It's been so long since I had a first kiss. I submit. I open my mouth and allow him to take control. His tongue ravages mine, devours me as if I'm some sort of vital nourishment and he hasn't eaten in a year.

Then, just as suddenly as he began, he stops. Robin scrambles off me to his feet and retreats to the other side of the room. He leans down, hands on his knees, trying to catch his breath. Looking everywhere but at me.

"Robin—" I start, realizing this is the perfect time to tell him the truth. Don't worry, dude. You're not gay. Or whatever they call it in Sherwood Forest. I'm a chick. One hundred percent woman. But he waves a hand at me, cutting off my words.

"Don't say anything!" he growls, his eyes fierce with anger. "Just leave."

"But—"

"Begone!" he bellows.

I'm half afraid he's going to hit me—kill me, even—so I don't address the fact that he, in his mind, just made out with a guy. I pick up my skirts and flee the tower, running down the stairs, through the passage, out the door and into the courtyard. Tears stream down my face as I pass the guard and run into the field. I don't know where I'm going. I can barely see. I trip again, falling to my knees in the dirt. Unable to run any more, I allow sobs to overtake me, wracking my body, tearing at my soul.

What have I done? How did I let this happen? I hope the gypsy's not looking down on me now, shaking her head, unbelieving that someone could possibly make such a mess of a simple time-travel trip. I mean, really! How did a quest to save my coworker turn into a drama of "As the Wood Turns" proportions? All I wanted to do was find the Holy Grail. I never expected to lose my heart in the process.

At this moment, on my knees in the middle of a 12th-century English moor, I don't care much about my mission. Or about my 21st-century life, for that matter. All I can focus on, all I can wrap my head around, is the rejection slamming into my stomach with the force of a championship boxer's fist. Rejection from a man I've totally fallen for.

Why didn't I just tell him the truth from the start? Well, okay, maybe not the whole truth and nothing but the time-traveling truth. But I could have at least shared the fact that I have female body parts.

Stupid, Chrissie. Truly stupid.

I stumble back to my feet, my eyes too bleary from my tears to focus on which direction I should walk. I've got to get out of here. Somewhere, anywhere. Alone. Away from this place.

"Christian, wait!"

I turn and see Robin run after me. I know I must look a total sight. Tear-stained face and red nose . . . I never look glamorous when I cry, like the heroines in movies always seem to do without any effort. They cry and they take on a beautiful sorrow—pale face, delicate tears. Me? I start looking like a water-logged Bozo the Clown.

I sink back to my knees, realizing I can't escape, can't run away anymore. I have to face this. I have to tell him the truth.

Robin stands above me for a moment, hands on his hips, then sighs and scrambles down on the ground next to me. He puts a hesitant arm around my shoulder, patting me gently. It's awkward, for sure, but I can't help but lean into him a little, a desperate attempt to absorb some of his strength.

"I apologize, Christian," he says in a soothing voice. " 'Twill not happen again, I swear it. After all, I am not the sort of man who lies with boys. I just—

you just—oh Mary, mother of God!" he cries, running a hand through his loose hair. "I am so sorry if I frightened you."

"I'm a girl!" I cry, unable to keep the secret a second longer. I rip out of his embrace and gesture to my body. "I'm not a boy or a man or a eunuch or anything that has even remotely to do with a Y chromosome. I'm female through and through and always have been."

"What?" he asks, disbelieving and incredulous. "What are you going on about?"

"Don't you get it?" I ask, tears in my eyes, a lump in my throat. "I just pretended I was a boy so you wouldn't kick me out of camp. Like you did with Much the Miller's wife. You say women aren't welcome and I didn't have anyplace else to go. I'm sorry. I didn't mean to lie. It's just—"

And that's all I can get out before his mouth is on mine once again, kissing me with a passion I've never felt before.

"God's teeth! How could I have been so blind?" Robin murmurs, pulling away for a moment to examine my face. His hands grip my shoulder blades. " 'Tis so obvious. You're sweet and beautiful and fair. . . ." He takes my face in his hands, his own inches away. I can feel his hot breath steam my lips as he studies me with his emerald eyes. "I've been fighting this ever since that day on the log. When you dove into the water to save me. I thought I was going mad. I'd never been one of those men who liked lads. But you, there is something about you, Christian—" He stops and cocks his head. "What is your true name then?"

"Chrissie," I say. "Well, technically it's Christine."

"Christine," he murmurs, reaching behind me to undo my ponytail, allowing red curls to tumble around my face. He runs his fingers through the strands in an almost worshipful caress. "Oh, Christine." He leans forward and presses a small kiss against my lips, then pulls away.

"What?" I ask, not wanting any of this to stop, even for a millisecond.

"I forget myself," he says, releasing me. "The mere fact that you are a woman does not mean you desire me. And I have never been the type to force my affections."

"Are you kidding me?" I ask. "I've wanted you since the moment I laid eyes on you. Do you know how hard it's been to act like a boy this whole time?"

"I cannot imagine, my dear," Robin says fondly. "Though I must say, you did a very good job of it. I feel like quite the fool to not have guessed."

"Oh yes, you are very foolish. Very foolish indeed." I playfully plant a kiss on his nose. He smirks and returns the gesture, adding a loud smacking sound effect.

I giggle, throwing my hands above my head and collapsing into the grass—all the weight and stress of my secret lifted from my shoulders. I feel light enough to fly. And certainly happy enough. What had I been so afraid of? He's not mad I'm a girl. If anything, he's overjoyed.

Robin pulls on my hand, bringing me back up to a seated position. I study his face. His smile has faded and in its place has come a serious, contemplative look. I open my mouth to ask him what's wrong, but before I can speak, he takes my face in his hands and presses his lips against mine.

Ooh, time for kiss number two. And this time there's no shocking secrets to interrupt us.

This is not the crush of mouths we experienced earlier, either. Now his mouth is soft, gentle. His lips are inquiring; they move in an almost reverential caress. I allow myself a small moan as he trails kisses along my cheekbone. He nibbles my ear. He's barely touched me and already my insides are completely melty. How can one man's kiss stir such insta-matic passion?

Kisses were never like this with Danny. He always treated them as an obligatory routine—a means to an orgasmic end. Warm me up with a few kisses, then move in for the kill. But Robin seems disinterested in hurrying to the main event. In fact, his soft groans make me believe he's enjoying the foreplay as much as I am.

In a way it's strange, really, to kiss a stranger like this, someone other than Danny. After all, Danny was my first. The one I thought would be 'til death. But I'm not dead. In fact, I can't remember a time when I felt more alive.

Robin's hands run through my hair, separating each strand, then lower to my shoulders, dusting my arms with light dancing fingers, tickling my suddenly sensitive skin. Slowly exploring. Caressing. Taking his time. I let out a gasp of pleasure at the tingly sensation his touch evokes.

He reaches my hands, intertwining his fingers with

mine while his mouth tastes my neck. Soft, featherlight kisses dance across my skin.

He lowers me gently to the grass. Somehow it's sweet-smelling, of honeysuckle. Musky, of desire. Hands still holding mine, he pulls my arms above my head, effectively but gently pinning me down. He crawls on top of me, separating my legs with his knee. I attempt to stay calm. To not squirm against him as desire takes hold. I can feel his erection rubbing against my thigh. Strong, hard—in sharp contrast with his caress. He's making an effort to be gentle. Holding himself back.

"Oh lady," he groans, confirming my suspicion of his current state of sacrifice. "You tempt me sorely. But, I do not want to be the man to . . . steal your honor."

I look up in surprise. Oh. He must think I'm a virgin or something. After all, women back in these times didn't hook up 'til they were married. Er, how am I going to explain this without sounding like a Sherwood slut?

"Don't worry," I encourage, freeing my hand from his grasp and reaching up to loosen his hair from its leather tie. It falls into his face and he grins, shaking it aside. "I'm a . . . widow." That was almost true, considering Danny may be technically still breathing. At this moment he's definitely dead to me.

Evidently satisfied by my explanation, Robin drags his fingers down the insides of my arms until they reach my breasts. He cups them in his hands, his fingers lightly stroking the tips. I squirm at the sensation, barely able to control myself.

"And to think I stuck apples down your dress," he

chuckles between kisses. His mouth lowers to my throat, to my chest. His fingers pull at the neckline of the gown.

"Yeah, well, I know I'm not exactly blessed in the chest department," I say, feeling suddenly a bit inadequate, exposed.

"Ah, be quiet, woman. You are more beautiful than my favorite star," he murmurs, taking my left breast in his mouth. I bite my lower lip to hold back a moan as my fingers claw at the grass, the dirt, anything within reach.

Robin's mouth is hot, wet—magic—as it teases my nipple into a rock-hard peak. His other hand finds my right breast, stroking it into submission. I involuntarily push myself against his thigh, desperate to relieve the exquisite torment his touch invokes. He pushes back. Solid, firm. "Oh God," he mouths against my breast. "I have to have you. Now."

And I, I realize, have to be had.

He abandons my breasts, mashing his mouth against mine, his tongue diving in with seemingly relentless desire. He grabs at my skirts, desperately trying to pull them up. I can't help myself—I reach to pull down his calfskin trousers. I remember wondering that first day if he had stuck a sock in his tights. I now realize he did no such thing. He's magnificent. Absolutely magnificent.

Unclothed and free, he pushes himself inside me. Filling me. Completing me. I gasp as our bodies become one. He's deep inside me now—solid, hard, mine. He moans, his face a mask of concentration as he struggles to control his desire. To slow his pleasure for my sake. I feel a strange sense of power well up inside of me. *I'm* making him feel like this. *I'm* responsible for his groans of pleasure. Little old me has made the legendary Robin Hood rock hard and ready to go.

His movements are gentle at first, rocking against me, pressing himself deeper, then pulling back, then deeper again until I feel he's found my very core. I match his thrusts with my own, arching my back in delicious agony at the sensations electrifying every inch of my skin. His hand reaches down to stroke my sex, fingers masterfully dancing over my most sensitive flesh and I bite my lower lip to keep from screaming.

At this moment, there's no past, no future. Just delicious sensations. Timeless, eternal. Here. Now.

I want to laugh. I want to cry. I'm frightened to death and elated beyond measure. I feel more comfortable and happy in his arms than I ever did with Danny in all our years together.

He starts thrusting again. Faster, harder, our bodies slapping against one another. Fire blazes through my insides. My skin is hot and dewy. My mouth is open. My eyes are closed. The sensation is better than anything I can describe. I'm blazing hot but shivering. I'm struck by lightning, but drowned in the sea.

I gasp and scream. Can anyone hear me? I don't care. I dig my nails into his shoulders as I'm consumed by the tidal wave of ecstasy.

A moment later he lets go, shuddering, crying out, as pleasure takes him over the edge. He collapses against me, his whole body shaking, his breathing hard yet shallow. I wrap my arms around him and squeeze him tight against me.

"Wow," I whisper. "That was . . ."

He lifts his head, his eyes sparkling as he studies my face. He smiles. "Aye. That was." He plants a small kiss on my forehead and then cuddles me into his arms. Close. Warm. Safe.

I relax into his embrace, completely and utterly sated. For the first time since Danny cheated on me I'm a woman again. Desired. Wanted. For too long I've felt worthless. Like I wasn't even sexy enough to keep my own husband interested. But being with Robin . . . suddenly I feel beautiful again.

"Wow, the other men are sure going to be surprised when they find out!" I say with a small laugh. I reach up to kiss his nose, wanting to lie like this forever.

A shadow passes over Robin's face and he runs a hand through his loose hair. He rolls off of me and onto his back, staring up at the sun.

I crinkle my brow, concerned. Did I say something wrong? I turn on my side, propping my head up on my elbow, and study him. "Um, are you okay?" I ask, reaching out to stroke his abs with my fingers.

He looks down at my hand and lets loose a sigh. "This is difficult," he says at last.

Uh-oh. Fear grips my heart. This is the moment when you know the next thing out of a guy's mouth is going to be something you don't want to hear. I'm not ready for this. I can't take any more rejection.

"Difficult?" I repeat, my whole body shaking with fear. "In what way?"

So help me, if he says it's not me, it's him . . . Or that he's still not over Marion. Or that's he's not looking for a serious relationship right now, blah, blah, blah. Whatever bullshit line guys come up with to inform you that they're just not that into you *after* banging your brains out.

" 'Tis not that I want to hide my feelings for you," Robin says, "but I have worked very hard to lead the men of Sherwood Forest over the last year." He kicks at the ground with his foot and then turns to look at me. "And I have won their respect, Chris. But were I to show some sort of . . . weakness . . . that respect may be placed elsewhere."

I narrow my eyes, kind of getting where he's going with this. I pull my hand away. The sweetness we shared suddenly evaporates, and a dark cloud hangs over our naked bodies.

"When we banded together in Sherwood Forest for the first time—when we decided to form our own small forest community—we all signed a sacred oath. Rules to live by, you see."

"And let me guess. One of these so-called sacred rules is no girls allowed," I say. Wow. Who would have ever thought Sherwood Forest would be governed by the same commandments as a ten-year-old boy's tree fort?

"Aye." Robin sighs. "You must remember, at the time, my original men had been murdered because Robert's woman whispered our secret plans to the Sheriff of Nottingham. And I'd recently been betrayed by Marion, though in a much different way. To me, women seemed nothing more than a distraction . . . and perhaps the path to our destruction. Men lose their minds, think with their cocks. If we were to keep order, I truly believed we should have no feminine distractions. I was quite insistent upon it."

"I see. And so you put it in this sacred code thing."

"Aye. Now, if the men were to learn I'd broken my own rule—one that I signed with my own blood—they would have every right to remove me from power. To cast me away. Then all the work we have done, all the progress we've made, will be for naught. I will lose everything I've spent this last year building."

"So, then that's it?" I ask, growing angry. I grab the discarded dress, wanting to cover my body, suddenly uncomfortable being naked in front of him. "Fuck me and leave me because you don't want to lose your job? That's a bit harsh, don't you think? And certainly it's information that should have been provided before the orgasms!"

"Chrissie, please!" Robin cries. He turns to face me, his face anguished. "Understand that this is not what I desire. Bloody hell, I want nothing more than to carry you into my tent and make love to you every night, casting aside any oath or rule made under God or man. I know I can trust you. But there is more to think of here than my own needs."

I sit up, yanking the dress over my head. "You're a bastard," I retort. "Just like every other man I've ever met."

Robin grabs my shoulders. "Wait," he pleads. " 'Tis

not as if I am banishing you from the forest. I am not as cruel or stupid as that. All I ask is that you keep up your pretense. Our pretense. Our secret. At least until I figure out what to do."

I scowl, hating the situation, hating him. Here I thought we'd just shared something special and now I'm being told I have to hide it all. I feel sick to my stomach.

"Please!" Robin begs. "Understand this has nothing to do with the way I feel about you. I adore you. I think you're wonderful." To his credit he does look upset. I can feel myself softening a bit. "But 'tis for your own good as well as mine."

I sigh. Too bad I'm not really a eunuch. Or a nun. Or, I don't know, a normal 21st-century woman who didn't travel back in time. Then I'd never have to deal with any of this. 'Cause really, what am I supposed to do? I can't exactly say "Fuck you, you bastard, I'm so out of here!" can I? I mean, where would I go? I'm still just as stuck as I was before.

And I do get what he's saying. He'd be sending very mixed messages to his men—first saying no women and children and then showing up and announcing that the camp eunuch is actually a girl who not only is staying, but staying in his tent. The men would be totally pissed. And he obviously *is* willing to break his sacred vow for my sake. Just not openly. At least for the time being . . .

What to do, what to do, what to do?

"Look, I really like you, Chrissie," Robin says, reaching over to take my hand in his. I can feel my reserves melting, my anger fading as he squeezes my fingers. "And I don't want to lose you. I will work out a plan if you give me some time." He searches my face with anxious eyes. "Please?"

Argh, argh, argh.

"Okay," I say hesitantly. "But we're not hooking up again until everyone knows the truth."

"Hooking up?"

"Um, you know." I gesture helplessly to the crumpled grass.

"Lovemaking?"

"Yes. Or kissing. Or any of that relationship romance stuff. We'll just be . . . friends."

Robin's face falls a bit. "If that is what you want," he says. "Though forsooth I think of you as more than that." He releases my hand. It takes all of my willpower not to grab his back. But then I'd be breaking my own rule.

I try to focus. Change the subject. Move on with life. "Great. We're all good then." I scramble to my feet, doing everything I can to ignore the huge lump in my throat. "Let's get dressed and head back to the castle. We've got to free that poor guard. And didn't you say something about treasure?"

Chapter Ten

The next few weeks in Sherwood Forest seem to fly by. We plan and execute more than a dozen robberies. Robin and I spend long hours together, working out our capers. We make a great team, actually; he's tactical, I'm creative (and have more movie plots to fall back on). The men start learning to rely on my advice, and they really listen when I have something to say, which is totally cool. Certainly it's nothing I've ever experienced in my 21st-century life.

The villagers now keep watch for our arrival, cheering at the first sight of Robin's trademark green clothing. They throw open their doors and welcome us noisily—thrilled at the opportunity to benefit from our crimes. We've made quite a name for ourselves and are basically local celebrities. (If this were the 21st century, we'd so have our own reality show. I'm sure of it!) Many a bard, some far more talented than Allan a Dale—though that's not saying much—sing songs about Robin and his merry men. In fact, these days you can't enter a local pub without hearing greatly exaggerated tales of our derring-do.

We rob rich men riding through the forest in carriages. We rob corrupt abbeys whose friars buy jewels with the money meant for ministry. We rob the tax collectors when they leave the villages and give the money back to those they just took it from.

The merry men that I met that first day, the ones who sat around the fire complaining about the world but not doing anything to change it, are different people now. At night they throw wild parties at camp, with lots of drink and food. During the day they are warriors, taking back what was stolen from them. They're happy and dedicated to the cause. They have something to live for. They're making a difference.

And so am I. For the first time in my life I feel like I'm doing something worthwhile. Something good. Each day I'm working to change people's lives for the better. It's certainly a more worthwhile career than my previous one of photographing already anorexic women and then doctoring them further with Photo-Shop. Now I'm fattening up children instead of convincing them they need to diet.

It's funny, really. When the gypsy first sent me back in time I thought only about helping Kat; I had no idea I'd end up helping the whole kingdom. Not a bad way to whittle away the hours before King Richard's return, I guess.

Oh, and the eunuch thing? Well, Robin may have been right on the money when he said it was too dangerous to reveal my true sex to the men. I'm realizing more and more that in this day and age women just aren't equal. They couldn't plan battles. Hell, if the men knew I was a chick they'd probably relegate me to cooking and cleaning—if they didn't kick me out of the camp altogether.

At the same time, it's not exactly fun to constantly be pretending I'm something I'm not. And my stupid idea of not hooking up with Robin until we figured out a way to break it to the men? What was I thinking? Working beside him each day, becoming closer and closer to him . . . he's fast becoming my best friend. And yet all day I fantasize about jumping his bones. It's pretty torturous, let me tell you.

One night, after a particularly rowdy bonfire party, I crawl into my tent to fall asleep. But I'm soon woken by a gentle touch. I open my eyes and see Robin kneeling in front of me. It's dark, and I can only see his silhouette backlit by the moon. But I know it's him.

"Wha—?"

He puts a finger to his lips and beckons me to follow. A chill trips down my spine at the idea of a midnight adventure. Of being alone with him for the first time since Locksley Castle. Without a word I rise from my bed and follow him out of the camp and through the woods. We walk for about fifteen minutes, until we come to a small structure made of fallen trees and covered with pine boughs. A cave of sorts.

"A nest," he proclaims proudly. "For us."

I crawl in through the small doorway, gasping in delight. Inside it's like a tiny bedroom, with piles of furs on the floor. It's cozy and warm and smells like cinnamon.

Robin climbs in beside me. "Do you like it?" he asks with a smile.

"I love it. It's very cozy."

"I built it for us. So we could have a place to be alone. Took me all day."

"I was wondering where you'd gone to. Thought you'd been slacking off," I tease. "Getting drunk with Friar Tuck or something."

"Never!" he cries in mock horror. "I'd be far too afraid to face milady's wrath. For she is a hard taskmaster."

"Yes, I'm pretty scary, huh?" I shape my hands into claws and swat at him. "Grrr!" I cry. "Death to slackers!"

Robin scoots back, feigning fear. "Aye, you *are* terrifying!" He laughs. "But luckily for me I still have my ultimate weapon!" He leaps forward, grabbing me, pushing me down into the furs and tickling my ribs. "And the taskmaster has a secret weak spot!"

I squeal with protest mixed with laughter as he finds every sensitive funny spot. He's right. Tickling is definitely my kryptonite. I try pushing him away, but he's far too strong.

"Okay, okay! I forgive you!" I cry. "Stop the tickle torture!"

Luckily he obeys and I suck in a breath. He's still on top of me though, his face inches from mine. I can feel his warm breath on my face; my insides are mush. And I remember too well how the last session of tickle torture ended.

Argh. It's going to kill me to say this, but I have to.

157

I can't succumb to this seduction. Even though I want nothing more than to feel his hands on me, stroking me, loving me, fulfilling my every need, my every want, with his touch.

But I must be strong.

"Robin, I thought we decided there would be no—"

He sighs, backing away to the other corner of the love nest and settling into a sitting position against the wall.

"Yes, of course," he mumbles. "I apologize. I would never ask you to break your oath of chastity."

I shake my head. Argh. He's so overly dramatic sometimes. "Please. It's not that I've taken some sacred vow or anything. It's just . . . well, I don't think it's a good idea to be sneaking around. If we can't tell everyone that we're lovers, then I think it's best that we only hang as friends. Then nothing Romeo and Juliet bad can happen."

"Romeo and . . . ?"

Oops. Forgot Shakespeare hasn't been born yet. "Um, just some . . . friends I used to know. They fell in love, even though their two families were at war. It ended up with a very messy double suicide. We don't want to go there."

"I see."

"Not that I think this would happen with me and you. You don't really seem the type to chug poison, and I'm certainly not the kind of girl who stabs herself when things get tough. Or was it the other way around? Anyway, this just seems smart. 'Cause, like, 'Oh what a tangled web we weave when first we practice to deceive.' You know?"

He doesn't. He looks at me blankly. Okay, fine. I'm

done spouting English Lit quotes. Except maybe to remind myself that "the lady doth protest too much."

I mean, really! Why am I pushing him away? We're alone. No one can hear us. There's very little chance of getting caught. And it's not like I don't believe Robin cares for me. It's not like he doesn't respect me. Over the past few weeks he's been nothing short of amazing. And he's never once tried to make a move after I asked him not to. Even here, in this little love cave, when I say back away, he does so without question.

"Dearest, I did not build this nest as a means of seduction," he says softly, interrupting my conflicted thoughts. "But simply as a place we could go to be alone. We are surrounded by my men at all times, with no chance to speak freely. I thought mayhap you would appreciate a hideaway. A place where you can be your beautiful self and not be forced to act as someone you are not. Forsooth, I imagine 'tis been difficult for you to continue the charade, to act like a man all the time, and I feel terrible for my part in forcing you to do so."

My heart flutters at his words. He's so thoughtful. He's noticed the pain I've tried to conceal and is doing his best to make it better.

"Thank you," I say, smiling at him, hoping he can read the unspoken affection in my eyes. "It's absolutely perfect, and I adore you for coming up with the idea." I lie back into the furs and stare up at the ceiling. Robin joins me, not touching, but close enough that I'd simply have to shift positions and I'd be in his arms. Tempting. So tempting.

I glance over at him. He's staring up, a pensive look on his face.

"What are you thinking?" I ask.

"Only that I am becoming quite attached to you," he says. "It worries me a bit."

"Why?" I turn over on my side to face him. "I mean, isn't it a good thing that your feelings for me have grown?" Eesh, what's wrong now? This guy has more issues than a politician on the campaign trail. And he doesn't know the half of it! Imagine if I told him that I'm living eight hundred years before I'll be born.

He shrugs. "Mayhap," he says. "But still I ask, what do I have to offer you?" He rakes a hand through his chestnut hair, loosening the ponytail. "I am nothing but an outlaw with no home. There's a price on my head. I could be killed on any given day. And I cannot even admit to my own men my adoration of you." He turns to look at me, and I see tears in the corners of his eyes. "Why would you have any desire to love someone like me? You, who are so beautiful and good. You deserve so much more than I can ever hope to give."

I frown. "I haven't asked you for anything."

"I know, I know." He reaches out and fingers a loose strand of my hair. I close my eyes, enjoying his soft touch. "But it does not matter. I look at you and see all that you merit. All that another could give you so much more easily than I. You deserve fancy dresses, jewels—to sleep in a real bed. You could be a lady of the court. Instead you choose to live a squalid, difficult existence in the forest because you care for me."

"You're right about that. I care for *you*—not courts and jewels and dresses," I insist. "You're more important to me than material possessions. Not to mention that my life here is more fulfilling. I mean, look at all the good we do together. How we've changed the kingdom. With you by my side I feel like anything is possible. How can you say that's not giving me all I deserve?"

He pulls me into an embrace and I crumble into his arms. He strokes my hair and kisses me on the top of my head.

"I am truly blessed that you feel that way," he says. "And can only hope someday I will prove worthy of your affections."

"You already are worthy. More than worthy. You truly are."

"It's strange," he says. "I feel so close to you, yet I do not really know anything about you. Where do you come from? How did you get here? Why do you speak with such a strange tongue?" He laughs. "For all I know, you could be a spy of Prince John's, one who will be my demise."

I make a face at him. "Of course I'm not. Don't be stupid. Besides, before I came you guys weren't even doing anything worth spying on, remember?"

"True," Robin agrees. "But even still. You know everything about me and I know nothing about you. Why you talk so strangely. Where your home is and what it is like. Why are you so reluctant to reveal your past?"

Uh, because it's the future? That'd be one reason. But it's not one I can exactly explain to him.

He's staring at me with an expectant look. I'd better come up with something fast.

"I, well—once I had a husband," I begin slowly. I guess he'll have to be okay with half truths, at least for now. "Danny."

"Aye. You told me you were a widow. How did he die?"

"Er, actually, I was sort of stretching the truth on that one. I mean, I wish I were a widow. Actually my ex-husband is still alive and well, and living in my homeland."

"He is alive? And he let you go?"

"Please. He did not *let* me do anything! I left of my own accord." I think back to the day I packed my bags and said I was out of there. Danny begged me to stay. He told me it was all a big, bad mistake and it'd never happen again. Problem was, I didn't believe him . . . on either account.

"Why did you leave? Did he hurt you?" Robin asks, face darkening and hands balling into fists.

"No. Well, yes. I mean, not like you think." I try to clarify. "He didn't beat me. But he cheated on me. He, um, had sex with another girl and I caught him in the act."

Robin narrows his eyes and shakes his head. "How could anyone choose another over someone like you?"

I smile. "It's nice to know you have a high opinion of me, Rob. But it's not a universally shared one, trust me."

"Then the world is truly insane," he declares. "For you are beautiful and smart and fascinating and everything a man could hope for in a mate."

"Ditto," I say, leaning over to place a kiss on his nose.
"Ditto?"

"It means I think the exact same of you," I explain, realizing I'd inadvertently lapsed into my movie allusions again. Luckily Robin's no ghost in Whoopi Goldberg's body. "You're handsome and smart and fascinating and everything I have always imagined a man could be."

Robin smiles and then reaches over to pull me close into his arms, and he cuddles into me, cheek caressing cheek. I relax in his embrace, knowing I'm breaking my own rules but no longer caring.

Because, at the end of the day, secret or not, right or not, impossible or not, I am falling in love with this man.

Chapter Eleven

We wake up the next morning still entwined in each other's arms. Robin tells me that we'd better get back to camp before we're missed, so I sleepily gather my things and we exit the love nest.

"Don't worry, my dear," he says, reaching over to squeeze my hand. "We can return soon. Tonight, if you wish it."

"Oh, yeah. I wish it. I wish it a lot."

Robin goes on ahead, instructing me to follow in a few minutes so we're not seen wandering in together, doing the medieval version of the walk of shame.

I watch him as he heads down the forest path, my heart filled with joy and affection. Who knew I'd have to travel eight hundred years into the past to find my soul mate? If only we didn't have to keep this pesky secret, then everything would be perfect.

Suddenly my phone rings.

"Hello?" I ask, as if I can't guess who's on the other end. There's only one person who calls me in medieval times, and I don't need caller ID to know who.

"Is he back yet?"

"Why, hello Kat! It's great to hear from you too. I'm doing quite well. Thank you for asking."

"Sorry," Kat says, not actually sounding all that apologetic. "Hi, how are you, how's bow-and-arrow world, all that jazz. But really, Chrissie, don't hold me in suspense. Is King Richard back from the Crusades yet? Did you get the Holy Grail? Can Nimue get us back from the future?"

"Don't you think I would have called you if something had happened?" I ask, though technically I'm not sure if this phone is equipped to make outgoing calls to the future. You probably need a different minutes plan. Like a Century Plan or something—with no "time" limits. Hardy, har, har.

"Yes, I suppose you would. So that means he's not? Where the hell is this guy? How long does it take to capture the Holy City of Jerusalem anyway?"

"Um, actually I think he's currently rotting away in a prison in Austria," I say, trying to remember my history. "Captured on the way back or something."

"Grr," Kat growls into the phone. "Well, someone had better free him quick. Is anyone working on that? Hey, I know. Maybe you could head down there and try to get him out or something? Speed things up a little? Maybe Rob and his boys would be able to help. Just think, you'd all be heroes of the land."

"You want me to stage an international jailbreak of

one of the most famous prisoners in history? I can barely manage to survive in Sherwood Forest."

"Well, it was just a thought," Kat huffs. "I mean, I'm desperate here. Guen's hooked up with this guy that she thinks is the reincarnation of her husband King Arthur, but the dude has a wife! Of course, I think the wife might be having an affair with this hacker named Lance, which could totally bring down the entire company if it's true. Anyway, it's all very weird. And strangely deja vu-ish too, for some reason. In any case, I think it'd be a lot better if we could just all get back to the twenty-first century."

"Kat, you're just going to have to sit tight. Try to stay out of trouble for once in your life. There's nothing to do but wait."

"Fine, fine. I guess I have no choice, huh?" She pauses, then adds, "How are things going for you, anyway?"

"They're . . . interesting."

"Oh?"

"Well, first off, Robin Hood's figured out I'm a girl."

"Did he kick you out of camp? Are you on the streets? Er, or paths, or wherever the homeless hang out in the twelfth century?"

"No. We, um, have sort of, well . . . I guess we're dating." Dating. That sounds so lame. Like dinner and a movie instead of wild, hot sex in a flower-strewn meadow. Still, that's a little TMI to tell someone like Kat. Even if she would enjoy all the juicy details, I'm just not a kiss-and-teller.

"Uh, okay. But, well, I thought you were married. What about Danny? Is this one of those 'what happens in Sherwood Forest stays in Sherwood Forest' type things? Don't worry. You can trust me to keep a secret."

Ugh. I forgot I didn't tell her that yet. I swallow hard. "Actually, Danny and I split up before I came back in time. I found him . . . well, I mean, we just weren't getting along."

"He cheated on you?" For someone so dense and self-absorbed, sometimes Kat could be very perceptive. "That bastard!"

The lump forms back in my throat. So annoying, that even with this new, wonderful affair I still can't help but choke up when I think of what happened to my marriage. "Yeah," I say, after swallowing it back down. "So we've been separated a couple months now."

"And now you're back in time, getting it on with Robin Hood!" Kat concludes. "How freaking awesome is that? Good for you, Chrissie. Don't let the bastard get you down. Have wild and crazy sex with a legend instead. It's good for the soul. I should know. Been there, done that."

"Yeah, well it's a bit more complicated," I say.

"Oh, yeah. It always is. Lance and I had to keep our relationship a total secret. Pretend we were brother and sister. And so the knights thought he was actually sleeping with Guenevere. Isn't that ridiculous? Then through this whole case of mistaken identity thing they concluded that the two of them were having an affair instead of me and him, and they sentenced Guen to burn at the stake. Of course Lance and I totally rescued her, but still—it totally destroyed the whole kingdom of Camelot. Way messy, let me tell you."

"Wow." And here I thought hiding our relationship was hard. Sounds like Kat had it a lot worse. "But in the end . . . ?"

"Oh, well, happily ever after, really. Lance and I are thick as thieves. And we don't have to hide anymore, which rocks. We're PDA-ing all over the twenty-second century, let me tell you."

"Sounds nice."

"So what's your deal again?"

"I have to pretend I'm a guy."

"Oh yeah, the whole eunuch thing. I remember now. That must be fun. Not."

"They all signed some stupid sacred oath. No women in camp. And if the men knew he was breaking his own rule by hanging with me, it could really mess with his leadership. And we're doing so well now with the robberies and stuff. The kingdom is thriving. The poor are getting food. It'd be a shame to ruin all of those good things just for the right to kiss him in public." I sigh. "But still . . ."

"It's hard. I know. You feel like he's ashamed of you. That the relationship isn't important enough to risk his job over. Lance had very much the same issue. King Arthur wouldn't allow his knights to date. I mean, how lame is that? Not that many of them followed that rule. Gawain had a different damsel every night. But Lancelot was so good and pure." She laughs. "Until he met me, obviously."

"I can only imagine."

"Anyhow, try to think of this as an adventure. Isn't sneaking around kind of exciting? I mean, it's like the thrill of an affair without another woman being hurt."

"It'd be more fun if the stakes weren't so high. It's not like his job has an unemployment plan if he's fired for sleeping with me."

"Right. Well, hang in there, Chris. Things could change at a moment's notice. Just be true to yourself and your own feelings. And hey, enjoy the sex! How is our legendary outlaw in the bedroom department, anyway? I figure it's Robin Hood—he's got to be packin' something decent in his tigh—"

"Oh, Kat? Hello?" I tap the phone against my palm. "Can you hear me now? I think you're breaking up."

"Yeah, right. Bullshit. You just don't want to go all TMI. Fine, fine. Keep the juicy details to yourself."

I laugh. "It was good to talk to you, Kat," I say, and am surprised I mean it. Somewhere in all her crazy babble the girl does talk some sense. Who would have thought?

"Good to talk to you too, Chrissie. I'll call back soon. Go start staging that Austrian prison break. I know you could pull it off. You gotta have faith, faith, faith—"

I click the End button to cut short her butchering of the George Michael song and stuff the phone back in my bag. Time to head back to camp before Robin comes back looking for me.

As I approach the vicinity, I hear excited voices.

"Robin! Take a look at this!"

I follow the sound of the voices and come across several men, including Robin, all hovering around

Will Scarlet, who holds an unrolled piece of parchment in his hands.

"What is it?" I ask.

Robin looks up from reading. "An archery competition," he says, his eyes sparkling. "At Prince John's castle. The prize is a golden arrow."

"A golden arrow?"

"The shaft is made of solid silver and its head of solid gold," he explains. "Could feed a village for a month, it could."

I scrunch my eyebrows and wrack my brain. This sounds all too familiar. "I think it's a trap."

The four men stare at me.

"A trap?" Robin asks. "For who?"

"For you, duh. To get you back for all the recent robberies. Everyone knows you're the best archer in the land, so why not tempt you with a competition to bring you out of the safety of the forest and into the open? You win the tournament and your prize is a jail sentence."

"That seems a bit of an elaborate plan to snare me."

I sigh. How do I explain that I know what I know? It's not like I can say I read about it in a book that's yet to be written. I'm all of a sudden feeling a very strong Cassandra complex here.

Then again, should I really be trying to talk them out of things? I'm not trying to change history here. And if history proves correct, Robin cleverly escapes anyhow. All's well that ends well.

"You could win this," Will Scarlet says, looking back down at the paper. "There is no man better with a bow than you, Robin."

"Aye," Robin agrees. "I think I shall enter."

"Um, hello?" I say, waving my hands in front of his face. "Earth to Robin! You can't just waltz into the castle courtyard. They'll arrest you. Hang you."

"You worry too much, Chris," Robin says, " 'Tis simple. We shall wear disguises. Will, allow me to don one of your scarlet cloaks. The Prince and his sheriff will expect men in green."

A red cloak? That's his big disguise? That's as bad as Superman fooling everyone with Clark Kent glasses. I mean, *Duh, Lois Lane.* You'd think she'd totally know.

"Well, I'm coming with you," I interject. If he's going to go be all foolish and stuff, he needs backup. And I'm the only one in this stupid camp sensible enough—well, at the very least knowledgeable enough about how it's all supposed to play out. Not that anyone ever listens to me.

Robin scowls. "I do not think it is safe for—"

"For what?" I ask sweetly. "I am one of your *men,* am I not?" Heh. Sometimes this eunuch disguise can work in my favor.

He shoots me an exasperated glare, but of course he can't say anything in front of Will and the other guys. "Fine," he says at last. "Let's go win this tournament."

Chapter Twelve

Tournament day is bright and sunny, the air crisp and cool—perfect weather for a New England harvest festival or apple-picking adventure. However, I can't enjoy any of it because I'm so nervous.

While Locksley Castle was just basically a medieval McMansion plopped in the middle of a field, Nottingham Castle has a whole city built around it and is actually quite impressive. Houses, inns, and pubs flank narrow but bustling streets. We pass a blacksmith hammering horseshoes into shape, a bread maker kneading his dough. We walk through a market square packed with makeshift wooden stands selling everything under the sun. Luckily, Robin seems to know the way. I'd be totally lost.

Finally we come to a large courtyard adjacent to the castle itself. You have to go through a second set of guards to get in, but luckily they're not checking IDs or anything. A good thing, too—Robin's great disguise is not much more than Will Scarlet's red cloak pulled far over his head. Not the best costume in the world, not by a long shot. It feels weird to be here without the other merry men. But Robin was worried that showing up as a group might attract too much attention. My role is to play his servant and watch for any signs of recognition amongst the sheriff's men.

The place is packed: peasants, noblemen and women, knights in shining armor, the works, all milling about chatting amicably with one another. There's an excitement in the air—like the kind you find before a football game—and I half expect souvenir stands with big foam fingers and number jerseys for the Sheriff of Nottingham.

Robin motions for me to follow him, and we head over to the stand where people sign up for the tournament. I watch as he pays some silver, and the guard tosses him a quill to list his name on the roll of parchment. I squint to try to make out what Robin's going to choose as his special top secret tournament name, but I can't quite make out his scrawl. There sure are a lot of names on the list though. Guess the golden arrow's a pretty big prize. Hope Robin's up for the challenge. Then again, I already know that he wins this—I've read the book. So why am I so freaked out?

Once signed up, we head to a small unoccupied corner of the courtyard. Robin takes his bow from me and inspects it critically.

"Think I can do this?" he asks under his breath.

"Definitely," I say with a confidence I don't entirely feel. Not that I think he won't be able to hit a bull's-eye; I'm just afraid that he won't be able to hit a bull's-eye without getting caught for who he really is. "You'll kick their butts. Especially that stupid sheriff. But be careful of performing too, too well. After all, you don't want them to figure out it's you."

Robin laughs. "I will take my chances with that," he says. "For how can I do less than my best?"

Of course. Typical man. Still, in a strange way it makes me feel kind of proud. Robin really rocks with a bow. "All right then," I say. "You give them everything you've got. If they recognize you, we'll just fight our way out."

"God's teeth!" Robin mutters under his breath.

I glance over at him, surprised. "Uh, you don't want to fight?" This could be a problem, as I'm ninety-nine percent sure the history books say we'll have to.

"No, no," he says, his voice a bit hoarse. "I'm sorry. I was not responding to your words."

"Then what's wrong?" I ask, following his gaze out into the crowd and up onto a dais where the royalty sit wearing shimmering rainbow-colored dresses and fanning themselves with dainty silk handkerchiefs. "What are you looking at?"

I glance back at Robin. His face has gone white. His eyes are wide. His lower lip trembles. What the hell is wrong with him?

I look up at the dais—at one particular woman, sitting in a favored place next to a well-dressed man who is obviously Prince John. She has jet-black wavy hair and large doe-like brown eyes. Her lips are plump and cinnamon-colored. Her dress is sky blue and embroidered with elaborate designs. Her wrists and neck and head are draped with emeralds, rubies and sapphires.

His stare. Her beauty. I put two and two together and I'm certainly not getting five.

"Is that who I think it is?" I ask, my heart catching in my throat. God, please don't let it be her.

"Aye. 'Tis Marion."

Sigh. It's her. Thanks a lot, God.

This is what, in the back of my mind, I'd been afraid of all along. Screw the sheriff and getting caught and running for our lives. That I can handle. The fact that she'd be here—that he'd see her and dissolve into a sopping puddle on the floor—is what really terrified me.

And now it's happened.

I glare up at Marion, the woman who left Robin high and dry, traded him in for a new and better life. Hasn't that sunk into his thick skull yet? Shouldn't he be over her by now? And what about me? Have I just been convenient to waste time with while they've been apart? Someone to occupy the hours, satisfy his needs? While all along, deep inside, he continued to mourn the loss of his true love. The pure maiden Marion.

I hate guys. Hate, hate, *hate* them. They never see what they have right in front of them. They only want what they can't have. Marion screwed Robin over. She sold him out for those fine diamonds around her neck. But does he hate her? Does he resent her for all she's done? No, he practically swoons at the sight of her. And where does that leave me, the girl who has been by his side this last month? The one who literally created his legend, started his fan club, and pushed him into his place in history. The girl who has proven her love and loyalty time and time again?

I'll tell you. It leaves me SOL.

Robin shakes his head and turns back to me. "Sorry," he mutters. " 'Tis just . . . I have not seen her in near a summer."

"Whatever." I'm too annoyed to hear his excuses. I've seen the look in his eyes. The longing. The love. He will never look at me like that. If Marion came off that dais and ran toward him, he'd push me out of the way to get to her, never giving me a second thought.

Once again, I'm second-best.

"Are you all right?" Robin asks, peering at me with concern in his eyes.

The last thing I need is his pity.

"I'm fine," I say, forcing a smile that I'm sure doesn't quite reach my eyes. Not that he'll notice. "Fine as rain."

"You do not look it. Forsooth, you look quite pale. Too much sun, mayhap?"

God, men are idiots. My heart is breaking and he thinks I have sunstroke.

"I'm *fine*," I repeat firmly, crossing my arms over my chest and gritting my teeth.

He stares at me for a moment, opens his mouth to say something, then closes it again as trumpets sound. Saved by the bell.

"I think the tournament's starting," I say, mostly to get him to stop staring at me.

He sighs and nods. "Aye," he says. "I must get in place. We will talk later."

"Yeah, sure. Whatever."

He heads out into the courtyard, to the spot where

the contestants are gathering. I glance back up at Marion, who is smiling and chattering to a girlfriend to her left, totally clueless to the drama going on below. She's gorgeous. I can totally see why Robin's so hung up on her. Pure white skin, dark eyes, high cheekbones. Spitting image of effing Angelina Jolie.

Bitch.

I sigh. Why did I ever think Robin would find me a suitable replacement for someone like her? I'm so homely compared to his former girlfriend. Ugly curly red hair. I mean, Little Orphan Annie much? Freckled skin, watery hazel eyes. And my body . . . I steal a look at Marion's breasts. Creamy white and full, with a good deal of cleavage in sight. Of course.

I force my eyes away from the beauty queen and try to focus on the tournament. A man dressed in a brightly colored silk tunic steps out on a platform, unrolls a scroll and clears his throat. The din subsides as everyone starts paying attention.

"My lords, my ladies, I welcome you here to this archery competition. We have gathered here today to test the prowess of our men. To see them compete against one another in a battle of skill. Who shall be deemed the best archer in the land? Who shall win this beautiful golden arrow?"

A blonde, blue-eyed *Price is Right*-type model type holds up the arrow in question, daintily bobbing up and down as she displays it to the crowd. The arrow catches the sun, nearly blinding in its brilliance. Wow, pretty sweet reward.

I send up a small prayer. *Please let Robin win. Please let Robin win. Please let Robin—*

"But we compete for more than a simple trinket," the man continues, "for today the Lady Marion has selflessly offered our victor a kiss from her own sweet lips. Truly, the arrow pales in comparison to such an honor."

What?!?

Please let Robin lose. Please let Robin lose.

Okay, fine, not really. I mean, I want him to win. I do. After all, I can't be selfish here. That arrow could feed a village for a month. But still, this has got to be the icing on my shit cake of a day. Him mooning over her from afar is bad enough. The idea of him tasting her soft lips, her gentle breath in his face . . .

I hope she ate garlic for breakfast. Or something equally distasteful. Not that he'd probably even notice.

I look over at Robin to see his reaction to the kiss reward announcement. Not shockingly, he's staring up at the dais again, his eyes glazed over, deep in thought. Or deep in love. God, I hate him. Why did I ever think he was the perfect man? He's just like every other sorry excuse for a Y chromosome, wants what he can't have.

" 'Tis time to begin. Let the contestants be introduced by their squires. First up, the Sheriff of Nottingham."

A burly black-haired man steps up to the podium, unrolling some paper in his hand. "The Sheriff of Nottingham, son of Sir . . ."

He starts droning a list of names. Oh, I recognize this. They did this before jousting in *A Knight's Tale*. Chaucer made up Heath Ledger's entire family tree so he could sound like he was of noble blood to compete. I don't know if this particular tournament calls for noble blood, but I'd better do something for Robby here, as I think son of Lord Locksley would kind of blow our cover.

". . . son of Lord Ashley, who was son of Lord Beckinsworth . . ."

"Er, do I need to do that for you?" I hiss at Robin.

"Aye," he says, still sounding way too distracted for my liking.

Hmph. It sure would have been nice if he warned me ahead of time. How was I going to come up with a list of fake English names on such short notice?

"Your man is up next," a skinny servant boy informs me, nudging me on the arm. Oh great. "Go up and introduce him."

I hesitantly step onto the podium, feeling the eyes of the crowd on me. I've never been one for public speaking—that was more Danny's thing. I was always more content to disappear in a crowd. Now it seems I have no choice.

"Uh, hello," I stammer. Eesh. If there was a mic in front of me, this would be the moment where it screeched feedback and everyone held their ears. "I'd like to introduce you to Lord . . ." Lord what? Lord what? I notice Robin's eyes drifting toward the dais again. Loser. Utter loser. ". . . Lord Jerkoff—inich," I finish. "Yes, Lord Jerkoffinich of the Kingdom Assholia." I notice a few raised eyebrows and whispers among the ladies regarding Robin's last name. I'd better be more obscure from now on. "His dad was Sir Elton of John and his father was Sir Sean of

179

Connery. His father was John of Lennon who had a father named Ringo of the Kingdom of Star. Very musical family, really." Hey, this is kind of fun! "His father was David of Beckham. You should have seen his balls—"

"Um, thank you, lad, I think that should be enough." The announcer interrupts. Darn, just when I get on a roll.

The next herald steps up to describe his contestant, and I exit stage right, heading to the refreshment stand for a mug of beer. If I have to stand here and watch Robin make googly eyes at Marion, I might as well get good and hammered. I down the first drink before they're even done with the family history stuff and order a second.

"D'you think your man has a chance at the prize?" a fellow barfly standing next to me asks.

I take a big slurp of beer before answering. Good stuff. My insides are already warm and I'm feeling less annoyed at Robin's leering. "Oh yeah," I say, with a wave of my hand. "He's the best in the land, for sure."

"Funny that," the guy mutters thoughtfully. "Since I do not think I've seen him at tournaments before."

"Oh! Well, he's just visiting. From far away. From, um, France." That's pretty far away, right? I mean, it's not like they have Lear jets these days to country hop.

"France, eh? I've competed far and wide in that country and I have not ever heard of such a man."

Oops. Maybe not far away enough. "Not France the country, silly!" I say with a laugh. "France the city."

"The city?"

"Sure. France is a city in . . . um, a little kingdom called . . . called . . ." Come on, Chrissie! Just make up a name! "America," I say triumphantly. Heh. I'm so smart. He'll never know where America is 'cause it hasn't been invented yet.

"America?" the man says thoughtfully. "I have not heard of that kingdom, I'm afraid."

"Oh, yea, that's 'cause it's very far away. Very, very far away. But put your money on America, man. They're going to be a world power someday. Of course, we'll never have the musical geniuses you English have, but the food will be much better."

"I see." The man has a slightly confused look on his face. Hm, am I not making sense or something? Maybe I should lay off the booze. . . . "And your man learned to draw a bow in America?"

"Yup. He's brilliant at it. Ab-sho-lute-ly brilliant."

I take another swig of beer and realize my cup is empty. Again? These mugs look big, but they must be deceiving. Danny told me once that at big chain restaurants when you buy a 16 once draft beer you're actually only getting about 14 ounces. He was very proud of his pint pour. He'd been trained by a guy from Guinness who taught him to draw a little shamrock in the foam. Even had a certificate declaring he'd poured the perfect pint.

Danny. Our life together suddenly seems very far away. Which, I guess considering I'm eight hundred years in the past, it is.

The other barfly motions to the bartender, who

hands me another beer. That was nice of him. I steal a glance while he's paying. He's dressed better than your average villager, in a royal blue silk tunic and tights, with a feathered cap on his head. He has a trim beard and blue eyes. Pretty handsome, actually. Kind of metrosexual. Not all rough and outlawy like Robin. I wonder if Robin used to dress this way when he lived a prince's life at Locksley. When he was engaged to that bitch Marion.

I take a swig of beer. Maybe I should flirt with this guy, get Robin back for staring at Marion all day. After all, what's good for the gander is good for the gooses. Or however that saying goes. I take another sip, warming to the idea. Maybe this guy would want a normal relationship. One where we didn't have to keep things on the down-low. We could sing from the rooftops how we loved one another like they do in Moulin Rouge and no one would smack us down for it or ask the guy to resign from whatever job he works at.

"What is your man's name again?" my new boyfriend asks.

"Well, he's not really my man," I correct. "He's like my boss." I don't want him to think Robby's my boyfriend or something. "I'm single, actually. Very single. And available." Sigh. This would be a lot easier if I wasn't dressed as a man.

"And his name?" he asks, ignoring my not-so-subtle come-on.

D'oh, what did I claim his name was again? I remember making up some kind of insult-type name on stage, but now for the life of me I can't remember what it was. The beer is doing funny things to my brain.

"Lord . . . Bastardi? I mean . . . Sir Wankership? No, no, sorry. Captain Dickface. That's right." No, Chrissie, that's wrong. Very, very wrong.

The man raises an eyebrow, but says nothing. Instead, he waves to the bartender to bring me another beer. Ooh, drink number two from the handsome stranger! He must like me. Nice guy. Nice, nice guy. I take a few gulps from the mug already in my hand and swallow back a belch before double-fisting the second brew.

Oh screw it.

"Can youthh keep ah shhecret?" I ask, lowering my voice to a whisper. I mean, this guy is totally solid and we're practically engaged at this point. What would it hurt? He's just some random archery tournament attendee, after all. I hardly think he's going to go squeal on Robin to the Sheriff of Nottingham or something.

"Aye." He nods solemnly. "I swear on my mother's grave."

I stare back skeptically. "Did you *like* your mother?" I query. People always assume, when guys make that kind of solemn oath, that Mother Dearest was the sweet-faced, aproned, oatmeal-cookies-and-milk-after-school type and not the hideous monster mine was.

"Very much. I was most happy as a babe on her breast."

"Um, eww. Wayyy too much TMI, mistah," I say, waving my mugs. "But okay. Hereth my shecret. The man over there is actually—"

I stop. Wait one gosh darn second. Does this guy think I was born yesterday? What if he's a spy, sent by Prince John, trying to find out info from me? I mean, he thinks I'm a dude, yet he's buying me drinks. So either he's gayer than a leather piñata or he's working to get me to reveal our true identities. Which ain't gonna happen. Not on my watch.

"Aren't you drinking?" I ask, realizing his hands are empty. Suspicious. Very suspicious.

He shakes his head. "I must keep my wits about me for the tournament."

"Oh. You're in the tournament?"

"Aye. I shall win it, too."

"I see. Pretty sure of yourself, aren't you?"

"Mayhap." He shrugs. "I have yet to see a man best me with a bow."

"You haven't seen my guy, obviously."

"And his name again?"

"Ah-ha!" See! I knew it. I totally, totally knew it! "You're trying to trick me. Well, it won't work. I won't tell you Robin Hood's true identity. Not on your life."

Oh.

Fuck.

For those of you who are reading this and are under the age of legal alcohol consumption, this is a prime example of why you should just say no. Beer is bad. Bad, bad, bad. Especially when you're trying to keep a big, big secret.

"Uh, what am I saying? Robin Hood?" I laugh loudly. "How silly of me. Of course, I meant Count Crapola of Toiletville."

"It makes no difference to me, lad," the man says

with a smile. "I do not know of either gentlemen you mention."

Oh, phew. I let out the breath I didn't realize I was holding. Phew, phew, phew. For a moment there I thought I'd just given out Robin's secret to someone bad. Like the Sheriff of Nottingham or something.

"Next up, the Sheriff of Nottingham."

"That's me," my friend says with a grin. "Wish me luck."

Uh-oh. I suddenly get the feeling that "Count Crapola" is in deep shit. And it's all my fault.

Chapter Thirteen

You'd think an archery tournament would be exciting and fun, but let me tell you, in reality it's kind of long and dull. It's not like a jousting match, say, where there are two rampaging beasts storming at one another with two armed men on board, crashing lances into shields in an attempt to throw the other man off. If a jousting match is like football, then archery is like golf. Or watching bowling on TV. Quiet. Slow. Tedious. Boring.

It's especially tedious when you're sitting here, drunk as a skunk and worried as hell about the fact that you just gave away your boyfriend's secret identity to the man who most wants to capture him and sentence him to death. I need to warn Robin that the sheriff knows all, but the guards won't let me near the competitors.

Come on, sloshed brain. Think!

Luckily for me, at that very moment, sloshed brain comes through and I have a brilliant idea.

I'll sign up to compete, too!

I jump up from my seat and rush over to the sign-up booth. "Is it too late to join the competition?" I ask the man behind the counter.

He nods. "Aye. You must sign up before it begins."

Damn. That blows. But I'm not ready to give up quite yet.

"Is that a rule set in stone? Or . . ." I reach into my little hanging purse and pull out a few silvers. I know how these Nottingham guys think. "Silver?" I ask, holding them up.

The man looks left and right, then snatches the silver out of my hand. "Consider yourself a competitor," he whispers, winking at me. "Two more silvers and I'll give you a bow to compete with."

I dig into my bag.

Once outfitted with a rather splintery bow and a quiver full of arrows, I head into the tournament area. Several contestants have already been eliminated, so I try to huddle with the rest, to keep a low enough profile so no one will know I joined late. I look for Robin and see he's up, pulling back on his bow and letting his arrow fly. It soars through the air and lands, of course, right in the bull's-eye. The crowd goes wild and I can't help but smile with pride. He's so good.

The Sheriff of Nottingham is up next. He easily hits the mark as well. He and Robin walk back to the group of men waiting. How am I going to get Robin alone to warn him?

A few more men try their luck, but their arrows are way off the mark.

"Psst, Robin!" I hiss, waving my arms in the air, trying to get the outlaw's attention.

He turns and catches sight of me. His face furrows into a frown and he walks through the other contestants to reach me. "What are you doing?" he asks, looking confused.

"I'm competing! Duh!" I say, rather annoyed. I know I just came in here to warn him, but still! I've been practicing with my bow. I have just as much right to be here as anyone.

"Competing?" He cocks his head. "What are you going on about? Why would you be competing?"

Oh, I see how it is. I'm good enough to carry his bow, but not good enough to compete next to him. Puh-leeze. As they say where I come from, Anything guys can do, girls can do better. Plus, I'm trying to help. Ungrateful bastard.

"Why, do you have a problem with it?" I ask angrily. "What, would you prefer I just sit around on the sidelines and watch you eye Maid Marion?"

He rakes a hand through his hair. "What are you talking about? Are you drunk? You reek of beer."

Ugh. This convo is going from bad to worse. I have to focus. Keep my temper. Try to act sober. "Look, Robin," I say, "I don't care about the stupid competition. I just signed up so I could get close enough to warn you. The sheriff knows who you are. Our cover is blown." Of course, no need to inform him of exactly why our cover is blown, right? Or who technically did the blowing. Nope, no need at all.

Robin glances over at the sheriff and then back at me. He shrugs. "There is nothing we can do about it now then," he says.

I stare at him in disbelief. "What are you talking

about?" I demand. All this work, just to get close enough to warn him, and he doesn't want to leave? "Of course there's something to do about it. There's, like, running away! Getting out while we still can! That's something we can do about it. A good something, in my opinion. I mean, do you want to be post-archery hanging entertainment?"

"Next up, Sir Christian of Hoboken," the announcer calls out. Oh great. I'm up. This is not good.

"We need to get out of here. Now!" I hiss. But before Robin can answer, the other contestants push me forward. I trip and almost fall flat on my face, righting myself at the last second. I'm now alone. Standing approximately one million miles away from a bull's-eye on the far end of the courtyard. Wow. They expect me to shoot an arrow that far? I don't think I could hit that mark stone cold sober, never mind in my bleary-eyed, drunken state.

I start to walk toward the sidelines, ready to give up the game, but the crowd starts booing, jeering. Grr. Something inside me, some long lost but deeply ingrained competitive streak, rises up. This is my one and only, once in a lifetime chance to compete in a medieval archery tournament. It's a story I can tell my grandchildren someday. And I don't want a story I tell my grandchildren to end with "And then I walked away like a coward."

You know what? Screw it. If I miss the target then it sucks to be me. At least I'll know I tried.

I pull back my bow and fit my arrow, just like Robin taught me. I line up with what I think is the bull's-eye—though truth be told, it's kind of unfocused in my current state of inebriation and with no glasses. Then I close my eyes and let the arrow fly.

Thwak!

I open my eyes, unsure of the sounds I'm hearing. Are those . . . cheers? I look over at the target, squinting in the sun, and see an arrow sticking out of it. In the exact center. Bull's-eye. Did I do that? How the hell? Seems impossible, and yet . . .

"Sir Christian of Hoboken moves to the next round," the announcer confirms.

Woo-hoo! I hit the bull's-eye! I rock! I totally and utterly rock! I raise my hand to high-five someone, but then remember high-fiving has yet to be invented. But dancing hasn't, so I do a little jig.

"Beat that!" I say to Robin as I walk back to the sidelines. I'm so in the zone now.

Robin's staring at me, utter disbelief written on his face. Not that I blame him. "That was amazing!" he exclaims. "I have seen your usual aim, and daresay Little John has felt the effects of it. And yet you hit the target from a fair distance."

I shrug. "I guess I'm just awesome. Maybe I'll beat you and then I'll be the one to kiss Marion. Hey, are any of the vendors here selling garlic-flavored food? Or maybe onions? I want to make sure my breath is real sweet for the ol' maid."

Robin frowns. "Look, I did not know she would be here," he says, taking me by the shoulders and forcing me to face him. "And I am sorry if her presence upsets you."

"It's not her presence that upsets me, it's the way

you look at her," I retort, wrenching my arms from his grasp.

"I was not aware that I was looking any particular way."

"No, of course not. Probably didn't notice the drool at the corner of your mouth either."

"Next up, Lord Jerkoffinich," the announcer says. Robin looks relieved. Saved by the bell.

"We shall talk of this later," he says, wagging a finger at me before walking back out onto the range. I watch as he pulls back his bow and lets his arrow loose. It sails comfortably into the bull's-eye.

He walks back, standing a small distance away from me and refusing to look me in the eye as the next archer steps up. Fine. He can be that way. I don't care. I really don't.

Soon, it's my turn again. Most of the other archers have now been eliminated. In fact, there's only me, Robin, the sheriff and one other dude left in the running. And the random guy just missed the target on his last shot, so if we all get bull's-eyes he's out. Not that I imagine I'll get another bull's-eye. The first time had to be sheer luck, right?

In an insane hope for lightning to strike twice, I repeat exactly what I did before. Aim, pull back on the bow, close my eyes, and let loose. I open my eyes again, just in time to watch the arrow soar into its target—much to the delight of the crowd.

Oh yeah, baby! I do a little victory dance. Who's your daddy? Who. Is. Your. Daddy?! I remember this time, however, not to ask the question out loud.

Robin and the sheriff both match my performance and the random guy is out, and so now we're on to the next round. Who will be crowned archer of the land? Who will get the golden arrow and who will get to lay a big smooch on Maid Marion?

The sheriff goes first and easily lands the bull's-eye. Gotta give the guy props—evil or no, he's a good shot. But I know Robin can best him. After all, all the storybooks say so. Or maybe I will.

Robin steps to the line and I notice beads of sweat on his forehead. He's in serious mode now. He wants to win. He pulls back on his bow and lets the arrow fly. I squeeze my eyes shut, not able to watch, then open them again.

Robin's arrow has not only hit the bull's-eye, but it's literally hit exactly where the Sheriff hit—splitting the sheriff's arrow in two. Ooh, ooh! I remember this part from the legend! How cool is that!

The crowd agrees, going about as wild as we Red Sox fans did when our team won the World Series for the first time since 1909. The sheriff (definitely a Yankees fan) narrows his eyes. He bends his bow over his knee and snaps it in two, then throws it to the ground. The crowd jeers at his unsportsmanlike conduct—John McEnroe of Nottingham. He storms to the other side of the courtyard, down by where the targets are set up and I see him whisper something to a guard—probably selling us down the river now that he knows he can't get the glory of a victory. The guard looks over at Robin and then at me. We'd better win this thing quick.

It's my turn now. I don't think even my luck will cause me to split Robin's arrow in two. But I'm willing to give it the old college try. I close my eyes and release my arrow.

Zoom! Thump!

Did I do it? I hear screams again . . . though not exactly the same as before. Actually there's only one scream—of pain? Mixed with laughter? I open my eyes, my mouth dropping open.

So, um, let's just say my arrow has not, this time, hit its mark. Well, not the bull's-eye, anyway. It has managed, however, to pierce the Sheriff of Nottingham in the butt. And he's presently screaming incomprehensibly at me, his face purple with rage.

"Uh, oops. Sorry about that. My bad!" Gulp. This is not good. I glance over at Robin. He's shaking his head in disbelief. He's going to kill me later.

"Ladies and Gentlemen!" the sheriff cries, his voice a bit hoarse. "Those men you see before you are none other than the outlaw, Robin Hood, and his manservant. They are wanted for crimes of treason against his royal majesty, Prince John. Seize them, guards! And throw them in the dungeon."

"I think we've just worn out our welcome," Robin says with a wink. At least he doesn't seem ticked.

"Uh, yeah. No doubt." I agree. "What are we going to do now?"

"Follow me!"

Robin takes off and the guards begin their pursuit. I follow, dodging spectators and somehow managing to knock over a cart of fruit. Apples and pears tumble to the ground, making our escape about as easy as running on a floor made of marbles.

"Close the city gates! Do not let them escape!"

This could be bad. Very, very bad. I knew we should have left when I first slipped about Robin's identity to the sheriff. At least then we would have had a fighting chance. But no! Robin wanted the glory of a win. Or a chance at a kiss.

The outlaw stops at a small door embedded in the castle wall and motions me inside. I crawl in. The passageway beyond is narrow and dark.

I follow Robin, and we race through a maze of twisty hallways. Windowless. Dark. Illuminated only by sparse torches. I have no idea how he knows where he's going, but have no choice but to trust that he does. Cobwebs cling to my face and I bite my lip to keep from screaming as a six-inch rat crawls over my foot. Luckily I'm no longer feeling the alcohol. Adrenaline—not to mention fear for my life—is a definite buzz kill.

"In here!" I hear voices down the other end of the corridor.

"Hurry!" Robin urges.

My heart pounds a mile a minute as we run. I hope he knows what he's doing. Where he's going . . .

We reach a spiral stone staircase leading up into the darkness. We charge upward, until we come to a rotting wooden door blocking our path. Robin grabs the rusty handle but . . .

" 'Tis locked."

"What?" I cry. This is not good. I can hear the voices of the men in pursuit, and they're getting closer. And now we're trapped. There's no way out except through the door.

Will they kill us on sight? Or will they capture us and throw us in the dungeon? Which will be worse? Will they torture us? I remember seeing a History Channel special on medieval torture and it didn't look like something I wanted to experience firsthand.

Robin throws his body against the door, but it doesn't budge. He prepares to heave again.

"This door is not supposed to be locked!" he cries, his eyes shiny with panic. The cocky, confident Robin is gone. He doesn't want to die, either.

"Wait!" I say, a brainstorm coming to me. Could I actually pull this off? Save the day?

"We have no time to wait!"

"No, I mean, I think I can unlock the door," I interrupt. When I was a kid, my mom was always tripping out and forgetting what time it was. After being locked out of the apartment fifty times or so, my brother and I learned to pick the lock.

"Give me your knife," I say, pointing to the weapon in his boot. He pulls it from its sheath and hands it to me. I get on my knees and study the lock, then jam the knife in and feel my way around. It's a very simple lock, thank goodness, as my skills in lock-picking aren't exactly Oceans' 11 quality.

"Just a turn here, and then—"

"You'd better hurry. I hear them on the stairs and that blade is my only weapon."

"Don't rush me," I mutter. "I need to concentrate. It's been twenty-something years since I picked a lock."

But he's right. The voices sound like they're only a few feet away. *Come on, Chrissie! You can do this!*

Bingo! I hear a click and push on the door. It swings open easily.

"Go!" I cry. "It's open!"

Robin pushes me through the door and then joins me on the other side, shutting and locking it behind him. I realize we're in a small sparely furnished room with a rickety ladder leading up.

"We're in the east tower," Robin explains. "It's on the far castle wall. We need to go up to the roof. There may be another guard up top, so let me go first."

The guards are pounding on the door, screaming. I don't know how long we have before they pull a Jack Nicholson and "Here's Johnny!" with an axe.

"Okay." I nod. "Let's do this."

Robin starts climbing up the ladder and I follow, praying that it will hold both our weights. At the top, he pushes open a trapdoor, and sunshine streams into the dank chamber. I have to blink a few times to get used to the light change as I scramble up onto the tower's lookout point. When my eyes become accustomed to the brightness, I see that Robin has pulled a rope from his pack (where does he get all these wonderful toys?) and ties it around the iron trapdoor handle, tugging on it a few times to test its strength.

"Oh, no! I'm not climbing down that!" I protest. I'm deathly afraid of heights.

"You will, or you will die here. And I am not about to let you die."

"But I can't climb down that. I'll fall." I look over the tower edge. We've got to be more than fifty feet up. And there aren't a lot of handholds on the tower wall. This so reminds me of the time my fourth foster family signed me up for an Outward Bound adventure. Except, no safety harness this time.

"Just hold on to me," Robin instructs. "I will do the climbing for both of us."

I realize I have no real choice. Face the bloodthirsty sheriff's men or the rappel from hell. I hold out my arms and Robin hoists me piggyback style onto his back and we start our descent. I grip him tightly, eyes closed, fear making my heart race.

"Could you . . . try . . . not to dig your fingernails into my shoulders?" Robin mutters, out of breath.

"Uh, sorry." I try to release my hold, to put myself in his care. He knows what he's doing; I have to trust in that. He's Robin Hood, after all, right?

We climb down. Down, down, down. How tall is this tower, anyway? It didn't feel so tall going up the stairs. I feel his muscles strain and sweat dampens his tunic. But he doesn't pause.

After what seems an eternity, Robin jumps and we hit the ground. I tumble off of him, whacking my knee against a tree stump. "Ow!" I cry, face full of dirt. I scramble to my feet, brushing myself off. My tights have ripped and my knee is bleeding, but nothing's broken. And we're on the ground outside of the castle walls. I have a looser definition for "We're okay" these days.

"Come on!" Robin urges, out of breath but somehow still good to go. Man, this guy is impressive in a crisis. Glad he's on my side. "We're not safe 'til we're in the forest."

We run down the path and come to a few horses, which are saddled and tied to a tree. Must belong to some of the spectators—though this seems as dumb as leaving your keys inside your car outside of Yankee Stadium. Robin unties two of them and helps me onto mine. I cling to the reins and whisper a prayer to whatever higher power happens to be listening, then dig my heels into the horse's flanks. He (or she? I didn't take the time to check my mount's anatomy) takes off and I tighten my legs so I won't fall off.

I've only tried the horseback thing a couple of times and I still have no real idea how to steer, so it's lucky the horse seems to know enough to follow Robin. I hold on for dear life as we gallop along, the wind whipping through my hair. I glance back for a second—a total Lot's wife move that almost causes me to slip off the horse—and see the castle and guards fade into the distance. No one appears to be chasing us. Phew.

Now that I'm safe and sound (well, as safe and sound as a horse newb on a galloping beast can be) I get a thrill of excitement tickling my belly. We just escaped from an armed castle! How cool is that? And I was an integral part of the escape. My misspent youth actually came in handy in saving our lives! And then there were all those bull's-eyes on the archery field. Bull's-eyes made by me. You know, maybe that's been my problem all my life. I was born in the wrong century. Maybe I was destined to live back in these times. Maybe I did live back here and I'm just starting to remember my reincarnated roots.

Or maybe I'm just a drunk who got lucky.

Sadly though, it wasn't mission accomplished. We didn't get the arrow. Totally sucks. To make matters worse, now I'm sure we're topping the Ten Most Wanted in Nottingham list. The sheriff's butt will be sore for at least a week, and I'm sure the memory of the humiliating and painful incident will last much longer than that.

We reach the entrance to the forest and Robin slows his horse. Thankfully mine seems tired enough to slow him/herself, because in addition to being useless at steering, I have no idea how to put on the brakes. Maybe I should get myself some horseback riding lessons while I'm here as well.

"I believe we have lost them," Robin says. "We can rest our horses a bit."

I sigh in relief, squirming in my saddle to get more comfortable. Thank god. I thought for sure we were doomed. I glance over at Robin, ready to burst with overflowing leftover adrenaline.

"That was an amazing escape, huh?" I cry. "I thought we were goners for sure. And you haven't complimented me on my excellent aim in hitting the sheriff. That's my second bum shot this month!" I bat my eyelashes, waiting for a reaction. "*Bum* shot, get it? You know, like, with Little John's bum? Getting him in the bum? Hey!"

Robin nods, distracted and quiet. What's going on with him? Please don't tell me he's still messed up from seeing Marion.

Sigh. In all the excitement of our escape I nearly

forgot about that bitch. Now it all comes rushing back. Of course he's upset. He didn't get to kiss her. The woman he loves. And I was the one who screwed up his opportunity. What would he have done if given permission to approach her? Would he have whispered a meeting place in her ear as she lowered her lips to press against his? Would she tell him it was all a case of misunderstanding and that they should resume their affair? Will he ever talk to me again if he gets back together with her? And if not, how am I going to deal with losing him?

My heart pangs in my chest and I feel a bit sick. I can't believe I put myself in this situation. Allowed myself to fall in love with someone who thinks of me as second best. Again. And this time I have no excuse. I may not have known that Danny was spending quality time in coffeehouse bathrooms with waitresses, but Robin's love for Marion is written in a thousand texts. I knew he loved the girl when I was six and watched the Disney version, for goodness sake. And yet, once again, as I always do, I acted on feeling instead of facts. I allowed myself to believe him.

Perhaps he does love me, in his own way. As a friend. A companion. But not as the woman he would die for. Not as Marion.

Tears sting the corners of my eyes and I angrily brush them away. It's not fair. It's so not fair.

I look at his back, bobbing up and down to the horse's gait. I trace the outline of his broad shoulders with my eyes, his chestnut hair fallen out of its normal ponytail and blowing in the breeze. He's so achingly handsome. But it's more than that. It's a tenderness I feel toward him. An overwhelming desire to crawl into his arms and be held. Why can't he feel the same about me?

We arrive at the camp and the men run up to us, their eyes alight, begging to know what happened at the tournament. Did we win the silver arrow?

"I'll spin you the tale of our adventure after dinner," Robin declares. "For at this moment I am too weary and hungry to speak."

We head over to the fire and sit down on our makeshift treestump chairs. Little John serves us steaming bowls of stew, but I'm not really hungry. Friar Tuck offers us overflowing mugs of beer, but I wave mine away. The last thing I want is to get drunk again.

"So, tell us what took place at the castle today!" Will Scarlet begs eagerly. "Did you win? Is the arrow in your possession?"

"Aye, I won. And Christian here won in his own right." He tells the tale of my two bull's-eyes and my real accomplishment—an arrow in the butt of the sheriff. The men cheer.

"Christian, surely you are a better marksman than Robin here," says Little John, slapping me on the back. "For I like more what you choose as your bull's-eye."

"Aye, Christian. Let's hope 'is rump is too sore for him to be rutting with any maidens for a fortnight," jeers Will.

Allan a Dale stands up. "This calls for a song!

Good Christian is a champion with a bow
He shoots it high. He shoots it low.

He turns the competition into a farce
And shoots the Sheriff in the—

"Anyway," Robin interrupts. "As amusing as Christian's accomplishments were today, he cost us the arrow."

I cringe. He's mad at me. And I guess he's right. I didn't mean to screw up the competition, but I totally did. Ugh.

The men all turn and stare at me. I can feel my face growing beet red. "Uh, yeah," I mutter. "Sorry about that."

" 'Tis a shame," Will says. "That arrow could have fed a village for a month."

"Aye," Friar Tuck agrees. " 'Twould have been a great prize to win."

Great. I suck. And here I thought I was totally cool because of that lock-picking thing. But there would have been no lock to pick if I hadn't screwed things up in the first place.

"Well, no matter," Robin says. He sighs then laughs. "We will have other chances to win treasure for the poor."

The men murmur their agreement. They're letting me off the hook!

"So Christian, tell us more about your lucky shot," Little John says, gleefully changing the subject.

"Well, first I had a mug or two too much to drink," I say with a grin. The gang, especially Friar Tuck, cheers. "And then I hit two bull's-eyes with my eyes closed. I still have no idea how. Lucky, I guess."

I proceed to relate the whole tale: the competition,

my mis- (or perfectly!) aimed arrow, our subsequent escape from Nottingham Castle. The men hang on my every word, cheering and toasting every narrow escape. I'm probably embellishing the tale a bit too much, but I don't think anyone minds.

Through it all, Robin sits on the outskirts, whittling a stick with his knife, looking sad and contemplative. Half of me wants to run over and throw my arms around him, pulling him into a warm hug and letting him know everything will be okay. Part of me wants to strangle him for not being able to forget Marion.

I'm exhausted and the men suggest I take a nap while they clean up from the meal. I've been through a lot today, after all. Thankful, I crawl into my tent and pass out almost instantly, and I don't wake up until the sun has set.

I scan the camp for Robin. I want to talk to him about what went on today—apologize for my jealousy as well, especially since it nearly got us killed.

The whistling of an arrow overhead interrupts my search—the signal that someone is entering the camp. The men scramble to their feet, drawing swords or grabbing bows. Robin motions for them to be silent as he steps forward.

"Who goes there?" he calls.

"Robin?"

The men gasp at the female voice addressing their leader, at its high-pitched Betty Boop-like tone. What the . . . ?

The speaker steps from out of the shadows and into the illumination of the fire.

Oh no.

You've got to be kidding me.

Maid Marion.

She's dressed in a pale blue silk gown with a darker blue cloak covering her head. Her eyes catch the firelight and sparkle like a cat's.

What the hell is she doing here?

She steps forward again, nodding at Robin and then giving him a low curtsey. He's just staring at her, dumbfounded. And I thought the drool this morning was bad. Now, here in the camp, he looks like he's gone into cardiac arrest.

Oh, this is just great.

"Where . . . I mean . . . how? What . . . ?" he stumbles, the cocky, often smooth-tongued man seemingly unable to form a sentence.

She laughs, and to my annoyance it sounds like Christmas bells tinkling in the breeze. Of freaking course.

"You left without your prize," she says, giggling a little as she reaches into a bag. She pulls out the arrow. The men all exhale a gasp, though I'm not sure if it's because of the sight of the arrow or the cleavage she revealed as she bent over to retrieve it.

The arrow gleams in the firelight, silver shaft flashing with an almost unearthly light. I try to remind myself how good it is that she brought it here. That it will feed many poor families who have nothing, and how that's more important than my petty jealousy.

"Thank you, milady," Robin says, bowing low before accepting the gift. " 'Tis most kind of you to travel all this way."

Okay, cool. Arrow delivered. Now she goes home, right? After all, we've got that "no girls allowed at camp" rule, right?

"Would you like to stay the night?" Robin asks. " 'Tis not a safe place, this forest, for a lady."

What? *What?* I squeeze my fists together in fury. Now he's suddenly okay with women in camp? Oh, look, my long lost love shows up, so throw all the rules out the window. Sure, it's fine for Chrissie to pretend she's an effing eunuch indefinitely. But now that Marion's here? Oh, she's a lady and the boys better understand.

Marion smiles graciously. "Thank you, Robin. 'Twas a long trip, and my horse would be much appreciative of the rest."

I glower. Long trip my ass. She just wants to hang with my outlaw.

"How did you find this place, lady?" Robin asks as he escorts her to the fire and brushes off a log for her to sit on.

"One of your guards assisted me," she says with a smile. "When I told him of my mission: to present the arrow to its rightful winner—the true champion, Robin Hood of Sherwood Forest."

"He should not have done that," Robin says, but not in the *Oh my god, I'm going to kill the guy* type of way. If anything, he sounds slightly amused. "At least, not without a blindfold. The way to this place is secret, for many wish to do us harm."

"I am afraid 'tis my fault. I told him I have very sensitive eyes," Marion explains, batting the peepers in question. "He took pity on me."

"Ah," Robin says, taking a seat right next to her.

Uh, hello? Has everyone here developed hysterical blindness all of a sudden? Woman. In camp. Am I the only one here who remembers that this is supposed to be totally against the rules? The sacred oath? I wait for one of the men to jump in. To remind Robin he's breaking his own rule. But no one speaks up. Except Marion.

"Why did you not come back for me after the crusades?" she asks. Her voice is disgustingly soft and sweet, like sugar covered with chocolate covered with honey. I secretly hope that ants show up and stream down her throat. Where are those Sherwood ants? You can never find good ants when you need them.

Robin sighs. "I did. I . . . saw you in the arms of another man. I thought perhaps you had forgotten me."

Marion pauses, seemingly shocked. Then she laughs. "Another man? You must have seen me with my uncle!"

What? That's the oldest excuse in the book! That's, like, what a politician says when he's sneaking his intern into a function. Robin's not going to buy it, is he? He is.

I look around, desperate for backup. Amazingly, it seems all the merry men have vanished. I feel a nudge at my arm and turn around. It's Little John. "Come, Christian," he urges. "These two have much to talk about. Let us give them some time alone."

"What?" I cry. "You guys are just going to turn a blind eye to all of this? What about your sacred oath? No women allowed!"

John looks surprised. "She's not moving in, lad. She merely wishes a few moments with our Robin. Considering he has been suffering over the lass for near a year, I think 'tis only right for us to be understanding." He pulls on my arm. "Come. Let us take a walk. Give him a chance to win back his chosen bride."

I take one more look at the cuddly couple. They're talking softly, faces only a few inches apart. I wrench my arm from John's grasp and run into the forest, not feeling the branches as they whip at my face, my legs. All I care about is getting away. Far, far away.

I can't believe she came back! What does she want from him? Will they fall back in love? Did he ever stop loving her in the first place?

I run and run and run until I realize I've come to the hideaway, the love nest that Robin built for us. Just looking at the structure fills me with fury and I kick and kick it until the roof gives way and collapses inward. I've destroyed the place where we shared that sweet night in each other's arms.

But that was just a lie, I remind myself. Me just fooling myself into thinking he actually loved me. That he actually cared about me. That I wasn't second place.

Selfish bastard. I can't believe he made me pretend I was a guy all this time, made me live a lie for him. All so he could keep his job. His dignity. And for what? When Marion showed up, his men seemed totally cool with him hooking up with her. If they only knew what a jerk he was.

I stop and look at the destroyed nest, now a blatant symbol of our shattered love. We shared so much. I told him things I haven't told anyone. And what am I left with? Nothing. Just like with Danny.

I collapse to my knees and let sobs overtake me. They wrack my body, stealing my breath. How am I going to learn to live without him? Whoever made up that bullshit about it being better to have loved and lost should get his head examined.

I hear my cell phone ring, followed by a crashing in the bushes as unseen animals flee the futuristic sound effects—they're clearly spooked by a sound they never should have heard in their short 12th-century lifetimes. Sorry, Jefferson Airplane. I really need to put the thing on vibrate.

I look down at the phone. At first I'm tempted not to answer. What do I have to say to Kat, anyway? Beautiful, vapid Kat who goes back in time and wins the legendary knight Lancelot without a care in the world. I bet Lance never lied to her, never cast even the remotest glance at Guenevere once she was in the picture.

But the phone keeps ringing and I realize if I don't talk to someone I'll probably go insane. So I reluctantly push the button and put the phone to my ear.

"Hello?" I croak. She's definitely going to know that I've been bawling like a baby.

"Chrissie? Is that you?" Kat's voice demands. "It doesn't sound like you. If you're some bad medieval person who stole Chrissie's phone, well, you'd better return it to her or I'll so time travel back there and kick your ass."

I start laughing. I can't help it. Kat's just so . . . so . . . well, Kat.

"No, Kat, it's me. Sorry. I've just been . . . I mean, I think I have allergies. Living out in the woods can wreak havoc on your sinuses."

"That doesn't sound like an allergy to me, girl," Kat says. "That sounds like you've been crying. So spill. What's going on out there in Sherwood Forest?"

Realizing she's the only person I have to talk to, I start spilling my story. The silver arrow. The contest. The accidental "I shot the sheriff, but I did not kill his deputy" moment.

And, of course, Marion.

"That bitch!" Kat squeals over the phone, so loudly I have to pull it away from my ear for a moment. "How dare she try to steal your guy?"

"Well, honestly I don't think she has any clue he's my guy. If he even is." I shrug. "She hasn't seen him in years."

"Uh, ye-ah. 'Cause she left him. Duh. She's got absolutely no right to show up now and try to take him back. That little Sherwood slut."

"Well, I mean, I don't even know if that's her goal," I protest, not having any idea why I'm suddenly defending Marion. "She came to the camp to bring Robin the silver arrow."

"Yeah, and the kiss she never got to give him, right?"

"You're not helping."

"Sorry. You're right. I'm sure it's all fine. You just have to trust your man."

"Easy for you to say. You have the most loyal knight in the history of knights. And you haven't seen how

Robin looks at Marion. It's like he's some lovesick cocker spaniel."

"Are you sure? Or are you just imagining it 'cause you're being insecure?"

"I'm sure." Am I? Am I really sure? Or have I been projecting? I try to think back to Robin at the tournament. No, I've got to be right.

"Have you talked to him about it?" Kat presses. "I mean, I totally accused Lance of cheating on me with Guenevere. They went to this cottage in the woods together and everything! And, like, with medieval cheating you can't even do a condom search, you know? But it turns out he was just protecting her out of a sense of duty. He never even thought of her in that way."

"But my situation is different. Robin and Marion were lovers."

"Uh, yeah, like a billion years ago. We all have exes, Chris. Even you. How do you think you'd react if Danny showed up at the camp?"

Ugh. She's got a point. How would I act if Danny was the arrow delivery boy? Would I immediately tell him to eff off? Or would I want to spend a few moments alone with him to talk?

Whoever thought Kat Jones would be the voice of reason?

"You're right," I relent. "Maybe he just wants to get some closure or something, find out why she jilted him like she did. Who knows, maybe he's dying of boredom back at camp as she titters on and on. Maybe he realizes what a self-absorbed wench she was all along and doesn't remember what he used to see in her."

"Yeah. Sometimes that's all it takes," Kat says. "I know when someone dumps me, I always end up putting them on this stupid pedestal in my mind. Every time I think of them they get more god-like and grandiose. And why? Not because they were anything special. I mean, you should see the losers I dated before Lance. Can we say, 'Living at home in their parents' basement playing videogames all day 'cause they're too lazy to find employment' much? But because they rejected me, I immediately filed them in the Better Than Me category in my brain. And then, when I finally run into them again, I'm like, what the hell was I thinking? This guy's a total dork. He has no power over me."

I wonder briefly if I'll think that about Danny when I see him again. Have I built up our relationship as something more special than it was just because he betrayed me? How much did we really have together? Sure, we dated since high school, but we barely saw each other the four years I was in college. And when we moved in together after graduation my day shift and his night shift completely conflicted.

With Danny there were no long talks, no shared emotional or intellectual ties. We had great sex and he made me laugh and together we were able to coexist. But did he ever take the time to know the real me? Did he even care about my hopes and dreams? Did I ever care about his?

Maybe Kat's right. Maybe it's the same with Robin. One talk with Marion and he'll realize he outgrew his childhood crush long ago. That now he wants to be with someone who he can really connect with. Who won't leave him for a jeweled necklace. What Robin and I share is special. We have long, deep discussions. We bond on a higher plane than I ever did with Danny. Surely he feels that way about me as well.

I hope.

"So, uh, I guess I shouldn't even bother asking about King Richie, then," Kat says, bringing me back to the conversation.

"Uh, oh, sorry," I apologize, realizing I've been lost in thought. "No, no sign of the guy."

"Totally lame. But okay. Well, we'll keep hanging here in the twenty-second century, I guess."

"Sorry."

"Meh, it's not all bad. I've gotten this great job as a fashion designer for this really amazing company. I'm bringing back a little twenty-first century to the masses. And trust me, they need it! These people think acid-washed jeans are the latest in couture."

I laugh. "Sounds like you've got your work cut out for you."

"You too, babe. But don't give up on Hood Boy just yet. I'm telling you. From what you say, he sounds pretty special. You don't want to let something like that go."

"Thanks, Kat," I say, almost reluctant to let her off the phone. It's so odd how this adventure has totally bonded me to a girl I used to hate. But she's different now. Or maybe I'm just finally giving her a chance.

We say our good-byes and, much cheered, I head back to camp. I can't wait to see Robin. To tell him how much I care about him. How I'm excited about our relationship and I want to make it work. How I totally understand why he'd need some closure with Marion.

But when I get back to the camp I'm dismayed to see that they are still talking. Eesh. How much closure does this guy need? From the outskirts I watch as they whisper, nearly face to face, in low voices. Then, to my shock and horror, Marion leans forward and plants a small kiss on Robin's lips. Worse, he doesn't get mad or pull away or anything remotely smart and deserving of my love like that.

Instead, he pulls her into an embrace.

Chapter Fourteen

I stare at the two hugging figures for a second, wanting to pull out every hair in my head—or, preferably, every hair in Marion's perfect mane.

Obviously Kat was wrong about the closure thing. On the contrary, these two look like they're about to totally hook up. Maybe they made peace with each other. Maybe Marion apologized or made some stupid excuse as to why she's ignored him this past year. Maybe the dumbass actually accepted her apology.

Maybe they're back together.

Maybe Robin and I are done, forever.

Tears blur my vision and I rush back into the woods, unable to watch the scene a moment longer. I knew it! I knew he still had feelings for her. He was just using me until she came back.

I should have known this would happen the second he suggested we keep our relationship a secret. I mean, hello? He was too ashamed to even tell anyone that we were dating! That's so got to be one of the golden *He's Just Not That Into You* rules. If he really loved me, if he really wanted our relationship to last, he would have sung it from the rooftops like Ewan McGregor in *Moulin Rouge*, consequences be damned.

Unfortunately, knowing this in my head doesn't make my stomach hurt any less. Or my heart, for that matter. As the song says, *love bites*.

I run and run and run, not looking or caring where I'm going or what I'm going to do once I get there. As long as I'm away—out of proximity of the lovebirds— I'll hopefully be able to breathe again. That, in and of itself, seems like it will be a major accomplishment at this point.

The forest thins and I step out into a darkened meadow. A full moon illuminates the landscape, casting stark, frightening shadows at every bend. I look around warily, feeling like I've just stepped into some cheesy slasher flick. The home audience is screaming at me, begging me not to go off alone into the night. Not leave the safety of the camp, while Jason Voorhees, Freddy Kruger, Michael Myers and Leatherface all lie in wait, having joined forces to participate in my ultimate demise.

Um, yeah. Imagination running wild, I know. But sadly it's almost more comforting at the moment to dwell on potential psycho axe-wielding killers than rerun my mental YouTube video of Marion kissing Robin for the ten-thousandth time in my brain.

I try to catch my breath, hands on my knees. What now? Where do I go? What do I do? I certainly can't go back to the camp. Not now and probably not ever. After all, it would be way too torturous to sit around and watch Robin and Marion falling deeper and deeper in love as each day passes. To sit and listen to his trite apologies. His excuses.

It's not you, it's me. Can't we just be friends? I need some space . . .

Yeah, I'd pretty much rather pull out my own toenails one by one than listen to that bullshit.

Problem is, if not back to camp, where do I go? I'm now stuck in the same situation I was in when I arrived in the 12th century. Out of time. Trapped in medieval England until King Richard returns, and who the hell knows when that may be?

I shiver under my thin tunic. It's cold out here on the moors, and in my haste to get the hell out of Sherwood all I grabbed was my camera bag instead of a much more practical warm cloak. At the same time, it's too dark to wander far. What if I tripped on a branch or slipped on moss or fell in a hole and hit my head on a rock? I'd be totally SOL.

Resignedly, I gather up some stray sticks from the forest's edge and clear a spot to make a fire. Luckily the merry men taught me to light one the old fashioned way—without a Bic. Otherwise I'd probably freeze to death. Nice thought.

It takes me a few tries—rubbing two sticks together to spark a fire is so not as easy as they make it out to be in the movies—but in the end I manage to get a small blaze going. The process of feeding the fire, bringing it crackling to life, is somewhat soothing and takes my mind off my situation temporarily.

But when it's lit and I sit down beside it, holding my now sooty hands out for warmth, all my pain comes rushing back, my brain flooding with instant replays and unwanted memories. My stomach aches and I feel like I'm going to throw up.

This sucks. I'm lost. I'm freezing. I'm probably going to be eaten by some random animal I don't even recognize, and once again, I've fallen for a man who would rather be with someone else. Who took me and used me and emptied me just because I was convenient, because I was there. And when he was done, he cast me aside. He reunited with his true love and left me alone once again.

Okay, I need to get a grip here. I can't keep playing the victim. I purse my lips and try to remember what the self-help books told me. How I need to own my own power, not give it away to someone unworthy. That my destiny lies in my own hands. That I am a complete, wonderful, beautiful goddess who doesn't need a man to complete her.

I am woman. Hear me roar.

So how come all I want to do is whimper?

I awake the next morning curled up beside the black coals of the burnt-out fire, soaking wet from the dewy grass I fell asleep on. Ugh. I sit up and try to brush myself off. Thank goodness no one's around to see me. I'm rumpled, tear-stained, and smell way too ripe—not exactly the beautiful goddess the self-help books want me to channel.

Still, the sun is shining high in the sky, casting glittery light on the wet grass. A nearby bird twitters gaily, perhaps blissfully happy about the early morning worm he managed to score by not sleeping in. A warm breeze tickles my face, sharing the sweet scent of honeysuckle and wildflowers with me. And to top off the Disney-esque moment, I notice an adorable little spotted fawn a few yards away, casually munching grass next to her big brown-eyed mother. I watch as they enjoy their breakfast, seeming not to have a care in the world.

Suddenly I feel somewhat better.

So what if Robin and Danny are both losers with a capital L? My existence is not defined by whether a man likes me or not. I'm a 21st-century chick, after all. I could live a completely fulfilling life without any man at all, if I so desired. I don't need some stupid guy bringing me down.

I stand up and toe the fire like the men taught me, making sure there are no glowing embers to annoy Smokey the Bear or to kill Bambi's dad. My sudden movement startles the deer and they glide off across the field in graceful leaps.

I look back at the forest, wondering what to do. Part of me, the masochistic, likes-to-be-tortured part, wants to race back to the camp and see if Robin and Marion are sharing breakfast together after a night of passion. But, I realize, this option will only prolong my heartbreak and intensify my grief. I must be strong. I must let go. I must prove I can live without him by my side. After all, I don't have much choice.

I square my shoulders, firming my resolve. I just

need to hang someplace until King Richard returns. I don't need to stick around Sherwood Forest to survive. I can find my own place. In fact, I can head right to Nottingham Castle. After all, then I'll be nearby when King Richard returns with the grail. Maybe I can even get the 411 on that whole thing. Someone must know his ETA, right? Even if they're not looking forward to it.

Sure, the last time I was there I had to run for my life, but that was me dressed as a boy. Surely if I throw on a dress and let down my hair no one's going to recognize me. Heck, maybe I'll even go get a job. Become self-sufficient.

Screw Robin and his merry men. I don't need anyone but myself.

I take stock of my surroundings and think back to the maps we used when planning our robberies. Nottingham should be south of here, and the rising sun to the east clues me in to which direction I should walk to get there. It's going to take me hours to get there by foot. But that's okay. It'll give me time to pep talk myself some more.

I'm good enough, I'm smart enough, and gosh darn it, Stuart Smalley, people like me.

Um, yeah. Maybe I should just take in the scenery.

Soon I reach a small village nestled against a grassy hillside. I realize it's the same town we brought our first robbery spoils to more than a month ago. Today it looks different than the sad, dilapidated village it once was. For one thing, the threadbare thatched roofs have been repaired and the crumbling stone wall has been rebuilt. Children play outside the village perimeter, running and screaming in glee as they chase each other and a scruffy-looking little dog. Sure, the people are still wearing rags, but they don't look as underfed as they did during our first visit. Today the faces are fuller, the eyes not as hollow. Okay, they're still probably not meeting the full RDA Pyramid of Nutrition, but they definitely seem better off.

Pride warms my insides as I take in the scene. A few peasant women giggle as they hang laundry. Two men shout a happy arrival, showing off a freshly killed deer. The town seems happy and healthy and secure.

And it's all because of me.

Yes, little old me, who never did any good in her whole life before now is responsible for all of this. The girl who always stayed in the shadows of her drug-addicted mother or abusive foster parents or loud, vociferous husband. The girl who took an innocuous job as a fashion photographer because she was too afraid of applying to be a real photojournalist. That girl stepped out of her comfort zone, as the shrinks would say, and really made a difference. Okay, fine, it sounds kind of corny, but the evidence here more than proves it. These people are a thousand times better off than before I came to Sherwood Forest. Tears have been replaced by laughter. Empty stomachs are full. All because of me and my plan.

I totally rock.

The washer women finish hanging their clothes and head back into one of the thatched huts. I examine the garments they left behind, a plan forming in my mind. If I'm going to find a job in Nottingham, first thing I'll need is a dress. No reason to keep up the eunuch act once there. At the same time, I can't bring myself to just take clothes off the clothesline. After giving so much to these people, the last thing I want to do is take something away.

I know, I'll buy one. I have ten silver pennies in my bag. That should be way more than enough.

I knock on the cottage door. It's a tiny dwelling, crudely constructed of sticks and a straw thatched roof. Not the most secure-looking building, that's for sure. Certainly wouldn't have been a problem for the barrel-lunged wolf of legend to huff and puff and blow it all down.

"A good morn to you, sire." A pretty young teenage girl (had I been expecting one of the three pigs?) answers the door, greeting me with a small curtsey. "You are one of Robin Hood's men, are you not? 'Tis a great honor to have ye knock on me humble door."

"Shh," I say, finger to my lips, not wanting to clue the whole town in that I'm here. After all, I'm trying to keep a low profile. If Robin comes looking for me, I don't want him to know where I've gone. Not that he's likely to expend the energy on a search. He's probably worn out from screwing Marion all night. "I don't want to cause a scene. I was just wondering if I could buy a dress from you. Maybe one from the clothesline over there?" I point to the laundry.

"A dress? What would ye be needin' a dress for?" the girl asks, looking a tad suspicious.

"It's a long story," I say. "Involving . . . well, one of our adventures." There. Be as vague as possible, all while sounding unbearably cool.

"Ach, you'll be usin' it to trick the Sheriff of Nottingham, aye?" the girl asks, her watery blue eyes wide and shining with excitement. I thought she seemed impressed before; now she's looking at me like she's from New Jersey and I'm Bon Jovi.

"Er, yeah. Something like that," I agree. "So, can you spare a dress? I will pay you well, of course."

"Aye, of course. In truth, I can do one better. Come inside." She pulls open the door and invites me in. I step over the threshold into a dimly lit living space. The girl asks me to wait and disappears into a back room.

I look around. The small cottage is sparsely furnished and dirt-floored, but it seems clean and the fire pit is ventilated enough so the air is not overwhelmingly smoky. Still, a fire pit in a straw-roofed house? That should so be against some kind of code.

The teen returns with a dress. My eyes widen as she holds it out for my inspection. This is not your typical scratchy linen, undyed peasant smock. She's offering me a fancy crimson-colored gown with bell sleeves, fluttery lace, and tiny sparkling beads seeded in the hems. Where did she—?

" 'Twas me mother's," the girl explains, pushing the dress into my hands. The material is soft, likely silk. "She was a fine lady, she was, back when King Richard ruled our land."

"Ah. And, um, your mother won't mind you selling her dress?" I ask. After all, I know how teens can be. And I certainly don't want the missus of the house to come home from a day in the fields to learn that the last precious reminder of her former life has been sold for beer money.

The girl casts her eyes to the floor and shakes her head sorrowfully. "She is dead, milord. Killed in a raid several months before Robin and his men arrived that first day. One of the sheriff's men demanded she give up the ruby ring my father had given her before going off to die in the crusades. My mother told 'im she'd rather die." The girl shrugs helplessly. "And so he killed her."

I cringe. "Oh. I'm so sorry. That's terrible."

The girl nods. "So if you be needin' a dress to outwit the sheriff, this is the one you should wear," she says, handing me the garment. The silk rustles as I take it carefully into my arms. "Me mother would be proud to have it go to such a good cause."

"I can pay you for it," I interject, feeling a bit guilty that the dress isn't exactly being used as she might expect. I mean, sure, I technically didn't lie. I will be wearing it in an effort to trick the sheriff and the rest of the court. But it'll be more of a "lying on my resume to get a good job" kind of trick, rather than the "steal the court jewels and give them back to the people to repay them for all they've suffered under Prince John's rule" type she might be hoping for.

The girl waves a small brown hand. "Nay, I will not accept your silver. Forsooth, you and your men have done so much for our small village already. Look outside, milord. Children who once were at death's door now play without a care. My friends and neighbors smile as they go about an honest day's work, knowing now that their sweat and tears will not be in vain. Before you came we had nothing. No hope. No future. Now we thrive once again. So I am more than honored to give you my mother's dress. 'Tis the very least I can do for all the happiness you have brought us."

Pride wells up inside me. Again, wow. We really made a difference here. That's so cool. I've never saved a child from starving before. (Well, besides "Eswin," the little boy from Guatemala I sponsor back in the 21st century for 'less than a dollar a day.' I'm such a sucker for Sally Struthers's pleas.)

"Do not insult me mother's memory by refusing my gift," the girl adds. She's very well-spoken for being fifteen years old.

"No, no. I won't," I assure her. "It's a beautiful dress, and I promise it'll be put to good use."

The girl smiles, and I realize she's missing a few teeth. Too bad I couldn't rob a dentist and donate his services or something. Oh well, there's only so much I can do.

She turns to tend the bubbling cooking pot over the firepit. I say good-bye and repeat my thanks, then slip out of the hut. But not before dropping three silver pennies onto a crude wooden table by the door. She'll thank me later.

Armed with a dress and a plan, I get directions to Nottingham Castle from one of the villagers and continue my journey. It's not as close as I would have liked, especially on foot, and the slow trip gives me way too much time to think. But I try to keep my mind off Robin and his betrayal, and instead concentrate on what yet lies in store for me.

The way I figure it, the castle is the perfect place to hang while I wait for King Richard to return. After all, it's where royalty stays when it's in town, so it's likely he'll show up there first, right? And there I'll be, ready to convince him to give me a drop of Grail blood so I can get the hell out of Nottingham forever. Hopefully he's amenable to the idea. I can't imagine having waited all this time only to be turned down in the end.

Then I'll be done. Mission accomplished. Nimue will somehow bring me back to the 21st century and Kat can come back from the future. I wonder if time will have passed or if, like in Narnia, a thousand years here is like a day.

Either way, Monday morning at work is going to be absolutely no fun. Total time-travel hangover.

It's dusk by the time I reach the towering gray stone walls of Nottingham. Luckily they haven't yet closed the drawbridge for the night and I'm able to get myself inside. I wander around until I find a small inn and rent a room for the night. But that uses up the last of my money. Tomorrow I definitely need to find a job or I'll be forced to rob the rich to feed myself.

Chapter Fifteen

The morning sun streams through my window and I open my eyes, ready to greet day one of the rest of my life. This is a new chapter. A new start. And this time I'm going to do things right. No more hanging out in the forest, pretending I'm someone I'm not, mooning over someone who doesn't really want me. Starting today, I get to be myself again. Well, the 12th-century version of myself, but at least I'm back in dresses.

I look around the medieval B&B where I spent the night. B #1 was moth-eaten and lumpy, and I'm not holding out much hope for B #2 being anything vegetarian. But that's okay. I'm rested and raring to go. Watch out Nottingham, Chrissie is in town.

There's no shower, obviously, so I can't exactly freshen up the way I normally would back home. But I do convince the innkeeper to supply me with a pitcher of water and a small bar of soap to sponge bathe. Then I don the dress I got from the village teen. It feels a little loose—her mother must have been a bit heftier than I—but it's attractive and courtly looking. (At least in my mind. Admittedly, I skipped Fashion 101 of 12th century England.)

I primp a bit more, though the polished metal serving as a mirror doesn't exactly give me a crystal clear vision of my appearance. I pull my unruly hair into a bun and pinch my cheeks like Scarlett O'Hara used to, in an effort to achieve that sans-Cover Girl glow. It seems so odd to be worrying about things like hair and makeup again. But at the same time, it's kind of nice. Not that I ever was some fashionista like Kat, but I do like to look pretty on occasion.

I head down the rickety wooden stairs, through the bar—I take the few cat-calls from the early morning barflies as a good sign, though maybe not *that* good considering they've probably been drinking since noon yesterday—and outside into the bright morning sunlight.

Nottingham is alive with activity—the sights, smells and sounds nearly overwhelming to my just-woken state. A hammer slams against an anvil as a blacksmith morphs a chunk of metal into a deadly weapon. Chickens and cows cluck and moo, respectively. The scent of freshly baked bread wafts through the air, mingling with a scent of something far less pleasant that I can't identify and I'm not sure I want to.

I smile. This place isn't half bad. In fact, it's kind of exciting, to tell the truth. All the hustle and bustle of peasants and tradesmen going about their days. Pretty maids batting their eyelashes at the butchers, trying to save a penny with a smile. Hunky men-at-arms wandering the streets, making sure everyone stays in line. I can definitely see myself waiting out Richard's return here. It'll be a brand-new adventure. A brand-new life. And I don't need Robin to live it.

I do, however, need a job. I glance around, wondering how to find out who's hiring. I mean, it's not like I can just hop on Monster.com to find that dream barmaid position I've always lusted after. And I don't see any Help Wanted signs displayed on the pottery seller's stand. Hmm. This could be more difficult than I thought. What if they start asking for references? Or employment history? I'm thinking listing "professional robber of the rich" as my occupation and Robin Hood as my professional reference might turn off a few of my available employers.

I wander the streets for a bit, taking in all the sights, wondering who I should approach. Suddenly, a soldier clad in chain mail and a bright red tabard steps into my path.

"Milady," he addresses me, bowing low.

I raise an eyebrow at the interruption. "Yes?" I query. I hope he doesn't recognize me as one of Robin's men. That wouldn't be good. But still, that's impossible, right? After all, if he knew who I really was, he wouldn't be bowing. He also wouldn't be calling me "milady."

"Your presence has been humbly requested by his Majesty, Prince John. You are to come with me."

What? *My* presence has been requested? And requested by His Majesty? His Majesty Prince John? How does Prince John know to request my presence?

Jeez, and here I thought I was doing well, keeping a low profile. And what if this so-called presence requesting isn't due to some standard "Welcome to Nottingham" program the tourism board voted in last year, but rather that they somehow recognize me from the tournament?

But the guard has a really big sword strapped to his belt, so there's really not much I can do about the request except grant it, following him into the keep, praying that my head will not be "requested" from my shoulders.

We enter the castle, pass a few guards standing at the entrance, then march down a long stone hallway. Funnily enough, it's the same passage that Robin and I sprinted through two days ago while running for our lives after the archery tournament. I remember the adrenaline thrumming through my veins as I followed Robin, ready to die by his side if I had to. Sigh. That already seems a lifetime ago.

The ache returns, accompanied by a panicky electric crackling through my arms and fingers. The thought that my relationship with Robin is over forever just kills me inside. It squeezes my heart into a vise and makes it difficult to draw breath. Crushing, suffocating pain. And there's nothing I can do about it. As much as I'd like to curl up into a ball and die, I know my life depends on being able to keep it together.

Boy, it's so much easier to break up in the 21st century, where all you're required to do is lie on the couch with a bunch of tissues, eating Häagen-Dazs out of the carton and watching Lifetime movies.

I force myself to focus on my present situation. After all, I'm inside Nottingham Castle, home base of Prince John himself. Maybe I can do some recon while I'm here, get a better idea of when King Richard might be showing up.

"So, uh, nice place," I say, trying to make conversation with the guard. He grunts in response. Evidently he's the tall, dark and quiet type.

We make a few turns and end up at double wooden doors, guarded by two sentries. They bow to my escort and open the doors for us. We step over the threshold and into a giant hall.

Hmm. Maybe the Merry Maids are on vacation this week? The floor is filthy. It's caked with dirt and littered with feathers and bones, like someone let loose a fox in a chicken coop and never cleaned up afterward. In the center of the room there's a large fire pit giving off more smoke than fire at the moment, and making the air worse to breathe than village coffeehouses before they banned indoor smoking in NYC. Still, the people here don't seem to mind the smoke, and several are right next to the fire, drinking out of pewter mugs and chatting excitedly with one another.

The walls are made of stone and cloaked with tapestries depicting knights in various stages of derring-do and ladies hanging out with unicorns. Pretty standard medieval fare. At the far end of the room sit two ornate thrones covered in gold and encrusted with jewels. On the right sits a guy I recognize from the archery tournament as Prince John. He's wearing a crown that's a bit too big for his noggin, and he's currently slouched over, chin in hands, an expression of extreme boredom and annoyance on his face. With his orange-colored beard and unkempt hair, he really does look a little like the cowardly lion who plays his character in the Disney version of Robin Hood. It'd be funny if he suddenly started sucking his thumb and wanting his mommy. Less funny if he had a real snake for an advisor. Sir Hiss always used to freak me out.

"Milord, this is the lady you asked to see," the knight says, bowing low, then pushing me forward. I find myself standing in front of the prince, not sure what to do. So I give a little curtsey, hoping I'm doing it right. At least this place won't be like the court in *Shogun*. In that book the samurais cut off your head for even the most minor transgression against proto- col. I don't think it will be like that in England.

Prince John gives a toothy grin and rises from his throne to greet me.

"It's lovely to meet you, my dear," he says, in a voice that sounds too high-pitched to be coming from The Royal Leader of England. If you're going to be king, you'd better hope for a deep, booming voice. I bet King Richard has one. He certainly did when he was played by Sean Connery in *Prince of Thieves*. Mmm, sexy.

"It's, uh, lovely to meet you too," I stammer, still not entirely sure what to say. "Was there . . . some- thing I could help you with?" The second the words leave my mouth, however, I realize the question could seem rude. But I'm dying to know why he's called me here. If it's because he recognizes me and wants to behead me or hang me or whatever, I'd like to get all the cards on the table now.

But he only smiles again, circling me like a prowling cat, then reaches up a hand to run stubby fingers down my cheek. Um, ew? What's with the touching? Hasn't he heard of the three-foot-bubble rule? Then again, this is a guy who thinks nothing of starving children to death in his own kingdom. It's not surprising he lacks rudimentary social skills as well.

"You are very pretty," he says in a voice that almost sounds like he's purring. "Very pretty indeed." Too bad he's a scrawny evil wimp, because I am so in need of these types of compliments at the moment.

"Thanks," I say with an embarrassed shrug. "I try."

"Two of my knights spotted you at the inn last night and returned with tales of your beauty. Now I see they did not lie," he says, his face inches from mine. Ew. He has so not brushed his teeth this decade. Maybe while I'm here I could invent toothbrushes or something. "But who are you and where do you come from?"

"Actually I'm new," I say, struggling to come up with an on the spot lie. "My name's Princess Christine, and I come from the far off kingdom of . . . Hoboken."

He seems to buy it. Phew. "And what brings you to our simple little court?" Prince John asks, grinning smarmily. I spy—is that a droplet of spittle hanging from the corner of his lip? I mean, I'm happy he thinks I'm attractive, but I'll stop before the droolworthy point, thank you very much.

"Um, my father thought I could get a job here. Maybe as . . ." I was going to say a barmaid, but then decide to go for better. It's not like I have to show a resumé or provide references. "A lady-in-waiting."

The prince grabs my hand and gleefully shakes it up and down. "Of course!" he cries, more excited than a Superbowl winner on his way to Disney World. "I'd be delighted for you to become part of my court."

Weird. According to the legends, this guy is supposed to be evil incarnate, the devious ruler who stole the throne from his Crusading brother and taxed the villages to near starvation. So, how come he's acting like a silly little kid? Methinks someone else has got to be the brains of this operation.

"My Lord, I must speak with you." I hear a booming voice echo from across the hall. I glance in its direction and see none other than the Sheriff of Nottingham step through the door. I look back at Prince John and see the guy's become a bit pale. Ah-ha. So the sheriff's the Dick Cheney of England. It all becomes clearer.

"Yes, yes, very well, Sheriff," Prince John mumbles. He reminds me a little of Woody Allen. "I would be most pleased to speak with you on any matter you wish. I was just inviting my new friend here to—"

The sheriff takes a brief look at me, then waves a dismissing hand. Phew! He doesn't recognize me from the other day.

"This is more important than a woman," he declares, marching up to the second throne—the more ornate one, of course—and sitting down. "Send her away and let us talk business."

"Yes, yes, whatever you say, Sheriff." Prince John throws me an apologetic look. "I'll speak with you later, my dear," he says. "Sir Gerard, take Princess Christine up to ladies' chambers!"

We're at the top of a flight of wooden stairs. In front of us is a massive wooden door with an iron knocker. I guess this is the ladies' chamber. My new home.

The guard knocks twice.

"Ladies?" he calls.

I hear a titter of laughter from the other side of the door, then the squeaky turn of a key. The door swings open and three young women spill out from behind. When they see the guard, who I guess, now that I look at him, is pretty handsome, they giggle some more and twist strands of their hair while batting their eyelashes at him. It's the oldest flirting trick in the book. Though, actually, maybe it's not old in this century.

"Hi, Sir Gerard," a blonde chirps. She gives him a come-hither smile. "It's so nice of you to visit our chambers."

"Indeed, Sir Gerard," adds a chocolate-haired maiden beside her. "We are most honored by your presence."

"Won't you come in for a moment?" suggests a third girl. "You must be very tired from your important duties as a knight."

Gerard blushes but stands his ground. Strong man. These chicks may be silly and giggly, but they're all stunning. Each would be a knight in shining armor's dream.

"I'd like to introduce you to Princess Christine," he says, gesturing to me. "She will be joining you for a time."

The women glance at me, then giggle some more. They seem friendly. Phew. At least they're not going to act like snobby bitches.

"Thank you, Sir Gerard," they say in unison. "Now, won't you come in?"

"Sorry, ladies, I cannot," the guard says. "I must return to my post. Some other time, for certain."

They let out cries of disappointment, but the guard waves them off and says his good-byes, retreating down the hallway like one of Odysseus's crew who has just been saved from the sirens.

But I'm stuck with them.

Worse, the second the guard leaves, the women's attitudes change. They look me up and down, disdainful expressions clear on each face. Oh great. It's a medieval sorority, and they're ready to haze me.

"God's teeth! What in the devil's name is she wearing?" one of them asks, picking at the sleeve of my dress. "This style has not been in fashion for near five summers."

"And her hair! Does she not know how to run a comb through it, mayhap?"

"Not to mention her smell," adds the third, pinching her nose with delicate white fingers. "Surely she has not had a bath in several moons."

Oh great. Just my freaking luck. It's the medieval version of the staff at *La Style* magazine.

"Yes, yes, I'm not a fashionista. I get it. Never

claimed to be," I interrupt. "But I'm here and you're stuck with me, so why don't you just show me to my room?"

All three women stare at me.

"You dare order us about?" asks the blonde.

I square my shoulders. I've been intimidated by tall, anorexic blondes my entire life. I'm done with that now. "I just did, didn't I?"

"And what, pray tell, makes you believe we should oblige you or your orders?" asks the brunette.

Ugh. This is not going well. I attempt to lower my hackles. After all, I need to make friends with these women. As obnoxious as they are, they're going to be my roommates until King Richard returns, and the last thing I need is to have *Real World*-style drama in my living quarters right now. I've got enough to deal with.

I think fast. How can I impress these women? What's the one thing at *La Style* that the shallow, bitchy editors respected me for?

Suddenly, inspiration hits and I throw the girls a dazzling smile. This had better work. I know *I'm* impressed by how far photography has come, and I'm guessing these girls are pretty vain.

"Because I can show you magic beyond your wildest dreams."

Chapter Sixteen

Hm. I'm getting skeptical looks from the peanut gallery here. What, they don't believe in magic? Or, um, more worrisome, what if they do believe, and believe only witches can practice it? The last thing I need today is to be burned at the stake. Maybe I should have thought of that before I opened my big mouth.

"Magic? What magic?" queries the blonde, thankfully sounding more intrigued than outraged.

"Show us," commands the brunette.

I roll my eyes. "Uh, hello? You think I'm going to go perform magic right out here in the hallway where anyone can see? Puh-leeze. Show me to my room, and once I'm all washed up and good and ready, I'll put on a little show."

The three women turn to one another to confer over my proposition.

"She could be lying," says the blonde.

"Yes, how can we trust her?" says the brunette, looking at me indignantly. "Look at what she considers acceptable dress!"

God, these women are even *more* vapid than my *La Style* coworkers. And that's saying something.

"Look, my fashion sense has nothing to do with my magical prowess," I interrupt. "You'll just have to trust me on that."

They whisper to one another and then all three turn to me.

"Very well," the blonde says. "We will allow you entrance. However, if you do not prove your magic you will be cast out on your arse."

"Deal." I put out my hand to shake on it, then wonder if that's a gesture yet to be invented. I drop my arm. "So, uh, lead the way."

I follow them over the threshold and into a large suite of rooms. The middle chamber is sort of a sitting room, with a large fireplace and several stools. Delicate, colorful embroidery in varying stages of production lies everywhere. Guess that's what they do for fun around here. Ugh. I hope they don't expect me to join in. I never was one of those craft-type girls.

Off the main room there are several bedrooms, the largest featuring a canopy bed enclosed in heavy drapes.

"Who sleeps there?" I ask, peering inside.

"Lady Marion."

"Oh." I frown. Ugh. I've got to share the suite with her? That's going to be a bit awkward. Then again, maybe she won't be back, now that she's probably all shacking up with my boyfriend.

The thought sobers me and I sink onto one of the

stools, suddenly filled with melancholy. I've now gone from having the time of my life as an outlaw, doing good deeds and falling in love with a man I considered my possible soul mate, to cohabitating with a bunch of superficial bitches who only care about themselves and the latest cut in gowns. Sure, it'll be nice to have a bath, but I already miss Sherwood Forest.

Funny thing is, if I'm being completely honest, I miss life with Robin even more than I miss life back in the 21st century. Weird, huh? I mean, who would think I'd prefer sleeping on the ground and peeing in the woods to a Starbucks on every corner and taxis at my disposal? (Well, sort of at my disposal, depending on what time I really need them and what corner I find myself on.)

If things had worked out with Robin, what would I have done when King Richard returned? Would I have said good-bye and good luck and went on my merry way? Or would I have stayed? *Could* I have stayed, I wonder? Would Nimue allow it? Is it possible? I guess I could have always brought Robin back to the 21st century like Kat was trying to do with Lancelot, but would I even want to? I like it here. The fresh scent of pine in the forest, the cheery chirps of sweet songbirds waking me each morning, the good, hard-working, honest people that live here—I'd miss all of that.

According to the legends, once King Richard returns, Robin gets back his lands. He and I could get married and live as the Lord and Lady of Locksley. Our children could play at our feet, just as Robin told me he'd done as a child. We could be loyal, kind rulers, and our people would love us. We could grow old together, be best friends and true loves.

I shake my head to get rid of the ridiculous fantasy. Even if I could stay in the past, it no longer mattered. History had played out the way it was supposed to, Robin hooked up with Marion. She is his true love, the one destined to be Lady Locksley, not me. She is the one who gets the happy ending.

And me, I'll just go back to NYC and live out the rest of my days in an empty existence. I don't even want to meet another guy. Who's going to be better than the one I had? The legendary outlaw with the wicked smile and heart of gold. There's no one in the 21st century that could be as worthy. As strong. As confident. As hot and sexy.

One of the ladies in waiting rings a bell, and a few moments later a scrawny, red-headed servant boy appears in the doorway.

"Fetch the bath," the woman instructs him. "This girl stinks like a pig who has spent its day rolling in mud."

"Actually I heard pigs are pretty clean—just FYI," I tell her, unable to resist.

She shoots me a scornful look. Hm. I'm not doing so well on the winning-friends-and-influencing people thing. I wish Kat would call. She'd totally know how to handle these wenches. After all, these fashion obsessed types are totally her peeps.

A few moments later two other servants appear, between them carrying a large wooden tub. They set it down in the center of the room. Other servants follow, each with a bucket of steaming hot water, which they pour into the tub. I watch, actually kind of psyched. After all, I haven't had a bath the entire time I've been here. Sure, I've dunked in the lake, but there wasn't any soap and the freezing cold water forced me to limit my soak time.

The brunette hands me a bar of sweet-smelling soap. Another adds a pinch of crushed flower dust to the water and soon the sweet scent of roses rises with the steam. How lovely.

The servants bow and exit the room. I look at the tub, then back at the girls. They stand, waiting, expectant. Um . . .

"Can I have some privacy?" I ask, trying not to sound as impatient and annoyed as I feel. But, come on! I'm so not stripping in front of these girls. You know the first thing they're going to do is start making evil comments about my small chest. Or my not exactly "abs of steel" stomach. And trust me, I'm not ready to relive the locker room days of high school, thank you very much.

They grumble a bit, but they do retreat to various rooms in the suite. Alone, I strip off my dress and dip a foot into the steaming bath. It's a tad too hot, but at the same time it feels awesome against my skin. I force myself to endure the heat and sink into the water, my insides warming and a sense of contentment washing over me.

This is more like it! I may miss forest life, but I've also missed a nice hot bath like this. Especially since there's only a shower stall in my tiny apartment back home. I can't even remember the last time I soaked in a real tub. I almost forgot how wonderful it feels.

I wash all my two thousand parts and then just sit for a while, until the water starts cooling and my fingertips get all pruney. Then I rise and gingerly step out of the tub, my head a bit foggy from the heat. As if on cue, a servant steps out from one of the rooms—was she watching the whole time?—and wraps a towel around me. Another appears with a new dress, a bright green gown with embroidered bell sleeves. Very nice. And here I thought I'd have to get back in my filthy one.

Once I've dressed, the three ladies spill out from their various rooms and gather around me with eager expressions.

"You have had your bath," the blonde says. "And something suitable to wear. Now deliver us the magic you promised."

I swallow hard. Showtime. I hope this works.

I walk over to my bag and pull out my camera. I flip the on switch, and to my relief the device comes to life. I wasn't sure how much battery power I had left.

"Behold, the magic mirror!" I say, waving it around with as much showmanship as possible. The three women stare at the device, evidently not sure what to make of it. I chuckle. Wait 'til these vain vamps see what it does.

"Magic mirror?" asks the brunette, cocking her head.

"Ask no questions now. I will demonstrate its power," I say grandly, channeling David Copperfield. "Who would like to go first?"

The three girls look at one another with uneasy expressions. Ha! They're scared. My act is working. Finally the redhead timidly steps up.

"I will," she says, her voice a bit quavery.

"Very well," I say, giving her a once-over. She's actually very pretty, though a bit pale. I wish I had the *La Style* makeup artist on call. Or some lights for that matter. But hey, I remind myself, these girls have never seen a digital camera before. I don't need to deliver magazine-quality shots. Still, I do have some professional pride.

"Now," I instruct, getting into photog mode. "Look at me. Yes, right. Now turn your left hip outward. Good. Hands on your hips. Dip your head a little lower. That's right."

My subject frowns and glances over at her friends. I realize they're giggling at her expense. She turns back to me, glaring. "What does all of this have to do with a magic mirror?" she demands. "God save you if this is some kind of trick."

I shake my head. "No, no—no trick. I just want you to look your best. Just stay with me here. Back in position." I adjust a few settings on the camera and hold it up to my eye.

Click!

The shutter noise and the bright flash causes the three girls to jump back in shock.

"What was that light?"

"Did it come from the mirror?"

"I think I may be blind!"

I smile. Wait 'til they see what I've done.

"Okay, the magic mirror has captured your image in its aura. Now you shall see yourself, caught in its mystical eye." I motion for my model to come over to me. She hesitantly steps forward, her eyes wide and looking more than a bit scared.

"I see green spots," she says, "dancing in front of my eyes. Did you blind me, witch?"

"Nah, that goes away in a minute. Don't worry," I

assure her. "Do you want to see your picture—er, reflection—or not?"

I hold out the digital camera, turning it so she can see the LCD screen on the back. She takes it in her hands and stares down at her image. Her eyes widen and suddenly she's squealing in a mix of delight and horror. She throws the camera back at me, as if it were a hot potato, and runs to the other side of the room.

The other two girls crowd in behind me to see what has frightened their friend so much.

" 'Tis her!"

"Captured in the mirror!"

"How is it possible?"

"She looks beautiful!"

"I want a turn!"

"No, I am first."

"No, me!"

I grin. Mission accomplished. I'm in with the in crowd. Accepted, safe. Bed, bath and beyond.

Chrissie, one. Medieval fashionistas, zero. If only Kat could see me now!

Chapter Seventeen

That night there's to be a banquet in the main hall, celebrating some random saint or another, and I'm to attend as a guest of honor. Which is pretty cool, actually. I mean, obviously I've never been invited to a fancy party held in a medieval castle before. (No, Jen's second grade birthday party at Medieval Times does *not* count.) If I'm going to experience 12th-century life, I might as well experience it to the fullest. And since I've already done the sleeping on the stone-cold ground as an outlaw in the forest thing, I think it's about time to see how the other half lives.

At least, this is what my Pollyanna inner voice tries to convince me. The devil on my shoulder is a lot less interested in the whole deal. Truth be told, I miss Sherwood Forest. I miss the Merry Men. . . .

Ah, who am I trying to fool here? I miss Robin. Plain and simple. And I can't help obsessing over what's going on with him and Marion. Are they tucked away in his tent this very moment, making up for lost time with some wild and crazy sex? Or are they cuddling in one another's arms, vowing eternal devotion? Does Robin think of me at all as he traces her soft, white cheek with his callused finger? Does he wonder where I went? Does he even notice I'm gone?

Did I do the right thing? Should I have stayed, fought for Robin? No. If you love someone, you have to let them go. Everyone who's seen *Indecent Proposal* knows that.

If Robin comes back to me, he'll be mine forever.

Yeah, right. I'm so not holding my breath for that one!

"Princess Christine," Susan, the blonde, says, coming into the sitting room. "We must get you dressed."

Heh. Princess Christine. I kind of like the sound of that.

I push all outlaw thoughts from my brain and follow Susan into one of the bedrooms. She presents me with a gorgeous gown and explains it's mine to wear to the feast. It's made of the palest blue silk and has tiny crystals seeded into the embroidered sleeves. It's so delicate—ladylike—that I just know I'll end up spilling mead all down the front of it before the night is over. And sadly, stain-removing Colorox Bleach Pens have yet to be invented.

I don the dress and Elaine, the brunette, combs and braids my unruly hair. Then Avelyn, the redhead, drapes a silver necklace around my neck. Susan grabs my hand to slip a few chunky bejeweled rings on my fingers.

"So, where is this kingdom of Hoboken that you come from?" Avelyn asks as she combs.

"Yes, you speak with such a strange tongue. It must be very far," says Elaine. "I have never heard anyone talk as you do."

"Oh, yeah. It's far. Really far. Across a huge sea." And oceans of time, too, but we don't need to go into all of that.

"How did you get here?" Avelyn queries, draping a matching cloak over my shoulders and attaching it under my neck with an intricate silver dragon pin. "Was it by magic?"

I think for a moment before answering, then nod my head. What the heck, right? Might as well keep up the mystique I've built up. "Yes. The matchmaker in my . . . kingdom . . . cast a spell and sent me here to find my true love."

The girls' eyes all light at the mention of true love. So predictable. Who cares about magic when you've got potential hooking up to talk about?

"I daresay you'll have trouble finding it in *this* castle," Elaine says with an exaggerated sigh. "Your matchmaker should have sent you to France."

"Oh? I figured there'd be tons of guys around. I mean, even that knight earlier. The one who brought me up here. He was pretty good-looking."

"Aye. There are many handsome knights residing in the castle, but most are disinterested in courting a lady." Avelyn shrugs. "They'd rather rut with village whores on flea-infested bales of hay than chastely pursue royal ladies worthy of their love."

" 'Tis not the knights' fault," argues Susan. "Prince

John has ruled that they must not approach us. He enjoys the idea of having a castle filled with virgin brides, should he ever decide to take a wife."

"That seems kind of unfair to you guys," I say. Wow. None of these women have ever hooked up with a guy? No wonder they're so bitchy. "Wait 'til King Richard comes back," I comfort. "I'm sure he'll sort everything out."

"It seems King Richard will never return." Elaine sighs. "He rots in that Austrian prison, for no one is interested in paying his ransom. They'd rather throw banquets and stuff themselves like pigs."

"We are ladies in waiting. And so we wait," says Susan in a long-suffering voice.

"We will likely die virgins, never knowing a man's love."

I roll my eyes. "That's dumb. You guys shouldn't have to sacrifice your lives just on the prince's whim."

All three stop and stare at me.

"Well, it's true!" I protest. "You choose to be here. To live like this."

Susan stares at me. "Choose? What choice do we have? To leave the castle and live in the village like commoners? Brown our skin and sleep in huts?"

"Hey, all choices have consequences," I say. "You have to decide what you want in life. And what you're willing to sacrifice to get it."

The chimes of a faraway bell effectively end the discussion, and the girls squeal and scamper off to their respective chambers. Evidently that's the call for dinner, and none of them are ready. They chatter excitedly as they don dresses and add accessories at a frantic pace. I feel like I'm in some kind of medieval sorority or something. I wouldn't admit this to anyone back in the 21st century, but the whole thing is kind of cool. After all, I've never been in the giggling, girly crowd before. I always insisted I had no interest in it. Still, after months of eunuch-dom in a filthy forest, hanging with the girls is kind of fun.

I look around the room. No mirrors. But I do have my camera. I set the timer and strike a pose that would make Madonna proud.

Click! The flash blinds me for a moment, then I step out of frame and go to check out the digital image it took. I raise my eyebrows in surprise. Wow! I look so different. So . . . ladylike! These girls are good! I could totally see them as the Fab Three in a new Bravo show "Medieval Eye for the Modern Guy." Or, um, girl, in this case. Whatever.

If only Robin could see me now. I wonder what he'd think. Not that I care. Really. I'm so through with that scene. In fact, maybe I'll go down to dinner tonight and meet a really sexy knight in shining armor. One of those chivalrous ones who will recite poetry to me as he feeds me peeled grapes. One that can stay friends with his exes, but who has no desire to hook back up with any of them.

Oh wait, these knights aren't allowed to have girlfriends. Just my luck.

I feel eyes on me and look up from my camera's viewscreen. Susan stands in the doorway, looking bashful.

"What's up?" I ask.

She closes the door behind her and comes over to sit beside me on the bed. "Can I speak freely?" she asks.

"Of course," I say, wondering what's up.

"What you said before, about choices. Do you truly believe it?"

"Yes. Definitely. Why?"

She blushes and stares down at her hands. "There is this boy," she says, and suddenly I realize how young she probably is. Couldn't be more than eighteen. "His name is Paul. He works at the stable, making horseshoes. He's an apprentice to a great swordsmith." She smiles as she speaks, and I can practically feel her intense crush radiating from her.

"And you like him," I conclude unnecessarily.

"Aye," she says, her face's pink glow deepening. "And he has given me reason to think he likes me as well."

"So what's the problem?"

"He is poor. Life with him would be hard. I would be banned from court and forced to live as a peasant woman."

"But you'd be with him," I rationalize.

"Aye." Tears slip from her blue eyes as she looks up at me in utter honesty for what I imagine to be the first time. "Princess Christine, forsooth, I know not what to do."

"I think you do." I place a hand on her shoulder and give her a squeeze. "I think you want to follow your heart."

"But the other ladies will not understand," she protests, glancing at the closed door. "They will think

I've gone mad. To give up a life of leisure to live as a peasant . . ."

"One, who cares what they think?" I ask. "And two, I think they might surprise you if you're honest with them."

Susan smiles through her tears and reaches over to give me a huge hug. "Oh, Princess Christine," she says, burying her head in my shoulder. "You are so wise and good. I am very glad you came here."

I stroke her head, feeling wise beyond my years. "I'm glad as well."

Fashionably late, we head down to dinner. The great hall has been transformed (and cleaned up, thank God!) for the feast. Torches and candles cast a fiery glow on long, row tables covered with plates and bowls overflowing with meats and fruits and cheese. On one side of the room sits a trio of musicians gently strumming their harps. Servants in grey linen tunics rush to and fro, delivering more and more food. Colorful, richly dressed courtiers lounge at each table, picking at their dinners. Judging from their waistlines, these guys aren't exactly downtrodden.

It's kind of sick, actually, to see so much food in one place. I mean, there's no way it's all going to be eaten by the small number of guests present, not unless they stuff themselves to the point of illness, which I guess is possible. But still! All this food, all this excess, and the common people are sitting in their villages starving. Babies are dying of malnutrition.

How can I be here? How can I enjoy this? It goes

against everything I stand for, everything I've worked to eliminate since I've been here. If the Merry Men could see me now, I'd be so ashamed.

"Princess Christine," a voice calls out. I look over to the head table and see Prince John himself is beckoning me. Oh great, just what I need to make my night complete. But hey, this is my job now. I'm an official lady-in-waiting and I'd better get used to the waiting part. I drop a curtsey and approach the table. The prince pats the empty seat next to him.

"Lady Marion is away this evening," he informs me. "So I humbly ask you do me the honor of taking her place by my side."

"Thank you, milord," I say, curtseying once again, trying to keep a poker face at the name of Marion. I can't believe she's not back yet. Did she decide to shack up with Robin for good? What do the men think of that? I mean, here I thought the "no women in camp" rule was pretty set in stone. After all, Robin made me hang out dressed as a boy for weeks. Does Marion get some special dispensation? God, I'd like to wring that stupid outlaw's neck.

"Princess Christine?" queries the prince.

I shake my head, forcing my thoughts back to the here and now. "Sorry, Your Majesty," I apologize. "You honor me. I'd love to sit next to you."

Okay, fine, "love" may be a tad too strong a word for my real feelings on the matter, especially as I see spittle on his mouth as he grins at my acceptance. Bleh! But really, what other option do I have? He's the prince. I came to his court willingly. I have to follow protocol.

Besides, maybe I can do some recon while I'm here,

I remember. Find out the 411 on King Richard and his expected return date, for one. I've been playing around in the forest way too long. I can now focus on the real reason I'm back in time.

A servant beckons me into my seat, holding my chair for me as I sit down. Another dumps a plate of some kind of bony roasted bird in front of me. I wave it away. He bows, then returns a few moments later with a haunch of some other sickly sweet-smelling meat. I can't help but hold my nose, bad manners be damned. After all, getting sick all over the head table would be much worse.

"No, no. I don't eat meat," I try to explain. He looks at me like I just said monkeys fly out of my butt, but shrugs and retreats, leaving me foodless.

"You do not eat meat?" Prince John questions, he himself viciously gnawing on some kind of dead animal or another. I swallow hard, forcing my stomach to behave. "Why ever not?"

Luckily, I've fielded this question before. Many times, in fact. "I don't like the idea of animals being killed for our own frivolous indulgences. After all, there are plenty of other things to eat in this world."

Back in the 21st century I usually follow up my argument with a heated discussion on hormones and unfair farm practices, but in this case that's all moot.

"How truly odd," the Prince remarks. "You are a fascinating woman, Princess Christine."

"You're not so uninteresting yourself, milord," I say, trying to compliment him back. It's hard when the guy in question has a string of meat hanging from the corner of his mouth. Um, ew. Gross.

"And you're very beautiful," he adds, in case I didn't realize that the first thing he said was a total come-on. He fancies me. Oh golly gee, great. Damn the ladies in waiting for making me look too nice. So now I've not only lost the hero, but I'm going to have to fend off the advances of the villain as well.

"Thank you, milord," I acknowledge, then quickly change the subject. "So, how goes the whole ruling the kingdom thing these days? Any word from your brother on his return?" I bat my eyes and smile sweetly.

John's face darkens and his eyes narrow. "My dear brother Richard is being held prisoner in Austria," he says at last. "We are attempting to raise the money to free him as we speak."

Mm-hm. Sure you are. That's why you're wearing piles of gold jewelry and hosting crazy feasts like this. Penny-pinching to raise the ransom money; real charitable of you.

"That's great!" I say, forcing my voice to sound completely naive: "So, when do you think you'll have enough to bail the guy out? I mean, it must be soon, right? Poor Richard. All alone in that dark, dank prison cell."

At least the guy has the decency to look embarrassed. "I'm . . . not sure," he says at last. "My advisors . . ."

"Your Majesty, we do not talk of state affairs to strangers at the dinner table," interrupts the Sheriff of Nottingham, picking that moment to take the seat to the prince's left.

Prince John blushes furiously. "Right, right," he

says. "I apologize, Sheriff. My tongue got away from me, I fear."

The sheriff nods stiffly and goes at his dinner. Guess now I know for sure who's ruling this roost. It ain't the guy with a crown on his head.

Prince John turns back to me and lowers his voice. "As you can see, 'tis not a subject I can speak freely on," he whispers. "But forsooth, I will do everything in my power to free my brother. I miss him dreadfully."

I cock my head in surprise. What? Now this part wasn't in the storybooks. (Though I guess I should be used to that by now.) Prince John's supposed to be the baddie, the one who wants to take over King Richard's kingdom forever.

"You . . . miss him?" I ask.

Prince John nods enthusiastically. "Aye, of course. He's my brother, and I love him dearly. He's a fine ruler as well. I never had the taste for power he has. If I had my way, I'd sit and embroider all day."

Uh, what? Did I hear him right? "Embroider?" I repeat, pretty sure I must have misunderstood.

His face reddens and he grins sheepishly. "The ale has loosened my tongue," he mutters. "But yes. 'Tis a . . . hobby—something I fair enjoy. However, I do not want to be teased for it." He glances furtively up at me.

"No-no," I assure him, trying to smother a giggle. I can't believe the big bad prince is actually a nancy-boy. "I think it's admirable that you don't let your sex or position keep you from doing something you love."

"Truly?" he asks with puppy-dog eagerness. His IQ can *not* be higher than his shoe size.

"Truly," I say. "In fact, I think it's very cool. I'd love to see your work sometime."

"Oh, thank you, Princess Christine," Prince John says, grinning from ear to ear like a little kid who just got praise for the A on his report card. Never mind that it was for attendance. "Not everyone in the court shares your mind in this matter, and it delights me to no end that you approve. If you'd like, after dinner I can show you some of my work."

"I'd love that," I say, smiling back. I'm warming to the prince. He doesn't seem that bad of a guy. He's not the super-villain the stories make him out to be.

I hear a commotion at the far end of the hall and squint my eyes to see. The guards are opening the far doors with great ceremony, and a lone figure steps through. A curvy, voluptuous, annoying figure I'd recognize any day of the week.

" 'Tis nice of you to join us, Lady Marion," Prince John says, jumping from his seat and clapping his hands in glee. "You have been sorely missed. I trust your father is well?"

Marion approaches the head table. She's dressed in a pristine white, impossibly delicate gown with silver trim. I bet she never drops food down herself, either. Bitch.

"He is, milord," she says, curtseying low. "I thank you for allowing me leave to visit him."

Ah, so that's the excuse she used in order to fly the coop and go hook up with my boyfriend. I should denounce her as a liar right here, right now. But that could endanger Robin and his men and I'd never do that, no matter how much I want to strangle the guy.

There's too much at stake. The entire kingdom's welfare depends on him.

Besides, you still love him, something inside me jeers.

Marion turns and notices me, and her eyes narrow suspiciously. Does she recognize me from Robin's camp? It seems impossible, but still . . . That's the last thing I need. To be denounced as one of Robin's merry men right before dessert? I'd probably be hanged before breakfast.

"I'd hoped for a bit of supper," she says coolly, masking her face again. "But I see my place at the table has already been filled."

Oh! She's just annoyed that I'm sitting in her seat. Phew. That kind of annoyance I can handle.

I jump up and gesture to the seat in question. "All yours, Marion," I say. "I'm stuffed, anyway." I'm not really, obviously, since I didn't eat anything, but I'm more than happy to be excused from the banquet.

Marion bows coolly to me and walks around the table to take my seat. The whole court has their eyes on her. And why not? She's gorgeous and poised and elegant—everything I could never be. Suddenly my once gorgeous dress feels unbearably frumpy.

But I have to wonder, why is she back? Did they have a fight? Did Robin tell her that he's in love with me? Or is she only back temporarily? Maybe to grab her stuff before moving out to the Forest Sherwood on a more permanent basis.

"Come over here and sit with us," call the other ladies in waiting to me from the left side of the room. They have their own long table piled with food, but none of them seem to be eating. Sure they all have full plates, but they push the food around with their spoons, never bringing a single bite to their mouths. Medieval anorexics, most like. I've photographed enough models at *La Style* to know the signs.

I take a seat at their table and grab a hunk of bread, gnawing on it, carbs be damned, as I watch the head table. The Sheriff of Nottingham leaves his seat and walks over to Marion, whispers something in her ear. She nods solemnly and he retreats back to his side of the table. Prince John looks at her in question, probably wondering what it was the sheriff said. She only giggles and shakes her head and doesn't answer. I wonder what that's all about.

After dinner, music and court jester types entertain as overflowing pitchers of mead are passed around. It's rowdy, loud, and everyone's getting pretty sloshed. When a servant offers to fill my glass I decline, remembering what happened the last time I drank, back at the tournament. I'm so not interested in a repeat of that little adventure.

I watch as Marion slips out of her seat, unnoticed by anyone but me, and heads toward an unguarded side door. Where is she going? I try to tell myself that she's probably just tired—though hopefully not from all that shagging with Robin—and is heading to bed early, but a nagging Spidey-sense tells me there's something more to her disappearance. The fact that she did not say good night—not even to the prince— is suspicious.

She's just probably going to the bathroom, Chrissie!

Maybe. But it wouldn't hurt to check out that theory, would it? So against my rational brain's better judgment I give her a little head start and then make for the same door she exited.

The door opens into a long stone corridor flanked by lit torches. I tiptoe down, not wanting to be seen. A door at the far end creaks open . . . and then slams shut again. I reach it a moment later and open it cautiously. I see it leads out to a small garden. I slip outside, careful to close the door softly behind me.

The garden is beautiful, bursting with flowers—on the ground, climbing up pillars and trellises—and I bet the place is gorgeous by day. The sweet fragrances alone would make a blind man enjoy spending time here.

I see Marion on the far side of the garden, still an angel in white. She sits down on a stone bench and places her head in her hands. What is she doing? Is she praying? Geez. Here I'm thinking she's some horrible girl up to no good and I've interrupted her time with God.

I'm almost ready to go back to the feast, when a tall, broad-shouldered figure makes me stop in my tracks. I duck behind a nearby shrub, and watch as the dark figure makes his way over to Marion. She looks up and then rises to her feet.

A shiver creeps through me as I realize the figure is none other than the Sheriff of Nottingham.

I watch in shock as the two embrace. Are they just friends? Or . . . I remember Robin talking about catching Marion kissing someone in the garden when he first returned to England. Her uncle? Ha! Could the sheriff have been her lover? And if so, then . . .

I strain to listen to the quiet conversation.

"So?" the sheriff asks, pulling away from the hug.

Marion laughs, but the pleasant tinkling of Christmas bells has long disappeared. This laugh is guttural. Almost evil-sounding.

"So I did it, of course," she says, sitting back down on the bench. "Such fools. They'd not let a strange man into their den for a thousand pieces of silver—"

"Yet a beautiful woman they allow in with open arms."

"Aye. I had no problem at all convincing the guard that I needed to see Robin. The arrow worked perfectly as bait. You should have seen his round, greedy eyes. They forgot even to blindfold me as they led me straight to Robin's lair."

My heart pounds in my chest as I take in the words. Oh my god. It was a trap. Marion didn't want to see Robin because she missed him or wanted to rekindle their relationship. She's been in cahoots with the sheriff all along.

"And what about your former intended, the traitorous Robin of Locksley?" the sheriff asks.

Marion laughs. "Are you jealous, my love?" she asks. "For he has no claim on my affections."

"As it should be," the sheriff replies, leaning down to plant a kiss on Marion's cheek. "But how did he receive you? With any suspicion?"

"Nay," she says, shaking her head. "Though, oddly enough, he seems to have finally gotten over his silly crush on me."

"Oh?"

"Aye. He tells me he's in love with another. Some

girl from a foreign land. It was quite disgusting how he babbled on about her."

Warmth floods my heart at her words. Robin told her about me? He told her that he loves me! I've been such a fool. Oh, why didn't I trust him?

"Jealous, my dear?" the sheriff returns with a snarky grin.

"Nay. He can rut his foreign whore until the day he dies," Marion declares. Wow, I can't believe I once thought she was some delicate lady. "Which, now that we have the location of his hideout, shouldn't be more than a moon."

"A moon? I shall not wait that long. Not when we are so close to victory."

"And what is your plan?"

The sheriff smirks. "First we shall go to the villages of Donham and Trent, punish those vile peasants who accepted stolen silver from the outlaws."

"But if you kill the peasants, who will be left to bring in the harvest?"

"No, Marion," the sheriff replies. " 'Twould be fool-ish to harm able-bodied men. We will take away their children, instead. Round them up and bring them back to Nottingham. We'll tell them if they keep aid-ing outlaws, they will never see their young ones again."

Marion smiles. "And then?"

"Then we shall launch our attack on Robin Hood's camp, kill each and every one of those traitorous out-laws that have wreaked such havoc on our land. And if we have any trouble, we can always use the children to bait another trap."

"An excellent plan," Marion says. "You are truly brilliant, milord." She rises from her seat and throws herself into the sheriff's arms. They start making out, big time, but I'm no longer watching. I'm running back, my mind racing.

I have to warn Robin and his men!

Chapter Eighteen

I rush down the hallway, desperately trying to remember my way out of the castle. The place twists and turns into dead ends and alleys to nowhere. It's kind of like the hedge maze in *The Shining*.

Voices around the bend force me to slow my pace. I must act natural, must not appear like I've been running for my life. Maybe whoever it is can help me find my way out.

I turn the corner and find Elaine and Avelyn hanging out in the hall, talking in low whispers. They turn to acknowledge my presence and wave a friendly hello. Thank goodness I managed to win them over earlier with the camera trick. The last thing I need is for those two gossips to inform Prince John and his sheriff that I'd pulled an Elvis and was exiting the building.

"Could you please tell me the way outside?" I ask, trying not to sound too eager.

"Outside? Are you mad?" asks Elaine as she squints at me with worried eyes. "The sun has already set. Surely you do not want to leave the safety of our castle walls."

"Who knows the barbarian filth you may encounter outside of Prince John's protection," adds Avelyn solemnly. "Scoundrels who would rejoice in the opportunity to soil a lady's honor."

"Ooh, yes—like Robin of the Hood," Elaine suggests with a wicked gleam in her eye.

"Aye!" Avelyn's face lights up. "Though for him, I would gladly sacrifice my honor."

"You would sacrifice it for far less, Avey," Elaine counters.

The two ladies giggle hysterically, and I resist the urge to roll my eyes. So silly. Still, I'm secretly pleased. My boyfriend is a total rock star, and now I know he only has eyes for me. How lucky am I?

Robin. My heart flutters as I imagine him sitting in the forest, waiting, hoping for me to return. Is he worried? Does he think I've been captured? Killed? Has he been searching for me?

I have to get back ASAP.

I force myself to laugh carelessly. "Nah, I'm not going outside for long," I inform them. "Just wanted to get a little fresh air."

"But we have walled gardens within where you can do that in complete safety," protests Elaine, who thinks she's being helpful. "D'you want me to show them to you?"

"Been there, done that. I think I was interrupting a romantic moment, though."

"A romantic moment?" Now I've got both girls' attention. The fashions may be different, but I can tell women haven't changed much in eight hundred years. "Between who?"

"Yes, Princess Christine!" Avelyn says, eyes shining. "You simply must tell us."

I grin. "Tell me the way out of the castle and I will tell you all I know."

The girls look at each other, then nod and turn back to me. "Very well. But we still do not advise you to leave the castle gates 'til sunup. 'Tis dangerous for a princess."

"Sure. No prob. I'll wait 'til morning. I promise." I cross two fingers behind my back as I say this, hoping that this gesture still counts, even though it's likely not yet been invented. "Now where?"

Elaine points her small, white hand down the hall. "Go down yonder, then take a left and then your next right. You'll see a wooden door adorned by a dragon crest. It leads outside."

"Thanks," I say, relieved.

"Now, do tell us! Do not hold anything back!" The two girls crowd me, faces alight with their eagerness for the big scoop.

I laugh, holding up my hands to playfully ward them off. "Okay, okay!" I cry. "Lady Marion and the Sheriff of Nottingham!"

Their squeals are so loud I'm afraid they'll alert the entire kingdom.

"That naughty girl," Elaine says. "She kept it from us this entire time."

"How dare she not share her secret romance with

her sisters?" Avelyn says, looking both pleased at learning the secret and offended that Marion had kept it from her.

I shrug. "Well, she's in the garden still, if you want to go ask her."

"Ooh, shall we?" asks Elaine.

Avelyn nods in delighted agreement. "Thank you, Princess Christine," she gushes. "For such a delicious tale."

"Yeah, sure. No prob. Any time." I wave them off. They scamper down the hallway to go catch their friend. If Marion wasn't a traitorous bitch, I'd almost feel bad for her. She's about to get outed.

They turn the corner and I pick up my pace, heading in the direction they told me, praying for no more interruptions. If the sheriff's truly attacking soon, I don't have much time to waste.

I arrive near the hideaway about an hour later. I've worked my stolen horse too hard, and he's foaming at the mouth and soaked with sweat. I slide off of him and give him a thankful pat.

"Sorry about that," I whisper. "We'll make sure you get some yummy carrots or something when this is all said and done."

"Who goes there?" A man's voice cuts through the night.

"It's me . . . ," I cry, ready to say Christian. Then I remember. I'm still dressed as a medieval lady. Maybe I should have changed back into my tunic and tights before coming here. No one's going to recognize me in my current ensemble. Except Robin, of course.

Little John and Much the Miller jump from the bushes, bows drawn and aimed straight at my heart. They circle around, suspicious.

"Another one! It's like bleeding ladies' night around here these days," Much exclaims.

"Who are you, and what pray is your business here, milady?" Little John demands.

I look from one outlaw to the other, wondering how I'm going to get out of this. I guess I've got no choice but to tell the truth. Hopefully they'll be understanding. Who knows, maybe they'll find it all a big laugh. Maybe.

"It's me!" I cry. "Christian! Don't you guys recognize me?"

They give me the once-over. "Christian?" Little John cocks his head. "But you're a . . . He's a . . ." Recognition dawns on his face. "Why are you dressed as a girl, Christian?"

"Well, I've got a confession to make, actually." Might as well throw all my cards out on the table at this point. "I'm not actually a eunuch at all. In fact, I'm one hundred percent woman. I just pretended to be a eunuch because you have that sacred code thing and I was afraid of getting kicked out of camp if people learned the truth." I laugh nervously. "Isn't that just so silly?"

Unfortunately for me, neither of the men looks very amused. In fact, they look downright pissed off.

"You have tricked us this entire time?" Much the Miller asks in an outraged voice, his fingers gripping his bow tightly. Uh-oh. This is not going as well as I'd hoped. Why can't they be happy about this, like they were when Much's wife got to stay the night? When Maid Marion showed up? Sure, Much's wife didn't get to stay longer, but—

"Robin will be sure to hear of your treachery, woman," Little John adds in a menacing voice I didn't know the jolly green giant could muster.

"Uh . . ." Ugh. What am I supposed to say? Should I admit that Robin was in on the secret most of the time? Or would that threaten his leadership at a time when he needs it the most?

I shake my head. This isn't about me. Not now. They can do with me what they like. My warning is much more important.

"Listen guys, I can tell you everything later. Right now, we've got more important fish to fry. You're in great danger! Where's Robin? I have to warn him."

Little John shakes his burly head. "Nay. You will not see Robin until you explain—"

"What goes on here?"

I breathe a sigh of relief at the sound of Robin's voice through the trees. A moment later he appears out of the brush, his eyes widening as he sees me.

"This lady claims she's our Christian," Little John says, keeping the arrow in his drawn bow aimed at my heart. "That she's been tricking us all along."

I hold my breath, waiting for Robin's reaction. Everything about us, our relationship, maybe even our very lives hinges on his next move.

He stares at me for a minute, and I'm not sure if he wants to kiss me or kill me. He opens his mouth to speak, then closes it again, then opens it. I watch him struggle to decide how to handle this volatile situation. He knows the stakes are high; his future—and mine—hang in the balance.

"I have known for some time that Christian—Christine, actually—is a woman," he says at last. " 'Twas I who demanded she keep it secret from you all."

Little John's face hardens. "You lied to us, Robin?" he asks, his angry voice tinged with hurt. "This whole time, you lied to us to protect a woman? You went against the sacred code we all signed when we banded together in the forest?"

Oh no, this was not good.

John throws down his bow in disgust. "You ask us to fight for you. To obey your rules and live under your command. To give up our lives if necessary to do what's right. And all along, you're flaunting your own indiscretion?"

Robin hangs his head. "I cannot make any excuses for my behavior," he says. "I only did what I thought needed to be done."

"Needed to be done? *Why?*" Much the Miller demands. "So you can sneak off and rut her senseless while the rest of us go without? I've sat alone in me tent each night, dreaming of me wife and child left behind in the village, all because of your insistence on us following the rule. And now I find out you've been breaking it all along?"

" 'Twas not like—"

"Are you denying that you lay with her while she was a guest in our camp?"

Robin lets out a frustrated breath. "No."

This is not good. This is so not good. Sure, I didn't want to be Robin's dirty secret anymore, but I also didn't want him to completely lose everything he worked for just because of me. Especially not now. When everything is at stake.

"Look, it's not Robin's fault!" I try to protest. Much raises his bow, and points it at me, a furious look on his usually friendly face.

"Quiet, woman," he demands. "You have done enough."

Little John sighs, his eyes sad, and turns to Robin. "I am sorry, old friend," he mutters, his voice laden with remorse. "But you know what I must do."

Robin nods solemnly. " 'Tis only right. I would not expect any less, and would do the same 'twere I in your position."

John nods and clears his throat. "Robin of Locksley," he proclaims, "You have been found guilty of violating the sacred code of The Men of Sherwood Forest. Now, in compliance with the laws you created and agreed to follow, you must be arrested and held prisoner until a council is held to decide your punishment."

"Aye, and you are relieved of your command as well," Much adds, more venomously than John. "Liars and traitors will never lead us. Who knows how else we may have been deceived? Perhaps you are in league with the sheriff himself!"

"I would never!" Robin cries, shocked.

"You swore also that you would never let a woman into our home, but we see your treachery now," Much interrupts. He pulls a knife from his belt and points it at Robin. "As John said, you are under arrest until we decide what to do with you." He turns to me. "You and your little whore."

He shoves Robin forward, and John reluctantly gestures for me to follow. They lead us into the camp. Several men jump up and surround us, asking what's wrong.

"Robin Hood is a traitor," Much informs them. "He and this woman!"

"Look, you're making a big mistake!" I cry, realizing this may be my one and only chance to warn everyone at once. "And we've got bigger problems to deal with! The sheriff is launching an attack against you guys very soon. We've got to stop him!"

"The sheriff does not know where we reside, lady," Much reminds me. "Unless 'twas you who told him."

"It wasn't me, you idiot!" I snap, narrowing my eyes at him. "It was Maid Marion. You know, the *woman* you all let in to your camp no questions asked? I'm not the enemy here. She is!"

"Quiet, or we shall gag you!"

"I will not be quiet! You guys have to be ready for this attack! They'll massacre you if you don't!"

But no one pays any attention to my warnings. Instead, they find lengths of rope and tie Robin's and my hands behind our backs. The cord cuts into my wrists. I bite down on my lower lip, trying to keep a poker face, refusing to give them the satisfaction of seeing me cry. After binding us, they push us into a small, musty-smelling tent and I hear them instruct someone to guard the door. The tent flap closes and we're alone in the blackness.

"Oh my god, I'm so sorry," I cry, tears finally

springing to my eyes. "I've ruined everything!" I sink to my knees and try to get comfortable.

"Don't be daft. This is my fault for lying in the first place," Robin answers. He lowers himself to the ground. "I am just glad you are all right. When you disappeared, I feared the worst. I have been scouring the forest for days searching for you. I thought mayhap you'd been eaten by a wild creature."

Even under these dire circumstances my heart warms at the idea of him looking for me, wondering if I was dead. He cares about me. He really cares.

But, I realize, now is not the time to kiss and make up. We've got to get the men to believe that this attack I've been babbling about is very real, and that they've got to start preparing to fight. All of our lives depend on it.

"Robin, what I was saying before—about the sheriff's raid—I wasn't just bluffing to get them to stop tying us up."

"How did you learn of it?"

"It's a long story, but basically when I left here, I went to Prince John's castle and applied to be a lady-in-waiting and they gave me the gig. Anyway, while I was there, Marion showed up during a banquet. I followed her out into the courtyard garden where she met up with the Sheriff of Nottingham." I swallow hard, not wanting to be the one to break the news. "They're evidently lovers."

My eyes, now adjusted to the darkness, search Robin's face for a hint of jealousy, but I see none. There's a little disappointment, maybe, but I guess that's to be expected.

Relieved, I continue. "The reason she came out here was to find out the location of your camp and to spy on the number of men and resources you've amassed. The sheriff figured a beautiful woman like her could convince the men to lead her to your camp without the obligatory blindfold and stuff. And, of course, he was right. So after she chatted you up, she headed back and reported her findings to the sheriff. Very soon they're going to launch an all-out attack—first on the villages and then they're coming here to destroy us all."

"That harlot!" Robin scowls, his eyes flashing. "This is grave news indeed. Our small army is nò match for the sheriff's forces."

"Yeah, I was kind of thinking that. Though at least now they've lost the element of surprise."

"True. Yet we are not much good stuck here in this tent, charged as traitors."

"Yeah, sorry about that," I say. "I should have changed back into my boy outfit before showing up. I totally forgot."

"Do not blame yourself. The truth had to come out eventually."

"Yeah, right. Eventually." I attempt a shrug. It's difficult with my hands tied. "But not right before our impending demise, rendering us completely helpless in the face of death."

"You are not making this any easier."

I sigh. "You're right. So what's the plan?"

Robin shakes his head. "Forsooth, I am at a loss. If they will not accept me as their leader then I cannot—"

The light bulb thing goes off over my head. "That's it!" I cry.

"Milady?" Robin cocks his head in question.

"You need to give up your leadership. Tell them you're resigning and give Little John command or something. Let him lead the battle."

The outlaw frowns. "But this is my band of men. I found them and trained them and—"

"Argh!" I cry. "Don't you understand the art of war? Your men are angry at you right now. They feel you have no right to lead. But at the same time, if you don't appoint someone else to take over while you're out of the picture, it's going to be chaos if an attack comes."

The outlaw bows his head, contemplating my words.

"Robin, sometimes you have to give up power to gain it. Don't you trust your men? Put your ego aside for a moment."

Robin remains silent, staring down at the ground. Then he lifts his head. "You are right, of course," he says resignedly. "Although I know not what you mean by 'ego.' But I do realize I am committing the sin of vanity. Better I relinquish command. Then we will have a small chance of survival."

"Exactly." I smile, more than a bit proud of the guy. He's certainly changed since the first day I met him. The day he refused to lend a hand to help that boy in the wood.

"John!" Robin calls out. "I must speak with you."

"When he's done with your mother," Much the Miller replies—quite unkindly, in my opinion.

"Please, Little John!" I beg. "It's really important."

I hear a loud huff and some movement outside the tent. A moment later the flap opens and Little John, accompanied by Much, peeks his head inside. "This had better be good," Much says before John can open his mouth. "Better than your mother, in any case, though that ain't saying much." He chuckles to himself and I can see Robin's face twist in annoyance.

Come on, dude. Stick with the plan. There are lives at stake here.

"Look, John," Robin says, thankfully keeping his cool. "You have been my second-in-command for as long as we've been together. You're loyal, trustworthy, and brave."

"Unlike you, who are a lying, cowardly son of a whore," Much notes.

I can see Robin's hard swallow. It's taking all he's got to keep the humility thing going.

Luckily, John finds his tongue. "Much, I would like to speak with Robin alone for a moment," he says. Much scowls but obeys, leaving the tent. John crawls in and sits down beside us.

"Speak, lad," he says. "We are now alone."

"John, I trust you with my very life," Robin says. "I always have. And now I must ask a favor."

John shakes his shaggy head. "Nay. I cannot let you free. I am sorry, old friend, but 'tis against the code."

"You misunderstand. 'Tis not the favor I seek," Robin says. "I am asking that you now take command of the men. Lady Christine has heard word of an impending attack on this place and the villages. I need you to prepare us for battle."

"You want me to lead the men?" John asks, raising his bushy unibrow. "You are willingly giving up your command?"

"Aye," Robin says, his voice resolute. "After all, 'tis in the best interest of us all. They need a leader they can trust. I violated that trust and thus am not fit to command. Not now. And we need immediate action."

"Me, the leader of the Men of Sherwood Forest?" John asks. I'm pleased to see a sparkle in his eyes. Maybe this will work!

"Aye. And a fine one you'll make. You're loyal, you're brave . . . I'd knight you if I had the authority, John. As I said before, I'd trust you with my life."

Little John bows his head. "Thank you, Robin," he says. "Your faith in me will not go unrewarded."

"Hey, speaking of rewards," I butt in. "Can you untie us at the very least? Keep the guard outside or whatever you have to do. We won't go anywhere. But these cords are killing me."

John thinks for a moment, then nods. "Very well," he says. "But do not let Much know I have done this." He pulls a knife from his boot and cuts our bindings.

I stretch my arms and rub my wrists, thankful to be free again. "So, about this attack . . ." I relate all I heard from the sheriff. "We can't let this happen. Especially to the villagers and their kids. They're totally innocent."

"Look, we have one advantage," John points out. "The sheriff doesn't know we know about the attack. So we have time to take action."

"What do you propose?"

"We send men to the villages tonight to warn the people. Tell them to gather what they need and then escort them to a safe location deep in the forest. In the meantime, we'll break down the hideaway here and move everything to a new spot. When the sheriff's men arrive, we will be long gone."

Robin nods eagerly at his burly friend. "This way we can protect the children and save our own skins. Good work, John."

The giant blushes at the compliment. " 'Twas nothing," he says. "Just a simple plan."

"It's genius."

"Of course, it means breaking our vow," John says. "We'd be working with women and children, inviting them to be part of our forest home."

Robin smiles. "My dear friend, I know now I was wrong to be so blind. And I am glad my men have compassionate hearts that can love and care."

John grins. "Well, then, I guess I best be rallying the men and telling them of the plan." He pauses, then adds, "Hope they'll listen to me."

"They'd be mad not to. This is the perfect plan, and I know of no one I'd trust to execute it more than you."

"Thanks, Robin," Little John says gruffly. "I'm sorry we had to throw you in here. And I'm really glad you've found happiness with your woman."

Robin smiles at John and then turns to me. "Aye. That I have, John," he says. "And it means more to me than anything else in the world."

I reach over and squeeze his hand, overwhelmed by his words. Maybe everything will really be all right.

John exits the tent. A moment later I hear him calling everyone to attention and explaining the situation.

Alone and unbound, Robin pulls me close to him, into his warm embrace. I collapse in his arms, feeding off his strength.

" 'Tis all my fault," Robin murmurs in my ear. "If I listened to you at the tournament . . . if we left before we were discovered . . . if I did not allow Marion free run of the forest . . ."

"Don't beat yourself up over this, Robin," I comfort, stroking his head. "You did what you thought was best. No one's perfect. We all make mistakes. We just have to make sure we learn from them."

"My biggest mistake was to shame you by forcing you to pretend you were something you are not," he says mournfully. "Can you forgive me that?"

"It's already forgotten."

"These past few days I have thought of nothing else," he confesses. "I searched endlessly for you in the forest. But deep inside, I knew that you had left for another reason."

"I'm sorry about that, too. It's just I—"

"Thought I would fall back in love with Marion," he concludes. "Yes, I realized that later. The way I spoke of her over the time you've been here . . . there would be no reason you would not think it possible."

"Don't get me wrong," I protest. "I didn't just leave out of self pity. I wanted you to be happy. And if you were happy with Marion, if you loved her more than you'd ever love me, I'd never want to force you to deny that just out of a sense of obligation." I shrug. "They have a saying where I'm from. If you love someone, set them free. If they come back to you, they're yours forever. If they don't, they were never yours to begin with."

" 'Tis a very noble saying," Robin says. "But truly it cannot be so simple."

"Well, I'm not going to lie and say it didn't hurt. To be rejected, considered second-best . . ." Tears spring to my eyes as I recall the pain, the hurt, the doubt I'd felt. "But still. For a while there . . . Well, I guess I began to believe I was special—that maybe, just maybe, you truly loved me for me, warts and all. And then Marion goes and shows back up and once again I felt like I was being relegated to second place. Which would be fine, I guess, if she's what you wanted. I mean, I can't be selfish here. I want you to be happy, and if she could do that and I could not—well, then I feel you should rightfully be with her."

"Shhh. Quiet, silly woman," Robin scolds suddenly. I look at him in surprise. "No wonder you cannot keep your men. You do not fight for them."

"What?" Now I'm confused. Here I'm being all noble and brave and he's criticizing me?

"In your kingdom of Hoboken you may think love is letting go. But here we value it too much to allow it to escape. We fight to keep what we love. Our lands, our family, our women. Did you not teach me that? 'Tis better to stand up against the evil in this land than let things stay as they are. How is it you cannot apply that to your own life? You would let another so easily win my affections? Do I mean so little to you?"

He's right, I realize, surprised. This "poor me" attitude I have held on to my whole life—playing the victim, the one who always loses—it's been nothing more than a self-indulgence to comfort myself rather than to allow myself to grow into a fully functioning adult. When my mother left my brother and I for three days without food, we sat in our rooms, hungry, never thinking for a moment we should go outside and find help. When one foster father beat me, I allowed myself to believe I deserved the punishment. And when things with Danny started going south, it only made sense to my addled mind. I wasn't deserving of a loving relationship. That's what I told myself. And so I allowed the distance between us to widen. I never questioned his late nights or the fact that we stopped talking. I sat home alone, feeling sorry for myself instead of fighting for my marriage. No wonder he ended up in another woman's arms. Not that it was my fault—he's a bastard to have done it. But I didn't give him any reason to stay.

"Seeing Marion again was hard, forsooth," Robin admitted. "Long lost childhood feelings dredged to the surface. But I knew well that if I never faced those feelings, never said to her all I needed to say, I could never get past them. I would be trapped in a cage of my own making forever and never find the freedom to love you as you deserve to be loved." Even through the darkness I can see Robin's gentle smile. "In the short time you have been here, Chrissie, you have become more to me than ten thousand Marions. As she and I sat by the fire and talked, I missed you. I wanted you to be there. I wondered where you went, if you were worried. Jealous. Marion spun a thousand fascinating tales, and yet all I wanted was to run after you, begging for you to understand. And then"—he pauses, swallowing hard—"she kissed me. I didn't know what to do."

"I saw the kiss. That's when I left."

"God's blood, I was afraid of that. But did you not stay a moment longer—to see me push her away and tell her that what had once been between us was over long ago? That I was in love with someone else? With you?"

"But if that's true, how come it took her so long to get back to Nottingham Castle? She didn't show up right away."

Robin sighs. "She begged me not to send her off, said that she'd lied to her guards and couldn't return right away. I didn't know what to do." He shakes his head. "I wanted her gone, but it seemed wise to keep her friendship—her goodwill. And then I was searching for you. . . ." He shakes his head. "Now I see she spent the time learning about our operations only to share that knowledge with the sheriff himself."

"Well, I guess there was no way you could have known."

"But I tell you true, Chrissie," Robin says earnestly. "Nothing happened between us. Because I love only you. More than anything in this world. I've been such a fool to make you lie to the men. To cover up something so right and so good. To make you ashamed to be who you are. If you can ever forgive me . . ." Tears cascade down his face like rain, and he makes no effort to brush them away.

"Of course," I say, trying to talk past the lump in my own throat. "I love you too. I'm sorry I didn't trust you. That I took off before getting your explanation.

That I didn't fight for your love. Now I know. I should have stood up for myself—and for us."

"Indeed, my love. Indeed." He cups my chin and pulls me close, pressing his lips against mine lovingly. "I love you Chrissie," he whispers against my mouth.

Chapter Nineteen

I awake the next morning to screaming. Robin's shaking me by the shoulders, his eyes wide and his expression grave.

"What's going on?" I ask, struggling to regain full consciousness.

" 'Tis the sheriff's men," he says. "They have come earlier than we expected."

"What? No!" I bolt up in bed, looking around the tent. The sheriff's men are here? Now? This morning?

"Come. We must get out of here," Robin commands, pulling me by the hand.

I follow him out of the tent and enter a battle zone. Swords clashing, arrows flying, men on the ground bleeding and begging for mercy—it's the worst thing I've ever seen.

Robin turns to me. "Chrissie, I want you to go," he commands. "Run far away."

"What?" I cry, disbelieving. "I can't—"

He glances around, his expression anguished. "This is a disaster. They outnumber us and will easily kill us all. And I cannot bear the thought of anything happening to you." He stares at me, desperation in his eyes. I realize I've become a liability, something he always warned the others about. A weakness. A distraction.

"Go," I say, pushing him forward. "Don't worry about me."

He gives me an agonized look, then turns and runs to the weapons tent. John throws him a bow and together the two men shout orders to others.

I duck behind a tent, searching for a viable escape route, wondering not for the first time what happens when one gets killed in the 12th century. Will I bounce back home, safe and sound? Or is this it? I try to decide which would be better. Sure, with the bounce-back theory I'd be comfy cozy in the present day USA, but I will have lost Robin forever. And I can't imagine living without him.

I look around. There's carnage everywhere. Our men are falling at a rapid pace. There's no way—no plan—that could have saved us from this attack. There's just too many of them. They're just too well equipped. We're dead. Doomed.

A noise behind me makes me whirl around. An armored soldier stands above me, wielding a huge sword. I'm caught. And likely dead.

I fall back, hands over my face in a vain attempt to ward off my death blow. The soldier draws his sword back to swing.

This is it. The moment of death. It's over. Forever. I send up a quick prayer to whoever's listening, apologizing for every wrongdoing I can remember from first grade on. I should have gone to confession before heading to the 12th century.

I think about Robin and pray that he makes it somehow. That he escapes and lives a long happy life. I figure maybe he has a chance. After all, this isn't how the story is supposed to end. . . .

I wait for my death, hoping it's quick. Hoping it's painless and that the soldier won't gut me and leave me alive with my entrails hanging out like you see in movies. But the death blow doesn't come. Confused, I open my eyes. The soldier is still standing above me, looking down. What is he waiting for? Just do it already!

" 'Tis you!"

Huh? I squint my eyes at him, confused. The soldier pulls off his helmet. My mouth drops open as I recognize the guy. It's the guard from Locksley Castle. The one I told Robin not to kill. The one we freed afterward.

"Oh, hey there," I say, surprised and overwhelmingly relieved. Holy small world, Batman. "How's it going? Off the castle-guarding gig, I see."

"I am Duncan of Carlisle. Once you saved my life," the soldier says. It's hard to hear him over the din of battle. He lowers his sword. "And I promised you the same someday. It seems this is destined to be that day."

I stare at him, shocked and disbelieving. He's really going to spare my life?

"Look," he hisses, his eyes darting to the battlefield behind us. "I will spare your life, but I must wound you somehow or someone else will surely kill you. A blow to the head will knock you out, but I shall make sure you live. If you wake, play dead until you are sure we have all left."

"No way!" I cry. "Then I won't be able to help. There's too few of us left as it is. We need every man. Robin, my beloved—"

"I am sorry, *girl,* but you have no choice in the matter. I must keep my promise to save your life." And before I can move, he lifts his sword and sends the pommel crashing down on my head. I swim into blackness.

I awake to the sounds of birds chirping too cheerfully, their tweets pounding into my already aching head. I sit up, for a moment not knowing where I am or what I'm doing here. Every muscle in my body aches and I'm covered in mud and grime. I look around and my mouth drops open in horror as visions of the morning flash back in rapid sequence.

The camp has been crushed beyond recognition. Bodies of formerly merry men are scattered throughout—pierced by arrows, slashed by swords, trampled by horses. The stench of dead bodies and unending gore under the hot afternoon sun invades my nostrils and I place a hand over my nose, scrambling to my feet in dismay. But it's not enough. I lean over and puke my guts out.

I desperately scan the area, a vain attempt to find survivors, but no one's moving. My heart pounds and my hands shake as I walk from body to body, checking each for signs of life—a faint pulse, a flutter of eyelash?

No one stirs.

Tears stream down my cheeks and I can barely breathe through my sobs. All these men. Their hopes, dreams, lives. Their mothers, wives, children. Everything has been cruelly ripped from them because they decided to help save their world.

This is all my fault.

If I had not suggested that they rise up—if I'd not told them the plan to rob the rich to feed the poor— then the sheriff would have had no reason to launch such an attack. The men could have lived out their days drunk and stupid in Sherwood Forest, never bothered by the local government. But, no. Because I'd read a few storybooks, because I thought I knew how the legend went, I destroyed these people's lives. I killed them. I'm practically a murderer.

And what about Robin Hood? My partner. My true love. The man who said he would die for me? I suddenly realize that while the notion of someone dying for me sounds romantic in theory, I certainly didn't want him to actually go through with it.

What if Robin's dead?

I scan the bodies again, searching for a telltale feathered green cap. There's no sign of him.

I run to my place of solace, the spot by the lake where he and I shared so many thoughts on so many nights. I collapse at its shore; tears streaming from my eyes, splashing into the otherwise still water, rippling out into infinity. My head pounds with both physical and emotional agony.

Robin, my love. Where are you? Could you really be dead? Could I really have lost you forever?

That guard did me no favor by sparing my life. Not if with his other hand he struck down the only man I will ever love. Not if now I'm destined to live a purgatorial, loveless existence, robbed of the one person who could make life worth living.

"Chrissie!"

Hope leaps into my chest at the sound of the voice, and I'm not sure I can believe my ears. And then I doubt my eyes—am I seeing a ghost? But no. He's real. Robin of Locksley. Robin Hood. Robin of mine. Standing in front of me. He's caked in mud and dirt, but he's here. He's alive. And he's looking at me with the same overwhelming relief I'm feeling while looking at him.

"Robin!" I cry, jumping to my feet and throwing my arms around him. "Oh, Robin! I thought you were dead!"

"Chrissie, my love! You live!" he cries, burying his head in my curls. "When I came back to see what happened to the hideout—"

"Came back?" I pull away from the hug, confused. "Where did you go?"

"Many of us not killed outright were taken captive. The sheriff wants to hang us in the castle courtyard, to show the kingdom what happens to outlaws. Little John, Allan a Dale, Friar Tuck, myself and Will Scarlet were all thrown into a barred wagon. Halfway to the castle, they stopped to give the horses a rest and the strangest thing happened. Duncan of Carlisle—the one whose life you made me spare at Castle Locksley, approached the wagon once the others had turned their backs. He said he would free me to repay the debt to his own life. I begged that he free us all, but he said 'twould be too obvious and they would come after us."

"He saved my life during the battle as well." I smile, rubbing my head. "Though in a much more painful way."

Robin looks impressed. "Then your foresight not to have him killed saved both of our lives."

"Not foresight. Just human compassion. And good karma."

"Karma?"

"Er, never mind." We don't have time to get into the Hindu laws of cause and effect at the moment. "So he let you free?"

"Aye. And I promised the others I'd return to rescue them before the hanging." He shakes his head. "So I rushed back here, hoping to find others to aid me. But you are the first living person I've found. It seems . . . all the others are lost."

His sober words erase the joy I felt a moment ago upon learning he was alive. "Oh, Robin!" I sob into his shoulder. "This is all my fault. If I hadn't roused the men into action, if I hadn't suggested we rob—"

"Shhh. Quiet, silly woman," Robin scolds, squeezing me into a tighter embrace. I can barely breathe he's hugging me so hard, but I don't mind. "You're speaking nonsense. You gave these men something no one else could. A reason to live. A sense of purpose. A noble cause. You saved starving children. You put roofs over people's heads. You gave the hopeless hope. We were a miserable band before you arrived. Now we are soldiers, fighting for our land and country."

"But we've lost. Most of us are dead, and those of us who are left are captured. There's no way to rescue them. I mean, look at what happened last time you tried to storm a castle. And now it's just the two of us."

"Aye, it does seem that two against an entire castle are not favorable odds," Robin agrees. "But I cannot leave the men to die at the hands of the sheriff. We must try."

I pull back from the hug to smile at him. He's changed so much since I first arrived in Sherwood Forest. The old, defeated Robin wouldn't risk a fight with three men on horseback to save a boy's hand. Now he's ready to lay siege to an entire castle to rescue his drinking buddies. He's definitely back to his old self—the Robin Hood of legend.

I've changed too, I realize. I'm no longer simply Chrissie Hayward of Hoboken. I've grown beyond the obedient magazine photographer who spent most of her life being walked on by others. I'm one of Robin's merry men. I'm a soldier for the cause. Sherwood Forest is my home, and I love our ragged gang as much as Robin does. If I have to die to save them, I will.

"I'm with you," I say, pressing my lips together in determination. "Whatever it takes, I'm with you."

"As am I!"

"And I!"

"And I!"

Robin and I whirl around at the sound of voices behind us. My eyes widen as I see a ragtag team of peasants marching toward us. There's at least a hundred men, women and children led by two merry men. I breathe a sigh of relief. We may not have saved our camp, but at least we saved the villagers.

"What happened?" asks one of the men, looking at the carnage with horror.

"The sheriff came early," Robin says, relating all that had happened. "Those not killed were taken captive. They are to be hanged in the castle courtyard tomorrow."

The villagers murmur amongst themselves. Then a bearded man steps forward. "We will help you get them back."

Robin stares at him. "You will?" he asks, his voice laced with his disbelief.

" 'Tis only fair," pipes up a sweet-faced woman. "You risked yer hides to feed us when we was dying of starvation. You stood up to the sheriff's men and saved the lives of our babes. We was glad to accept your charity, but now 'tis time we pay you back."

Another steps forward, a boy, probably only fifteen. "We are not warriors, sir. But we are many. And we will fight with everything we have to help rescue your men."

The woman nods. "You have taught us that we can fight back. That we can make a difference."

"And we're ready to make that difference now. To throw the bastard Sheriff of Nottingham out of power and restore England to its rightful glory!"

The bearded man raises a fist in the air and the

crowd cheers. The noise is almost deafening. Did I say there were a hundred people? It sounds like nearly a thousand.

Robin stares at them, tears rolling down his cheeks. He gets on his knees, humble, and bows his head.

"Thank you, Lord," he says in prayer. "Thank you." Then he rises to his feet, jumps on a nearby boulder to get some height and starts addressing the crowd.

"I welcome you all," he says. " 'Tis a proud day for England indeed. Now here's what we're going to do."

Chapter Twenty

In a videogame I used to play with Danny they called it Zerging—named after a little creature called a Zergling that's cheap to make and can be sent, in massive quantities, to rush an enemy's base, defeating them with sheer numbers rather than strength of arms. Danny used to always create a million of the tiny buggers, bringing down my carefully constructed space stations every time.

But Zerglings are made of pixels not people. And so Robin's suggestion that we basically storm the castle and rescue his men is not one I can comfortably go along with. "Too many people will die," I whisper into his ear. "There have already been enough wasted deaths today as it is."

"Then what do you suggest?" he asks.

I think fast. How can we stage a castle rescue with no casualties, launch a war even Gandhi would approve of?

That's it! Wow, what would I do in the middle ages without movie plots to fall back on? "We'll do a sit-in," I announce. "A peaceful protest."

Robin and the rest of the villagers look at me as if I'm absolutely bonkers. "What do you mean?" he asks.

"Look," I say. "There's a lot of us here, but there's no way we're going to be able to storm a castle on our own. No offense, but you guys are mostly farmers, armed with pitchforks. You can't go up against trained, armed guards. And I like you all. I don't want to see you get killed trying to help us. So, instead, we'll go sit outside the castle and shout stuff. Dance. Play instruments. Whatever."

"A siege? You want to try to starve them out?" Robin asks. "That could take a long time. And the hangings are tomorrow morning."

"No, no." I shake my head. "The sit-in is just a distraction. All the guards are going to be watching us, waiting for us to make a violent move. In the meantime, a few men will go around the back. Remember that castle wall you told me about, Robin? The one you climbed to find Marion? You can lead our most-trained men in through there and go rescue the prisoners. Since most of the soldiers will be keeping an eye on the ruckus outside, there likely won't be a huge guard contingent to deal with."

Robin nods his head slowly. "You know, Chrissie, that could actually work."

The men and women nod and murmur in agreement. Robin squeezes my arm. I feel a sense of pride well up inside me. For the first time in my life I feel a strange sense of confidence. Like William Wallace, aka Mel Gibson, speaking to his men on the Scottish moor before the battle of their lives. Although, come to think of it, that didn't end so well. Obviously, old Bill the Scot had needed me and my movie plots.

"They may take our lives," I yell, suddenly inspired. "But they'll never take . . . *our freedom!*"

I wait for a following whoop of cheers, but all is silent. I stop screaming "Freedom" and scan the crowd. They're looking at me skeptically. Hm. Maybe it's the lack of blue warpaint. Oh well.

"Are you with me?" I demand. "Are you ready to join forces and fight to regain all that has been taken from you? Well, not fight exactly. More like . . . sit. Are you ready to . . . sit . . . to regain all that's been taken from you? Are you ready to sit to save country and king?!" Hm, maybe this would go down in history as the Armchair Revolution.

"You are all free people," I add. "Making the decision to join us on this quest to sit. If you are not fully ready to . . . sit . . . please leave now. Go home to your warm beds and do not think about the opportunity you missed. . . . to sit for . . . *FREEDOM!*"

A few scattered cheers this time. Hmm. I've got to get these peasants on the *Braveheart* bandwagon.

"Doesn't the word 'freedom' mean anything to you?" I ask. "Does the idea of slavery and oppression turn you on instead? Would you like to be under Prince John and the Sheriff of Nottingham's rule forever?"

"Nay!"

"No! We want to live freely."

"Down with Prince John. And his lousy sheriff!"

"Right," I say. "So, um, when I say 'freedom,' that's

your cue to shout and scream and rally the troops. Okay?"

Nods of agreement all around.

"Okay, let's give this a try." I draw in a deep breath. *"Freedom!"*

A few cheers, a smattering of claps. I sigh.

"Freedom!" I cry again, raising my fist this time.

More people. A dull roar of cheers.

"I said . . . *freedom!*" I try one last time. "And, um, *a chicken in every pot. and a . . . horse . . . in every . . .* um, *stable!*"

Now the crowd erupts in cheers. Who'd have thought they'd be more turned on by Herbert Hoover than William Wallace? I can't believe these people would rather eat chicken than taste freedom. Sad, really. But hey, at this point, whatever works.

Robin squeezes my arm and I turn to look at him. He's gazing at me with loving eyes. "You're magnificent," he whispers.

"You should really be doing this," I tell him. "I'm not a leader. . . ."

"What are you going on about, woman? You have rallied your people. You have suggested a plan that could actually work." He leans over to kiss me lightly on the cheek. "You are truly wonderful. And I am honored to be under your leadership."

I smile, for the first time in my life feeling confident and valued. Robin is right. I do make a kick-ass leader. I feel like I was born to do this stuff. Maybe the gypsy knew something I didn't when she told me my destiny lay in another era.

'Cause I certainly can't imagine going back to the 21st century now.

The thought troubles me, and I turn back to my makeshift army. "We march now," I inform them. "And make camp a ways off tonight. First thing in the morning, when the men are brought out to the court-yard to be hanged, we sit on our butts."

Everyone yells their assent, and we start walking. Robin and I lead the group. But the joy of accomplishment I had moments before is permanently damp-ened. Because all I can think of, suddenly, is the idea of going home. My true home—in the 21st century.

If we survive this, if King Richard returns, if I get the blood from the Holy Grail, what then? I'm as-suming the next step is me being transported back to the 21st century to hand it over to the gypsy, right? And that means leaving here. Leaving Robin. Maybe without warning.

I glance over at him and my heart aches. I love him so much. More than anyone ever. Danny was nothing compared to what I feel for Robin. How can I leave him? And what will I be going back to? My empty apartment with bills stacked from floor to ceiling that I can't pay? Messy divorce proceedings? A superficial job that I hate? In the 21st century I'm no one. Here I have a role. A place in history. A man who loves me.

What am I going to do?

"What are you thinking about?" Robin asks, reach-ing over to take my hand in his. His thumb strokes the back of my palm.

"Nothing," I lie. How can I explain this to him?

That I'm still not exactly who he thinks I am? What would he say if he knew I came from another time? "Just about how much I love you," I add, smiling at him. He squeezes my hand and smiles back. My heart plummets. What am I going to do?

We make camp at nightfall. Some of the villagers have tents, but others make themselves at home on the ground. One village leader offers Robin and me a tent, which at first I refuse. Then he tells me it's his honor to supply it and would be greatly offended if we didn't take the thing. So we do, setting it up a small distance from the rest of the camp.

Robin's exhausted from his ordeal and falls asleep almost immediately. I'm restless though, still thinking about the future, and I toss and turn, wondering what I should do. As if on cue, my cell phone starts vibrating. How does that thing still have battery power? Nimue must have cast some spell on it. I hope if I do have to go back to the 21st century I can keep that spell . . . I'm always forgetting to charge the stupid thing.

I slip out of the tent so as not to wake Robin, and walk out into the field, and answer it.

"Hey, Kat," I greet, for who else could it be?

"Hey, Chrissie. How's it going? Did you work everything out with Robin? Are you still doing the love that dares not speak its name thing, or are you out of the closet, so to speak?"

Wow. I almost drop the phone. "Aren't you going to ask me if King Richard's back with the Holy Grail?" I ask, slightly incredulous.

Kat laughs. "You must really think I'm a selfish bitch, huh?" she says.

I immediately feel bad. "No. Well, actually I used to. But not anymore. Since I've been talking to you via time-cell continuum . . . well, you've sort of become a friend, actually." And I mean it, too. Though whoever would have thought Kat and I would become bosom buddies?

"Thanks, Chris. That means a lot. I think you're pretty cool yourself. After all, you left everything behind to rescue me, even though you didn't even like me. Not many people would do that and I'm grateful."

"No problem," I say, feeling it isn't the time to explain that I was sort of forced into going on this mission. "Actually, Kat, I love it here. I'm glad I came."

"Yeah? That's cool. I liked Camelot okay too. But I'll be happy to get home to my own bed. It's been way too long."

"Not me. If I could stay here forever, I would."

"Really?" Kat exclaims. "You like it that much?"

"Yeah. And there's Robin, too. I can't imagine leaving him." I briefly explain all that happened over the last few days. Maid Marion, the battle, me channeling Mel Gibson and Thoreau.

"Wow. You've been a busy girl!" Kat says, sounding impressed. "And now you're leading an army to besiege a castle? Eesh, I thought I was productive learning how to ride a horse!"

I laugh. "Yeah, well, for some reason medieval life agrees with me."

"Well, hm. Maybe you could stay? I wonder if that's

allowed. I mean, it seems stupid to come back to the twenty-first century if you like it there better, right?"

"But what about the Grail? I have to bring a drop of blood from the Holy Grail back to Nimue so she can bring you back to the twenty-first century."

"Oh yeah. I forgot about that little detail." Kat's silent for a moment. "I mean, I don't want you to ruin your life to save mine, but still. Things are pretty hairy here in the twenty-second century. I don't know how long before we've worn out our welcome." She sighs. "Ugh. What to do?"

"Well, don't think of it now," I say. "I'll continue on this mission. Who knows, I may die in this rescue attempt tomorrow and Nimue will have to get someone else to retrieve the Grail."

"Don't say that, Chrissie. You'll be great, I'm sure. It sounds like you've got a terrific plan there. You'll knock the sheriff on his fat ass."

"Uh, nonviolent protest, remember? Meaning, without violence. No ass-knocking allowed in this campaign." I laugh. "Though, maybe I should make an exception for our dear sheriff. After all, he's probably still sore from that arrow I shot into his butt."

"Right." Kat giggles. At least she thinks I'm funny. "I totally think you should. In any case, I'll call you tomorrow night. I want to hear all the gory details. Well, maybe not the gory ones. But some details. I think." She laughs. "Anyway, good luck."

We say our good-byes and I hang up the phone and head back to the camp. I crawl into our tent, hoping for sleep. But Robin's awake.

"Where did you go?" he asks sleepily.

"Just for a walk," I say, slipping my phone in my bag.

"Come here," he says, stretching out his arms. I crawl into his embrace and he wraps himself around me. I allow myself to melt into him, to take his strength, his love.

He finds my lips and starts kissing me gently. "I have thanked the Lord a thousand times today that he spared your life in the attack."

"Actually, it wasn't the Lord. It was that guy at Locksley that I told you not to kill," I remind him, wanting to force my point home about avoiding senseless murder.

"Fate weaves a complex web indeed," Robin says, separating my curls with his fingers. "And you have great foresight."

"Nah, I'm just a softie," I say.

"Aye, soft and fair." Robin presses his nose to my shoulder and breathes in. "And sweet. So sweet."

"I don't know about sweet." I chuckle. "I could definitely use a bath."

Robin silences me with a kiss, his lips moving against mine, exploring, tasting, sparking an intense ache deep inside me. We haven't made love since that first time in the field. But there's no reason to hold back any longer. I trust him. I love him. And I know he loves me.

He eases me down, laying my head on the coarse, makeshift canvas pillow. Propping himself on his side next to me, he continues to cover my face with soft kisses while his hand traces my body, lightly running over every inch of skin. I moan in pleasure as his touch evokes an exquisite torture between my legs.

I've waited so long for another chance to feel his caress. Too long.

He helps me out of my dress, pulling the garment over my head so I'm naked and open to him. Exposed. Vulnerable. But I don't feel any shame. Because the way Robin's eyes take me in, the way his breath catches in his throat, all convinces me beyond a doubt that he thinks I'm the most beautiful girl in the world. And at that moment, I feel like it too.

His fingers trace my hips, graze my stomach, find my breast. He circles the tip, coaxing it into his power. I arch my back at the electric sensation now coursing through me, trying to enjoy the moment but impatient to feel him deep inside of me. For us to become one. He leans down, finding my other breast with his mouth—licking, tasting, savoring. I squeeze my eyes shut and toss my head back. It's almost too much.

"I must have you inside of me," I murmur, not caring if I sound too bold. I've been afraid too long in my life. Now I know what I want and am not too shy to ask for it.

"Mmm," he agrees, reaching down to pull off his trousers. I yank open his belt and lift his tunic over his head, running my fingers down his now exposed perfect six-pack abs.

His face contorts from easy pleasure to determined passion. He pushes me back to the ground, forcing my legs apart and climbing on top of me. Robin is not a fumbling boy, awkward and shy. He's a man. In control. Ready to take what he needs.

And I'm so ready to give it.

He presses himself inside me and I let out a cry as

our bodies join. That precious moment. The ultimate power of connection. The feeling that together you can accomplish anything.

Robin steadies himself for a moment, his face a mask of concentration as the sensations must overwhelm him. I smile up at him, encouraging and loving. He relaxes and grins back, reaching up to tame a wild curl from my face. Then he leans down, crushing my lips with his, demanding possession of my mouth.

We rock against each other, moving as one, physical pleasure only trumped by the sweet singing tingles of love, trust, and devotion. God, I want to be like this, one with this man, for all eternity.

Suddenly he pulls away, opening his eyes for a moment, ceasing his thrusts. He looks at me, capturing me with his glow-in-the-dark emerald eyes. Studying my face with an intense curiousness, longing, and love. They say a picture is worth a thousand words. His gaze must be worth ten million. Then he smiles, the most sweet, gentle, loving smile, his eyes crinkling at the corners. He playfully leans down to kiss my nose.

"I never knew I could love someone so much," he whispers. "It's terrifying, yet wonderful."

I nod, too caught up to speak, a lump in my throat and tears threatening. The overwhelming love I feel for this man, it makes me want to die, right here, right now, so I'll never feel another way again. But then I'd never get the future moments. The joys of life, even the pain. I want to share it all with him. Everything.

He begins to thrust again, gently, passionately, and I'm savoring each sensation. Before I know it, I find myself over the edge, sweet release crowning me and bathing me in a warm sea.

He comes soon after, biting down on his lower lip not to cry out and amuse any nearby peasants. He collapses atop me and I rejoice in the weight of his body, pressing down, filling me. I could lie like this forever. One with him.

"I love you, Robin," I murmur, pressing my face into his shoulder, squeezing him and not wanting to let him go.

"I love you too, Chrissie," he whispers back, pulling out of my embrace so he can look into my eyes. He smiles down at me and I want to laugh and cry at the same time. "So much."

Eventually we realize we must separate, and he rolls off of me and onto his back. I cuddle up next to him, my head on his chest, my fingers lightly tracing his stomach hairs.

"I'm worried about tomorrow," I tell him as we lie intertwined in each other's arms. "What if something goes wrong? What if you die? I can't bear the idea of you dying."

He puts a finger to my lips. "No talk of death, Chrissie," he says. " 'Tis unlucky. And besides, I'm not going to die. I need to stay alive to take care of you for the rest of your days."

His words sober me. What am I going to do? What if I have to go back? What would he think if I just disappeared off the face of the earth? Would he waste his life searching for me, swearing he'll never love again?

I can't do that to him. I love him too much. I have

to tell him the truth. And there's no time like the present—er, past—to tell him about the future.

"Robin, we need to talk," I say cautiously. "There's something I must tell you."

"Anything, love, for 'twill not change how I feel about you."

Hm. I'm not sure about that. But okay, here goes. "This is going to sound strange, but . . ."

" 'Tis no stranger than the mystery of love."

"Shh." I shush him with a giggle. "I'm trying to talk here."

He laughs. "Sorry, milady. Please go on."

"You always ask me where I'm really from. And I always tell you a faraway kingdom called Hoboken. Well, Hoboken *is* very far away. But it's also . . . um, not of this time."

"I'm afraid I do not understand."

I take a deep breath and let it all spill: "I'm from the future, Robin. Eight hundred-some years in the future, to be exact."

He laughs. "Do not mock me, Chrissie."

"I'm not. I'm serious." I pull from his embrace and sit up. "I'm from the future."

He shakes his head. "You are talking madness. 'Tis impossible."

"I would have agreed with you before it happened to me."

He stares, half amused, half disbelieving. "And were I to believe your wild tale, tell me why did you travel back through time? Just to meet me?" he adds, teasingly.

I shove him. "You wish."

"Then why?"

"It's, um, a long story, actually."

"We have all night."

He's right. And the more details I give him, the easier it will be for him to accept the truth. So I tell him. About the medieval faire. About Kat. About the gypsy. About my destiny supposedly lying in another era. When I'm finished, he still looks skeptical. Not that I blame him. I'm not sure I would believe me either.

" 'Tis a fantastic tale," he says. "And I want to believe you, of course . . ."

"Look," I say, whipping out my cell phone. "This is a phone. And . . ." I rummage through my bag. "Here's a camera."

He studies the 21st century items with awe.

"Watch, I'll take a photo of you," I hold up the camera and point it at him. The flash in the darkness of our tent makes him jump back in shock.

"What in God's name?"

I motion him over and show him the digital preview. "See, there you are. It's called a camera. In the twenty-first century my job is to take photos of people."

He stares at the camera, then up at me. "You are telling the truth," he says slowly. "You are truly from the future."

"Yes." I nod. "I truly am."

He stares down at his hands for a moment and I can almost see smoke coming out of his ears he's thinking so hard. I wait, silent. I figure this is a lot to soak in and he needs a few minutes.

Finally he looks up. "Well, I suppose it matters not

where you come from," he says, his eyes shining with tenderness. "As long as you are here with me now."

Ugh. Now here comes revelation number two. This is not such a fun discussion.

"Uh, that's the other thing I'm worried about," I admit. "You see, I was sent back for a reason. To bring back a drop of blood from the Holy Grail so that Kat can get herself back from the future. I'm like a courier. So when King Richard shows up and I get the blood, I have to take it back. And I don't know if it's possible, once I get to the twenty-first century, to return here."

A shadow crosses Robin's face. "You mean, you would leave me?"

"Well, it's not that I'd want to, but—"

"After all we talked about? About love being the most important thing? You would just go and abandon all we have built together?" He sits up in bed, suddenly shoving his feet into his trousers.

"Robin, you've got to understand—"

"No, I do not. I will not." His face darkens with rage. "How can some quest be more important than us being together? You're no better than Marion."

"That's not fair. She chose to leave you. I have no choice."

"There is always a choice. You just have to be willing to accept the consequences. Which clearly you are not."

And with that, he scrambles to his feet and exits the tent. I bolt after him, desperate to convince him that I want nothing more than to stay. Doesn't he see what a bad position I'm in? It's not like this is my fault, my choice. There are more people than just me involved in this. Kat, Lancelot, Guenevere. I can't just abandon them in the future because I fell in love, can I?

I want to run after him, but realize I'm stark naked. The time it takes for me to throw on my dress gives him enough leeway to make his escape. My heart aches in my chest as I watch him jump on a horse and gallop off. Where is he going? Just to clear his head? To get away from me? Hopefully he'll return in the morning. We need him for this scheme. I need him for so much more.

Part of me now wishes I'd never told him the truth. But no, it's been a secret for far too long. He deserves to know. But now I've inadvertently hurt him. Led him to believe I don't care about him as much as I really do.

What am I going to do?

Chapter Twenty-one

I can't sleep. I think part of me is hoping Robin will come back, crawl into the tent and take me in his arms and say he realizes what a complicated position I'm in and will support me in any decision I make. But of course this doesn't happen. Instead I toss and turn, alternating between sweaty hot and freezing cold. It's almost as if I'm sick. I guess I am, in a way. At least my heart is.

At dawn I crawl out of the tent and walk over to the cooking fire. Most of the peasants are already awake and preparing to break down camp and head to the castle. I scan the area, but see no sign of Robin.

"Has anyone seen Robin Hood?" I ask around, getting the same answer each time. *Not since last night.*

Where is he? How can he just take off? Sure he's pissed at me, but don't his people matter? Little John, Friar Tuck, Will Scarlet—they're all to be hanged by mid-morning if we don't rescue them. Isn't that more important than a lovers' quarrel?

I square my shoulders. While I want nothing more than to run back into my tent and cry my eyes out, I know I have to be strong. These people need a leader for their protest. Robin might be gone, but he'll follow through with his plan to save his men and he'll need the diversion.

"Okay, let's get everything packed up," I announce. "Next stop, Nottingham Castle!"

The peasants cheer, waving their hands in the air. They're ready to sit and shout and dance for freedom. I contemplate teaching them the Macarena. God, I hope this isn't going to be another massacre.

But as a leader I can't let any doubt show. "For England!" I cry. "For freedom!"

Cheers all around. At the very least they're now on the *Braveheart* bandwagon.

We head out, marching to the castle. Soon we see it looming in the distance. It looks bigger than I remember. More foreboding. As we get closer I can see archers on the rooftops, ready to fire on anyone who gets too close.

I turn back to look at the villagers and swallow hard. Okay, here goes nothing.

"Everybody sit!" I order.

Everyone does. Hundreds of men, women, and children all plop down on their butts in sync. I lower myself to the ground, suddenly realizing I should have brought a blanket or something. The ground's soaking with dew.

"Okay, now some of you get up and dance," I order. "And some of you sing at the top of your lungs."

The villagers comply and soon we're having what looks like a medieval rave in front of Nottingham Castle. I look up at the walls. The guards have multiplied and they're watching closely, probably confused as all hell.

But then the drawbridge starts to lower.

My breath catches in my throat as I see armored men on horseback behind the drawbridge, ready to march. Have they merely been sent to see what's going on, or are they going to kill us all? Is my plan a success or a complete disaster?

The mounted soldiers gallop across the drawbridge and onto the field. The villagers start murmuring in fright, frantically searching for their makeshift weapons—pitchforks, staves, shovels . . .

"No!" I cry. "Keep singing and dancing and sitting. Do not give them reason to attack you!"

The soldiers are getting closer. I swallow hard. *Please let this work, please let this work.*

Suddenly the soldiers start pointing at us, backing away, almost as if they're frightened.

The mounted knights struggle to maintain holds on their horses who are bucking with fear. Then the leader gives an order, and they all turn tail and gallop back behind the castle walls.

Are they afraid of us? How could they be afraid of us? It doesn't make sense.

I turn to see what the fuss is about and suddenly realize why the castle guards are fleeing. They're not scared of my peaceful protest. They're scared of the huge royal army behind us, brandishing flags with an orange lion emblazoned on them. King Richard has returned! And evidently he's ready to kick some ass rather than sit on it.

The best part? Robin's with him. And he's looking at me with a huge grin on his face.

If life were like a *Lord of the Rings* book, this is the part where there'd be a fifty page über-boring battle scene. No offense to *LOTR* fans—hey, I like Legolas as much as the next girl—but this castle's run by sniveling Prince John, not the Lord Sauron, and so they give in pretty easily. Most of the prince's guards formerly served King Richard anyway, and they aren't about to keep on the obvious losing side. A few of the sheriff's men put up a bit of a fight, but nothing that a royal army and a flock of peasants can't handle.

It turns out that Prince John *is* actually overjoyed that his brother is home, and he gladly hands over the throne, declaring he'll now have much more time for his embroidery. The sheriff's arrested and thrown into the dungeon until he can be tried for treason. So is Maid Marion. No more jewels and fancy gowns for her! Not that I'm gloating or anything. Well, maybe just a bit.

It takes forever to wash all the caked-on dirt from my body, but finally I emerge from the bath feeling gloriously clean. A maid helps me into a beautiful royal blue gown, a lot like the one I wore to King Arthur's faire to begin with. Wow, that seems a lifetime ago.

Avelyn and Elaine help me fix my hair, pulling it into two Princess Leia buns and setting a veiled dunce cap-like thing on my head. I think I might look a little silly, but they insist it's the height of fashion and that Robin will think it's very sexy. While they primp, they ask a billion questions about my favorite outlaw—how did I meet him, what's he like, is he a good kisser? After all, the guy's infamous, and obviously even medieval women have a thing for bad boys. They're both totally psyched that Richard's back. Now they can start dating again.

"And you will never believe it!" Elaine says as she slips a chunky silver bracelet around my wrist. "Susan left the castle!"

"Aye, she evidently had a lover in the village," Avelyn adds. "And now they are to be wed."

"I thought at first she was crazy to leave the castle," Elaine says. "But she seems so happy. So very happy."

I beam, thrilled beyond belief. You go, Susan! The first feminist. I'm so glad she had the guts to go after her and Paul's happily-ever-after.

Finally, after what seems an eternity of girliness, I'm pronounced gorgeous and led downstairs to officially meet King Richard. The girls giggle their good-luck wishes at the door to the throne room. They're not allowed inside, but that's okay. They're content to flirt with the outer guards anyhow. I send up a silent prayer that they will soon get their own happy endings.

I step inside. The place has already been cleaned

up. When Prince John was in charge, it was a sty.
Now it looks like a movie set—exactly how a royal
palace should look.

I walk slowly across the room 'til I reach the throne
where King Richard is lounging. He has this aura
about him—he just *looks* like a king. Trim beard,
steel blue eyes, a plain but richly cut red tunic. And
his crown fits properly on his head. I can't tell you
how much that helps.

Robin stands by Richard's side, dressed in a royal
green silk tunic. His hair has been re-cut into a page
boy, and it shines with a just-washed glow. He looks
gorgeous and amazingly clean. Funny not to see him
all rough and unready.

I stop and bow low, then think better and curtsey
deeply. After all, this guy's the King of England, not to
mention I've got to ask him the hugest favor in the
history of favors.

"Rise, Lady Christine," Richard says in a deep bari-
tone. I remember that in *Prince of Thieves*, the Kevin
Costner movie, Richard is played by Sean Connery.
The real Richard kind of has the same deep foreign
voice thing going on, but in the face he more resem-
bles Roger Moore. Funny.

I scramble back to my feet, not as gracefully as I
would have liked. Ah well, not enough practice, what
can you do?

"Robin has told me of your recent adventures,"
Richard says. "I am greatly in your debt for all you
have done for my people while I have been away."

Wow. The King of England is in debt to me. How
cool is that? And it could certainly be helpful. I smile.

"Thanks. It was nothing, really. Plus I had a lot of help. Robin, his men. Really it was a team effort."

Richard smiles. "According to Robin, none of it would have come to pass without your guidance."

"Robin Hood is very kind," I say, stealing a look at the outlaw. He gives me an uncertain smile. I sigh. There's still so much unsaid. I really need to speak to him alone.

"Uh-uh," Richard corrects, with a wave of his hand. He's wearing several awesome rings on his fingers. "'Robin Hood' no longer, milady. It is Robin, Lord Locksley that stands before you this day."

"Really?" I cry, turning to Robin. "You got your castle back? That's so great!" I have to resist the urge to throw myself into his arms and hug the lights out of him. I know how much the castle means to him. And now he won't have to live in the forest!

"Yes, King Richard is most generous," Robin says formally. But I can see a sparkle in his green eyes. He's psyched.

"I'll say. That's way cool. Thank you, Rich—er, King Richard." I must remember courtly manners here. There's no use getting too friendly with Richie Rich. "What about Little John? Much the Miller, Will Scarlet and the rest of the men?"

Robin smiles. "They have agreed to pardon me for my crime. And as reward for their loyal service to King Richard, they will be given lands of their own."

"Very nice." I smile, happy that everyone's friends again.

"And you, Lady Christine," Richard continues. "I should like to reward you in kind."

I raise an eyebrow. "Oh?"

"Aye. Simply name it and it shall be yours. Be it half my kingdom."

Heh. Tempting. Always in movies that offer is made. Hardly ever does anyone take the king up on it. They always want something stupid and inconsequential. Like John the Baptist's head on a platter. I mean, come on! Half a kingdom here, people! Me—queen of half of England!

But now I can't take him up on that generous offer either. 'Cause I know exactly what I have to ask for.

"Can I whisper my request in your ear, Your Majesty?" I ask, not wanting any of the various courtiers to hear me. After all, I'm sure Richie here wants to keep secret the fact that he stole the Holy Grail from the Church.

"Certainly, my child." He looks a little titillated.

I climb up on the dais and tell him my request. His eyes widen. "How do you know of that?" he demands, now looking a little PO'ed.

"It doesn't matter. And I won't tell anyone, as long as I get what I need. Which should be no skin off your back, right? I mean, dude, I could have taken half the kingdom, right? Consider yourself lucky."

Richard considers my proposition for a moment, then nods his head. "Very well," he says. "It shall be done."

Woot! Mission accomplished. Kat is going to be so thrilled.

That night Robin escorts me to the suite of rooms that King Richard assigned him, and we curl up into one another on the canopy bed.

"How do you fare?" he asks, stroking my cheek.

I smile, stretching my arms above my head and then snuggling closer against him. "Right this second I couldn't be cozier."

"I am so sorry for last night. Running away like a coward. I just could not bear the thought of losing you."

"I know," I say, stroking the stubble on his cheek gently with the back of my hand. "It's not that I want to be lost, believe me. If I had my choice I'd stay here with you forever."

"Do you mean that, truly?"

"Yes. I love you, Robin. You're the best thing that's ever happened to me. I love our life here in Nottingham. And it's only going to get better from here on out. Why would I want to leave all this behind?"

"Well, then," Robin says, clearing his throat. "I think you should go."

"Wh-what?" That was so not what I expected the guy to say.

"You told me once that in your land—in your . . . time—if you love someone, you should let them go. Well, Chrissie, I know that you have to go. And though 'tis unbearably painful, I must let you."

Tears fill my eyes and I cuddle closer to him, seeking all the warmth and comfort his body has to offer.

"I will figure out a way to return, Robin," I promise. "Someway, somehow, I will find you again."

"I know, dearest," Robin says, taking my head in his hands and kissing me slowly. "I believe that with all my heart. That's the only reason I can do this."

We make love slowly; I'm crying the whole time. Every caress, every kiss feels like a knife inside me.

It's lucky we seldom know the last time we'll make love to our partners. Feeling that person inside you . . . If you knew the person you loved was tomorrow going to walk out of that door and get hit by a bus—or meet someone new who they wanted to dump you for—you might find that last time too much to bear. I understood that now.

Every heavenly sensation of our lovemaking is accompanied by a suffocating feeling of loss, every ounce of pleasure doused by a pound of pain. In the end, we simply stop, crying in one another's arms. We're too emotionally drained to speak.

Finally, I've found the man of my dreams and I'm forced to leave him for some silly mission. It's not fair. So not fair.

Somehow I eventually fall asleep. I dream I'm walking through King Arthur's Faire, carrying the vial with the Holy Grail blood in my hands. I approach the gypsy tent and pop inside.

Nimue sits there, exactly as I saw her the first time, by her crystal ball. She greets me with all-knowing, wise eyes.

"Did you bring it?" she asks.

I hold up the vial. "Of course."

"You have done well, little one. I am very proud of you."

I start to hand over the vial, then suddenly change my mind, an idea forming in my brain. Robin told me once if you loved someone you should fight for them. And suddenly I'm ready to put on the gloves and get dirty.

"Look, Nimue," I say. "I'll give you the blood. But you have to give me something too." I've seen enough episodes of *24* to know how to set up a trade.

"That was not part of our deal," Nimue says stiffly.

"Well, then, I'm changing the deal."

"And what is it that you want? Riches? Shoes? What is it you twenty-first century women find more precious than gold?"

"I don't want money! I want to stay back in the twelfth century. To be with my true love. You told me long ago that perhaps my destiny lies in another era. Well, it's true. My destiny, my future, is not here. It's with Robin."

There. I said it.

"So you would rather let your friend languish away in the twenty-second century to fulfill your own selfish desires?"

"No. I want to help Kat. That's why I got you the stupid Grail blood to begin with. Jeez, I gave up half of England for the stuff. But I'm also done being the sacrificial lamb in everyone else's happiness. And now that I've found it, I'll be damned if I'm going to let that slip away."

Nimue smiles, her blue eyes crinkling at the corners. "You speak well, Chrissie," she says. "You have much changed since you first appeared at my door. The timid mouse has grown up to be a tiger."

"Uh, thanks, I think." She's right of course. The shy, unassuming photographer who came to King Arthur's faire with Kat is nothing like who I am today. I'm strong. I'm self-sufficient. I'm a leader. And I have a man who loves me enough to die for me. Not that I'd ever want him to.

"Did you really think I'd force you back to this century when I knew all along you belonged in the past?"

I cock my head in surprise. Whoa. I wasn't expecting that answer! "You knew?"

"Remember," Nimue reminds me, "I am the one who first told you that you would be the gentle soul who tamed an outlaw's thirst for revenge."

"That's right," I say, thinking back.

"If your destiny truly lies in this other place and time, there is no reason for me to keep you here. You have accomplished your mission. You have saved your friend, and she will now be able to safely return. Of course I will allow you to stay in the twelfth century." She glances into her crystal ball for a moment, then back up at me. "You will live long and have many children," she prophesies. "In fact, you already have your first inside of you."

"What? I'm pregnant?" I look down at my flat stomach, unbelieving at first, then back at Nimue. "And I can stay with Robin?"

"Aye." Nimue smiles. "Now, begone. Go back to your love, for he wakes by your side." She waves a hand and the room swirls into blackness.

"Chrissie, Chrissie! Wake up!"

I groan as I feel a hand nudging my shoulder. Reluctantly I open my eyes. Robin is leaning above me, concern in his eyes.

"What?" I ask. "What's wrong?"

" 'Twas the strangest thing. You started to fade for a moment."

"Fade?"

"I cannot explain it. Perhaps you were traveling to your homeland. I got frightened. I realized this might be the moment I lose you forever and I did not get a chance to say good-bye."

I smile, remembering. Obviously it was no dream. I wonder what people in the 21st century will think when I don't return. Will anyone miss me? Will they launch a search? Maybe Kat will be able to make up something believable. I wonder if I'll still get to talk to her from time to time on my cell phone. . . .

I realize none of this matters now. Not really. I have a new life, a new and glorious beginning with the man I love. All my dreams have come true.

"Robin, you don't have to be frightened. I'm not going anywhere. I did what you said. I fought for our love. And I won. You've got me for as long as you want me."

"Do not toy with me, Chrissie. I cannot bear it."

"I'm not. It's true. I've accomplished my mission and I've bargained my freedom. I can stay here with you forever."

Robin smothers me with a hug, squeezing me hard. Suddenly conscious of the baby growing inside me, I push him gently away and whisper our secret in his ear. His eyes widen and he stares at me, indescribable delight written on his face. Then he cuddles into me, placing a hand against my stomach, stroking the burgeoning life beneath. I curl my hand into his, feeling so happy, so wanted, so loved. So right.

I'm a Hoboken Hipster in Sherwood Forest. And this is where I belong.

Do you think historicals are a thing of the past?
Did you get caught up in THE MATRIX?
Did you devour Crimson City?

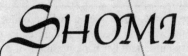

…It's time for something different.

Three new books.
Three new adventures.
Three new reasons to love romance.

Wired
LIZ MAVERICK
JULY 2007

Moongazer
MARIANNE MANCUSI
AUGUST 2007

Driven
EVE SILVER
SEPTEMBER 2007

A Connecticut Fashionista in King Arthur's Court

MARIANNE MANCUSI

Once upon a time, there lived a fashion editor named Kat, who certainly was not the typical damsel in distress. But when a gypsy curse sent her back in time to the days of King Arthur, she found she'd need every ounce of her 21st-century wits to navigate the legend. After all, just surviving without changing history or scuffing your Manolos takes some doing!

Luckily, she's got her very own knight in shining armor, Lancelot du Lac, on her side...even though she's not quite sure she wants him there. After all, shouldn't he be off romancing Queen Guenevere or something? Will Kat manage to stay out of trouble long enough to get back to her world? And what will Lancelot's forbidden love mean for the kingdom of Camelot?

WHAT, NO ROSES?

MARIANNE MANCUSI

Unless Dora Duncan can stop it, it's going to be another St. Valentine's Day Massacre. A year ago, her (now ex) boyfriend Nick stood her up at the worst possible moment. That was when she gave up important TV reporting. And things have been a whole lot quieter. *Too* quiet. Until now. Now she's gotta go back in time and stop that very same Nick from messing up the time-space continuum. She has to travel back to a place where everybody speaks easy and cuts a rug—and this Chicago ain't no musical. Here, there are tommy guns and torpedoes, guys and dolls, gin joints, flappers, stoolies, rats and a whole lot more; and prohibition means anything but no.

- -

NAOMI NEALE

METHOD MAN

Becca Egan is quickly working her way up the Yes Ladder when A. J. Daye rescues her from a "git it, hit it, and forgit it" lounge lizard. A pro pickup artist, A.J. knows all the lingo. He offers to teach Becca more secrets of The Method— a system to woo women into the bedroom in less time than it takes to say "strawberry-kiwi daiquiri."

Soon Becca is acting as A.J.'s wingman and learning way more about men's dirty pickup techniques than she ever wanted to know. But when the game starts to dictate her life, she realizes it may be time to ditch The Method and start playing by her own rules.
